DUKE

DUKE

• A NOVEL •

SARA TILLEY

PEDLAR PRESS | ST. JOHN'S

COVER ART John Haney and Carey Jernigan, *Ghost Barn* (2012)
Acrylic, salvaged barn wood, and solar-powered LEDs
102″(h) × various horizontal dimensions
Installation view at Fieldwork, Perth ON, May 2014
Photograph (detail) by John Haney
DESIGN Oberholtzer Design Inc., St John's NL
TYPEFACES Archer, Berkeley plus Claredon, Scala Jewel
PRINTED IN CANADA Coach House Printing

LIBRARY AND ARCHIVES CANADA CATALOGUING IN
PUBLICATION

Tilley, Sara, 1978-, author
Duke / Sara Tilley.

Includes bibliographical references.
ISBN 978-1-897141-68-7 (pbk.)

I. Title.

PS8639.I554D83 2015   C813'.6   C2014-906913-8

First Edition

This is a work of fiction. Names, places, dates and events are
used in a fictitious manner. This book, a novel, should not
be considered an accurate historical record or a biographic
account of any persons, alive or dead.

ACKNOWLEDGEMENTS
The publisher wishes to thank the Canada Council for the Arts
and the NL Publishers Assistance Program for their generous
support of our publishing program.

 Conseil des arts du Canada / Canada Council for the Arts

 Newfoundland Labrador

*I got my own thoughts
filling in the holes
of how it's written*

*& I am sure
what I imagines
is a thousandfold worse
than the Truth*

— Duke, page 294

For my father, Robert Tilley

BOOK ONE

· THE RIVER ·

Tonight I'll be in Dawson City   yes sir yes sir
famous Dawson City   where you can see the good
          & the bad, all mixed
famous Dawson City   where the saloons never close
          & neither do their women
(that's according to Clare   har har)

famous Dawson City   the Gold Rush Capital
the Klondike's Jewel   the Shiny City of Dreams Where
the Law Does Not Rule   Mythic, Majestic & Oh So Pretty
that's my girl   DAWSON CITY

we passed through Lake Laberge this morning, so big it looked
like the ocean & made me powerfully lonesome for N. F. L. D.,
though we've no mountains anything like this at home

imagine, a lake 30 miles long, the waves so big when we first
came to its lip we had to tie up on a sandbar & wait for the wind
to die down for fear of capsizing, & I'm not talking about a little
boat now, this is a 200 passenger steamer, boy, & she's not too
top-heavy neither   in the gusts off the lake you could feel

the belly of the boat shimmying up on the sand, the bars high &
soft & easy to get stuck into & then guess who would have to
get out & push, not the passengers, no sir, but us

us   Timber-Feeders, Stokers: Boiler-Men   we rough
lot what sleeps in the hold, not in cabins with little beds & white
sheets & pillows & a wash basin & armoire & window

every chance I gets I'm up on deck checking out The Sights but
Clare don't as he's been up & down the Yukon about a million
times before   & what was once Majestic is now A Bore
          I sang a few bars of Love Divine, All Loves Excelling,
& fair ruined it   I don't have much voice, that was always
Kate & Alice, James, Bob & Ernest's domain
& M—'s   not the rest of us

at Five Finger Rapids we nearly didn't pull through & even
Clare was shook   in the middle of the Rapids there's this
dirty big island what makes the passage awful close for a steamer
the size of the S.S. Dawson   & the current's so strong if
you fell off the boat you'd be dashed to pieces against the cliff
before you drowned

the noise of that water is Deafening

the captain saw me out on deck & it must have been obvious to
him this was my first trip up, due to my Awe of the Scenery
          he called me up & we stood together, me & him, & I was
glad I'd only been on her a week & hadn't built up too much of a
layer of grime yet, the captain himself in a pristine, pressed
uniform, at odds with his ancient, greying boater, the ends of
straw fraying round the brim & the ribbon dulled from what

might once have been scarlet to a kind of bright dark brown, like
the colour of dried blood

he explained how to manoeuvre her   —you have to look
at it like billiards, figure out how to angle the boat into the
current just enough to cause a repercussion of momentum in
the opposite direction to keep you in the middle of the channel
as you barrel ahead full force

the captain backed her up & waited for his chance, told me to
watch & see how it was done   the current got us on the
quarter too hard & the tail of her swung back, hit the cliff face
with a bang that echoed off itself into a smaller bang & then
another   like a rock dropped down a dry well shaft
the iron railing around the stern got bashed to pieces   the
lifeboat tore to wood shavings & rushed downstream past us
              I cursed & the sound was foreign to my mouth but it
came out easy just the same
—remain calm, Tilly
—yes, captain   are we sinking, though?
—no, man   now look to your crew chief down below, see
what needs doing, I do not pay you to stand about as my ship
goes to Hell, is that understood?

I understood him right enough & hurried off, not sure if I should
salute or bow or what   that dirty straw hat did not diminish
his Authority   he seemed so calm it was like nothing had
happened save my vexing him

amongst the rest, though, it was different   two ladies
fainted & were taken to their cabins & there was a boy who
was cut on his leg & needed sewing up, though from the rail

smashing or just prankster adventuring on a boat, I don't know
        nonetheless we all got a start to see that iron railing curl
up like a bit of paper   all hands got on the drink real hard
that night & for the next two days much of the ship had a powerful
headache, which made us work that much harder though without
much talking or whistling as we might normally do

Clare switched up with me for the last few hours of my shift
today so I might see some more of the river
—after all, I plan to do this trip a few hundred more times, Dukey,
& you don't know what you're planning
—not true, I'm going to look for Bob
—yes, I know, but what then
—then I'll do what he does
—so take the shift off, watch the water   you'll appreciate it
when you're up there, sniffing him out

there was something queer in his voice when he said that but
I didn't ask after it & then he went down below before I could
say anything back   that's Clare for you, boy, he don't take
no for an answer & you either Love or Hate him for it   or
you continually alternate between the two opinions depending
on the mood you're in

the water gets shallow again   the American next to me is
talking Hell's Gate
—that's what they call this spot you know
& it's not long till I finds out why   the captain lands us up
on a sandbar   the space between them here is narrow &
with the angle of the sun I guess he couldn't see the path straight
—fucken Hell's Gate   my mate says, under his breath
—does this happen often?

—not with all captains, but with that one there, you're lucky we
didn't tip
—I was up with him on the bridge when we sheared the lifeboat
off the side of her back at Five Finger   I say
—were ya now   how's his breath?
—fine I guess
—fine   ya duffer
—how long till we get off of here then?
—fucken Hell's Gate   from the feel of that slide in, could be
a day or more

& I see you, Dawson City, slipping further & further away
as do some others looking forward to your Charms, judging by
the cloud of curses now hovering over the deck   as does
the S. S. Dawson herself, longing to return to her Namesake

someone hustles me along to join the other crew men, waist deep
in the water wading with cables to shore, to try & pull ourselves
clear   the water shocking cold   so cold you can't
hardly feel it after a second or two

Dangerous

I put the cable over my shoulder, linked now to the other men
as on a chain gang   the cable heavy & cutting into my
wet shirt   a groove carving itself under the steel
rope (am I bleeding? best not to look!)   someone at
the front yells Pull   the sound of Grunting, Cursing,
Straining & sometimes a dulled Thunk! when a mate slips in
the sand & falls

there are Many Hours of this

I am numb to the core & my legs are gone to liquid & it is only resolve that keeps me upright at all, let alone pulling the cable yet somehow I don't go arse over teakettle

M— called that quality the Tilly Stubbornness, that we all would Persevere Pigheaded once we set our mind to something
most all of us have it & you can tell it's coming on by the wrinkling of the chin when we sets our jaws tight around a problem

the Tilly Stubbornness will let your body pull past its own strength   it will keep you upright past your own legs' determination   & can be a trial to live with, as I am sure M— would attest

finally a break is called   we stagger back to the boat, change into dry clothes & drink ourselves warm   get a bit of grub in   my hands are shaking so bad I waste half my Soup before it makes it to my lips   I got a dark bruise through each shoulder like the straps on overhauls, but there's nothing for it except to Curse

then it's back into the water, pulling, it's like a bad dream except not so bad this time because Clare is in front of me on the cable singing Friggin' in the Riggin' so I have something to cling to as my body keeps straining & shivering & the boat doesn't budge & the ladies gather on the deck in their florid floppy hats & stare at us with varying expressions from shock to titillation at the content of Clare's lyric   my jaw locking tight on the purpose ahead of me so as not to die of shame from them ladies having their fill of us, wet & struggling, with Clare's good tenor voice ringing in the gulf between us:

—He used to cool his favourite tool
in a glass of the Skipper's brandy!

their male counterparts, for the main part, also stare, & smoke
their pipes, except for a handful of them, who have joined in the
struggle & have taken up the cable like we have, & this gives
them status among us, which we shan't forget should any tension
later arise, as is wont to do between Working Men & their
Societal Superiors when stuck in close quarters under the stress
of a grounding of indeterminate length with plenty of Liquor to
lubricate the riling up of their Passions & with several of the
Fairer Sex at hand to further Amplify the Situation

though I have been conditioned by Father to think myself one
of the Higher Ranks, I know that I am not

Here, On the Cable, ordered on, not of my own free & noble Will
Here On the Cable, chained to it, Struggling
Here is Where My Station is
Here is My Calling

I shall ask no better than to put my Shoulder to the Cable my
whole life long

On the third day a ship comes by   we see her from far up
the river like a Mirage you might see in a Desert, & I blink a
time or two to make sure   but right enough there's a dot
on the water that soon has a proper shape & you can make out
it's a good-sized rig-up too

she's coming towards us & up rises a mighty cheer   a man
or two falls down in the excitement, their legs giving out from
the thought of being saved   & them so weak they nearly
drown & have to be hauled back to the boat by other men near
as gone

by this time half the passenger men are in the water, pulling
also, & it is these who are the first to fall   we carry them on
our shivering backs to their cabins where I suppose they might
have a Hot Toddy & a lie down on their bed under numerous
white wool blankets with a Steward coming to knock on the door,
inquiring if Sir might need anything   for our part, we
Working Men rush back to the hold & change our clothes again,
though like most of the rest I don't have anything left that's
completely dry & have to choose from varying degrees of damp

to wetness   we have taken to stripping off right away &
diving into our bunks under our blankets in a cloud of Curses

it is not what I imagined my Life would be like, when I was a
Lad

you must stay curled up tight for the first few minutes under
the dry blanket & then slowly your feet & hands start to thaw
          it hurts like Sin but it means you're not losing anything
               & then you curl up harder & shove your fingers deeper
into your armpits & suck the heat from one part of you into
another till you can bear to put the fresh damp kit on & get up
          I would just as soon stay naked as daybreak curled
under my ratty bit of blanket than ever get up again, but Clare
says —If we don't rise & shine, Dukey, they're going to have all
the grub gone & you for one my son look like you can't afford to
miss out on Cook's famous slop tonight   & then he's
whistling Irene Goodnight & waltzing out the door, bunging his
head off the frame when the boat lurches forward

—they're pulling us off, they're pulling us off, he sings —I'll see
you in my dreams!

& a second cheer goes up, under our blankets, because he's
right of course   that lurch means they're starting to haul
us off the sandbar & we won't have to get into the river again &
push   I got a few tears but am not Sad   pure Numb
& Grateful   too much like M— for my own good, Aunt
Sus would say

I force my arm out of the covers though my shoulders don't
want to move none too good & grab my Union Suit & haul it

back into the warm little cave I've made, the cold damp wool of the suit already starting to suck some of the Hope from me but Grin & Bear It Duke Be More Like Clare & Whistle Your Way Past The Discomforts of Living Like They're Nothing But a Cloud of Nippers

I wrap the blanket around my shoulders & shove my feet into my boots, an abuse they scream about   Clare must be some kind of God to go whistling out of here like he's impervious   though he's King of Bluff I know from cards & I suppose I admire him for it, being the transparent sort myself

Ernest used to joke I got my skin put on inside out by accident   Everything Shows   (well I prefer that to being like him: An Iceberg of a Man, with Heart Twice as Cold!)

I head up to the deck first thing, to see the progress, even though Clare is right about our slop going quick, I know   the Bonanza King has us cabled up & is starting to get us free of the bar   I wave at the men working on deck of the other boat & they wave back, glad to help   then I go get some grub & squish in next to Clare who's in the middle of enthralling the surrounding population with tales of his Previous Adventures in Dawson, Where the Laws Are Near As Loose As The Women

that stuff would make a man's ears burn, but the rest are mostly laughing

November 23, 1899

Father said —Do not touch your Tender Parts
It is a Mortal Sin now that you're Grown

(& how was I to know he'd come into my room in the morning
without knocking, as has happened but three times in my whole
life: One Birth   One Death (both of the same Soul)
          & once for a Fire in the Store)

—when you were a boy you were smacked for that very act, but
you don't recall it now, I suppose
—no Sir
—smacked on your arse, draped over my knee, & I didn't spare
you, though you were only three or so   Keep your Hands
to yourself or it's back over my knee you go   Don't think
you've Outgrown that Consequence, my Son, just because
you're Nearly Grown   Not while under My Roof, & Not
Ever Afterward, as your Mortal Soul depends on it, you hear?
          Do you wish to Burn Alone in Hell Forever, Son? For
that is what you're after
—I'm sorry, Sir   I don't hardly do it   this was the
first time   well, since that other time, I suppose

—let it be the last time, or by the Power of God I will cast you out
        I'll not have that filth under my roof   there's Women
living here, remember that

I wrung my hands in front of me as though to punish them
        like they acted of their own accord, them dirty dogs, in
spite of the rest of myself   —I shall obey

he tapped his left foot on the floor two times & closed the door
                what did the taps mean

~~touching the Tender Parts as he calls them makes them less~~
~~tender~~

~~it makes a Change that is a Rush of Blood & Love filling me up~~
~~Everywhere, my Skin like to Burst with it, Non-Specific Love for~~
~~Everyone & Everything that sometimes forms into A Face, A~~
~~Place, A Breast, An Ankle, Meadow Flowers, The Taste of~~
~~Rhubarb Pie, The Light At Dawn in October, who knows, right~~
~~before I Feel That Total Feeling, That Feeling Like a Geyser~~
~~Shuddering Through Every Cell In My Body & Up Out Through~~
~~My Member & then My Brain Goes to Quiet Places Where There~~
~~is Nothing but this Calm that has No Dark Part to it & I can Rest~~
~~There a Mite & Life Seems Easy & Good~~

~~It is a Thing A Boy needs now & again, so he do not turn Mean~~

don't tell me the others never did it!   Bob must have for
sure & I do think Jim & Cousin Clare must be Expert, they had
their 'lessons'   they just never got caught by Father
he never would come in our room unless lives were in the
balance

Father got His Rules

(I wonder what was At Risk today that he did Break Them?
        he did not say what he wanted after he seen me

did someone Die?   maybe one of them that went
Stateside?)

(Oh Father, don't go up into the Attic
DON'T EVER GO INTO THE ATTIC)

We pull up into Dawson in the middle of the night & before we reach the shore you can already hear the Ruckus   laughter & shouting & music all pouring out across the water & the saloons lit up like rum puddings, the glow from out of the windows looking so cozy & warm to us what just spent three days in the water, though this isn't half so high-sniffing as Leominster & but a speck to Grand Vancouver

as soon as we are docked the folks begin crowding the gang, all of us wanting to get to town as soon as we can   Clare tells me hang back as we have to wait for the passengers to disembark & sure there's close on to two hundred of them, time enough to tidy up

—slick your hair down some, Dukey, or you'll frighten the petticoats offa the whores (me blushing to hear that kind of talk & even redder at the thought of seeing those type of women up close & IN THE FLESH)

—sure you knows half the girlie passengers on her are Working Women, don't you, Cos?
& Freddie on the next bunk is laughing   —yes, but they

aren't on the clock till they sets down their pretty little feet in
the shit of Dawson's thoroughfare
—poor Duke never seen a woman's Parts before   better
come with me to court my Bess   what do you say?
I got my colour up   —I have seen a Part or two
—their hands don't count, Boy, nor their ears
(Freddie is guffawing)
—I ain't in it for nothing like that   I say
—My Cousin Sweet, I have to see to your Education, & Bessie's
better than a Schoolteacher as far as that goes   tell you
what, let's stop off at the Flora Dora first, have a swallow to get
your Courage up   we can head out for my Dove straight
after   wait till you see her figure, gives new meaning to
the word Generous   you'll be moaning in your sleep
tonight, my little man

Clare douses my head with cold water to make me shriek &
laughs when I hit out at him

—you have no shred of kindness, do you, Clare
—just want to see you get your fill & ain't no woman coming near
you if you resembles a filthy porcupine

he tips back his flask into his mouth, & I watch his throat
chugging the Whisky down

—give me a drop, you wretch
—we'll fill you up in town   let's have some fun   unless
of course with your preachy frame of mind you find that fun's
impossible
—seems he leans that way to me, says Freddie   & I only
known you for a week yet

we line up with the Deckhands   the last of the Passengers
in their clean pressed trousers are filing down the gangway
ahead of us   gathering on the shore like a flock of Sheep
turning this way & that   unsure of where they are or where
they might be headed   & sure when I get out on land I feel
the same, though I put it down to the sway in my legs that think
they're still on water   easy to tip over walking on this
tricky dirt & fall into the muddy thoroughfare on your fresh-
scrubbed face   & I will admit a time or two I nearly
take a tumble

still it is wonderful to see the glowing windows in the buildings
with the fancified painted fronts & plain logs for sides, tricking
you, the same building Rough or Fancy depending which way
you look   wood walkways between them to keep you up
out of the mud   a thousand souls all pushing their way
forward under the cloth banners hung over the thoroughfare
advertising the bounty of Goods & Services one might acquire,
should one have the Capital   & I can see how Clare's talk
of this place as Working Man's Heaven might not be so far off
                they got everything from Boots to Haircuts, Tailors,
Tanners, Haberdashers, Dog Mushers, & Good Times of All
Kinds advertised in the air above the street   banners
flapping like sails when the breeze blows through
it keeps a person looking up
& it seems a Universe, Entire, is here unto Herself

the wooden boardwalks are raised up high & I can see this
could be a treacherous town to be spit-drunk in, what with the
fall to the muck below & that muck soft enough to sink into &
pass out   & plenty willing to crawl down after & take a
wander through your pockets, I'd reckon

       we head to the Flora Dora, which boasts Seventy-Five
(75!) Dancing Girls   the place across the way has ten
more than that   a dozen of em hanging off the upper
balcony like baskets of geraniums, got up in bright dresses with
lacy collars going low as I only saw before in James's stereoscope,
with the cards come straight from Paris (truth told, a card or two
had No Garments At All to speak of, beside Shoes   a sight
I shall not soon lose hold of!)

Cousin Clare is rubbing his hands together, smacking his lips
        three fingers of whisky tipped back straight away & the
bottle at his elbow

—thanks, Tom   he says to the Barkeep   & is my girl
Bess still in the same place up Paradise Alley?
—you didn't hear?   things changed since you came through
last   they passed some law says all the Scarlets have to ply
their trade the other side of the river   to keep the town
Upright
—Dawson ain't been upright since it crawled out of the womb!
—well they're tryin to counterfeit its purity   so if you want
a lay you have to catch the ferry over & find it in Louse Town
—I am amazed, Tom   things sure change a lot when a man
been laid up a few months
—you're better now, though?
—back in old form
—French Pox?
—I cannot lie
—that's the price you pay for enjoying Life, I suppose
—I went for some Bargains & should have stuck to the Good
Ones   you pay more but they're clean, eh
—true enough

—poor Bess shunted over the river!   I've a mind to cry!
—that's the way of it, boy, it's all Bona Fide now   you can
  eyeball our dancers till sunrise but ain't none of them allowed
  to touch your member or they can shut us down   & you
  know there's a man or two in here plain-clothed waiting to
  catch any discrepancy
—bit of a tease then, the way you got em all done up
—that's what we're selling now   A Tease   & liquid fire
  for your furnace, of course
—top up my cousin there, Tom, with some of that   I think
  his furnace went out back in '98 sometime, n'ar flame to speak
  of in the likes of this one

my eyes are bugging out at all the Sleepy-Time Gals there is to
see   their Shoulders, & the Curving they Descend To
Dear Lord, shield my Eyes!   them Arms   all gleaming
white   gleaming so bright I can barely stand to look
around me for the glare & for thinking of Jennie   a
little Slip between my Lips   Clare don't know the
whole of all about me   the smell of smoke & lamp oil &
toilet water off them Ladies making it a chore to draw breath

—Clare, I think I should go back onboard   I got a headache
  something powerful
—have another drop of Painkiller

he grabs my glass & tips near half the bottle in

—sure you haven't even seen the famous Flora Dora dancers yet

so I sit down there on his left-hand side & sip at my Whisky,
which has got the sting of Homemade something awful

the player piano blaring out good dance hall waltzes so that my
toes start tapping on account of themselves   a man what
looks like he got drug through about ten wars hefts a filthy
burlap sack onto the bar next to my elbow   I can feel the
vibrations through my arm when it lands   I pry my eyes
off the sight of two Ladies who are sitting with a Gent in one of
the boxes to the side   they should be cold, not wearing
much of anything except fancy shoes & stockings & dresses
with no sleeves & scarcely skirts   one shawl between the
two of them   their arms & throats & faces glowing pale in
the kerosene   paste jewels sparkling in their ears

the thud of the sack   Barkeep hands the filthy man a big
brass bell with a handle so used to service the shine is gone

—another lucky day, eh, Manning
—get the bottles lined up, Tom   this'll be a mad old night,
I'll guarantee

Clare grabs my thigh   —take note of this, Dukey, & hold
onto your hat

& out goes Manning to the street, ringing his bell   Barkeep
opens up the poke to let the glint of Gold peek out   rough
rock, not like the stuff of wedding rings
                I'm feeling Drunk
        a bag of Gold just sitting there by my arm, as big as a
child, sitting on the bar & dully shining   the bell going
counterpoint to the waltzy music
                Clare counting down from ten as the man rushes back
with a swarm of folks full double what's already in the bar to
begin with

—best get out of the way, Duke, & stick to a corner   this
fella got Bonanza Fever & those mates might kick your teeth in
if you get between them & the drink

cheers rise up to drown out all the other sounds in the place as
Barkeep Tom pours out the Painkiller for anyone who wants it
              —Compliments of Mr. Manning   & he's pouring so
fast the Whisky slops out of the glasses   & if a man had a
mind to, he could inebriate hisself just by licking up & down
the length of the bar

Clare grabs me by the sleeve   —this is the perfect moment
to make our escape
—I don't know about it, Clare
—what you don't know could fill an Encyclopedia or more
I aim to raise you up proper here on the river   Let's Get

Clare drags me down to the riverbank   & though it
seems my feet are eager to follow, my guts do not relish sitting
aboard another boat & crossing current with so much Whisky
now sloshing about inside

Clare chuckles at my pale constitution   —quit playing the
sorry sap now, Duke   I hope them Flora Dora girls got
your appetite up some
—why did I get on this boat with you, You   (my curse goes
unfinished as I retch over the side, this ferry being a smallish
vessel, susceptible to the rise & fall of the river)
—poor old Duke, we'll find you a nursemaid in a minute
—you'll be the death of me, Clare
—if I am, boy, you've led A Sorry Kind of Life

another retch or two sees us across, & now I got nothing inside
me to object to what might transpire

Louse Town is smaller & you can tell much newer than Dawson
Proper   most of the girls are standing outside of canvas
tents, though a few got cabins & there's a bigger place or two
on up the road   some Gals we passes by looks roughed
up & maybe drunk, but most looks like regular girls to me, not
being got up in sleeveless outfits like the dance hall ones but in
their usual garb, skirts to the mud, coats buttoned to the chin
(it's a cool one)

—how do you know who's working & who's not   I haven't
got the sense to spot the difference
—if they're standing outside they'll take your coin, or if the
curtains're open

we pass a trio of fair-haired girls who look to be sisters
          they stop their chat & give us a gander but don't seem
none too put out when we keep moving past

—there's some here don't look White, are they Native to this area
—Dear Duke, here we see the Colours of the World unfold
          the miracle is that one woman's like another when she's
got her skirts up   or most are   my Bess, now, my
Bess is Gold

he stops a pace & sidles up to the nearest Dove   one who
is dark as brown bread & with black hair, blacker than M—'s

Clare takes her hand & kisses it

—fifty cents, Sir, for the full treatment, twenty for handiwork, ten
for watching if that's your game
—where can I find Miss Bessie Ford?
—she ain't got nothing I can't provide
—ten cents for directions is pretty easy money   if we have
our Energy we'll come back & see you afterwards for the
handiwork you advertise
—fifteen cents will get you where you want to go   but make
sure you bring your Friend back, he looks new
—new as a new-arsed baby
—I like those for a change

he hands her the money & she puts it somewhere in her skirts,
taking her time with the action & looking at me all the while
          my Blood is Burning   still staring at me, she pulls
Clare closer & whispers the directions in his ear   he holds
her by the waist to hear, & when she's done he pulls her hard in
to him so as to make her gasp

—why thank you Miss   we're much obliged   & he's
grinning like a cat in a cod liver barrel

off we go down the road   I feel like this is a Dream what
don't match up with My Real Existence   I am watching my
feet follow Clare's swagger & his whistle   my feet, eager
for Damnation, take the rest of me along against my Will

we turn to the right & knock at a log place what got no sign or
anything, the whole building not much bigger than our kitchen
at home   a girl answers, looks to be fifteen, though maybe
younger, with mousy hair tied back from off her forehead
          she lets us in & gives us chairs & Whisky   there's

hardly any light in here & I guess that's good for Trade   in
the dim I can make out a regular living setup, nothing fancy,
just table chairs & cookstove, & doors to two rooms off to the
right what must be just big enough to lie down   or maybe
you stand to do the Deed with Scarlets, how should I know?
          Clare's got the young one by the hand   —where's
Miss Bessie, girly?
—she's in back with a gent, near finished though
—I need her attentions something terrible   tell her Clarence
is here
—& what of your friend, Sir, do he have a need?   she got her
eye on my lower Self, which then begins its Stirring   my
voice is shrunk up   —I don't need much at present but to
sit a spell, I'm feeling poorly
—this soul don't have his courage up yet, so don't annoy him,
Clare says   —maybe he'll have a change of heart in a
minute
—I'll keep watch from the corner, Sir   you call out Mellie &
I'll tend you straight off

her hand drapes damp & heavy across my shoulder for a
moment, & I flinch   she sulks off to the shadows where
she recedes until just her eyes are reflected in the lamplight
          two shiny orbs that won't leave me be with their glittering
even as I stares at the tabletop

Clare fishes for his tobacco   this blonde woman comes
out of a bedroom with an old one half in his trousers, & Clare
quickly lays his pipe down

she is done up like I pictured Doves, before I got here
          Stockings   & a Robe that falls open in the front to

show her Chemise made of Openwork Descending Low Between
Her Mounds   (which are perhaps the largest I have seen
to date, on any female!)   all of her is large & curved &
Womanly   Clare is up, she laughs to see him, kisses the old
one on the cheek & boots him out the door right quick

Bess!   a big-boned girl in a light pink robe looking to
me like a carnation in full bloom, right before it begins to go
brown around the edges

—my beauty!
—come over here, Clarence, I've missed you, you were gone too
too long this time

he's got her by the waist & backed up to the wall across from me,
putting his hand under her skirts while she opens up the top
part to let his face in   her own face red & smiling
               she's got right pretty golden hair going down around
her shoulders but with the pox scars something bad   &
don't she look like she Loves her Employment   Clare
hefting up her thigh & taking handfuls of Breast & licking them

     & I know I'm bound to go to Hell for watching
     & bound again for wishing I was brazen enough to grab
     someone like that

I latch onto women with my eyes only & try to tell myself it
don't count as Sinning, though my eyes are just as greedy as
Clare's roaming fingers now buried deep under that girl's
clothes as she bites his ear & lets her Bosoms fully loose
          holding onto them herself & squeezing, like maybe she's
forgotten Clare altogether & is lost in her Solitary Pleasure

Oh My! Oh Yes!
Clever Bess!

Reaching Down
To Lick
Her Own
Nipples
With An
Incredible
Flexibility
Of Her
Neck!

—Bessie   sweet Bess   Clare's moaning & working away
on her & she's got her head turned toward me at the table, her
mouth on her own generous Breast (There is Enough for Us All)

my blood now going hot & fast in Hell's direction   her
eyes on mine & I'm nothing but a boiling tide, trying to prevent
myself from looking, but I have no Dominion over my Body
right now

—come to my room now, darling   you don't got to pay extra
tonight   I don't like these gigglesticks getting their jollies
off us
—I like it here, Bess, let him stare   I got you in a happy state
          why spoil it
—oh Clarence
—oh Bessie
—you know the trick, don't you   fuck me fuck me
—I will, I'll fuck you hard
—yes, fuck me

—yes, Bessie darling, but first I'll suck you
—fuck yes, oh yes yes yes Clarence yes
her head pressed back against the wall, face red & shiny & he's
kneeling on the floor with mouth upon That Secret Mound
(though Bess don't appear to keep much stock in Secrets)
        & I swear she ain't even touching the floor anymore,
banging on the wall with the back of her head in a kind of
waltzy rhythm   one! two-three   one! two-three
Clare starts in on some kind of moaning like he's calling the
spirits up & begins to kiss her there again   & though she
says she don't want me watching she's got her eyes on me, like
I am part of her Excitement

—Fuck yes yes ya ya

Clare holds back the folds of skirt & pauses in his ministrations
so that I can see all I care to   I swear it is deliberate, this
display, & she's crying out now like Death has visited her
        skull keeping time on the wall   one! two-three

I tip back the glass & concentrate on the burning down my gut
lest I go blind from all this Flesh & from Bessie's eyes boring
through me

—yes Clarence   fuck yes

when I look to the far corner, that Mellie also got me in her
sights   she sees me looking & moves into the light,
her blouse undone, pinched girl's Bosoms pale, with lavender
veins snaking toward her small brown Nipples   her
youngster's voice whining high   —Mister, you ready
for me now?

I stand up quick & lurch out the door with my hat held before my Member   I suck in a deep draught of the night air, what smells of all those who've Pissed in the Thoroughfare tonight or Cast Up their Accounts here

O! CIVILIZATION!

I stagger back down to the Ferry   that dark girl is still there, looking cold, though she appears not to remember me when I go by, & is just standing there singing some wordless tune to herself & jingling a rope of tiny bells looped around her left ankle

it sounds like Good People Music

I stand on deck & try to stomach the motion of the waves   my body is on the boat & my head is still in that cabin, still with Clare, holding open the Secret of his Bessie for me, using his Clever Tongue

I think of Mellie's sad girl's chest   I got a few tears

the jingle jangle of the Dark Dove's music trails away to nothing as the Louse Town Ferry crosses back to the other side

I want to rid myself of everything I ever done   if only one could Expel the Past as quickly as their Whisky

Clare may think my furnace got put out but there's a flame still   a tiny flame that's burning   there's things I should never have done, things I should never have allowed to continue, once begun   those kinds of things I feature every grown man must have, inside, that keeps them trying to scrub their Conscience clean the rest of their Lives   or else keeps them Running

when I get back to the other side I decide on supplemental Whisky as a Mind Eraser & head back to the Flora Dora
        what with Gold Poke Man I plan on getting a drink or two without spending any coin & that's a nice enough way to end the night

tis not as happy as I hoped, though, as some kind of fight quickly breaks out, though I don't know if it's from the Whisky running short before each man gets his dose or due to the rise in temperature when the Ladies with the feather fans step up on the platform by the piano & start throwing their legs around

men are swinging ill-aimed fists at one another & the feathered Ladies keep on dancing & somewhere in Louse Town Clare is deep inside Bessie's petticoats, so I got no one to turn to who can help me out of this

a shot is fired & women scream & another shot shatters the chandelier   my heart is pretty near beating out my ears & I fear its total failure   the Mounties are dragging away whoever they can lay their hands on & shouting at us all to restore order or be barred from the saloons of Dawson forevermore, which settles most of the rest down right quick

(This is a Fine Healthy Country & a Wily One at that
            Every Thing that is Bad is Here
            It is a job to Be Good)

—give me another Whisky, Barkeep, for my nerves
—we are clean out, Sir, my apologies   but you can have a
Sarsaparilla on the house

& I don't want to look at no more Ladies   not their feathers
or their Bosoms taken into Their Own Mouths   I am
plumb tired of Sinning with my Gazes   & I heave myself
up off my stool & press past the men what the Mounties left
behind as harmless & stagger out into the night

in the other saloon across the thoroughfare the same situation
appears to be repeating itself & I suppose all men's the same
          there's a Madness can set in when too much Drink & Flesh
abound for you to see straight

them Mounties look grim   they're pulling mates out of both
bars & piling them in the middle of the road where they sits
moaning & swinging out occasionally with their drunken fists
          when they get kicked in the hands they learns right
quick to stop & settles in to their lot & mostly goes to sleep

I stumble past the piles of fellows & through the mud toward
the river   my guts betray me so's I have to stop & expel
the Whisky & the Sarsaparilla, what don't agree with me one bit
          the foul sweet liquid spewing out onto the road without
warning

I feel like I'm a real Rush Lad now, as I reckon every man what
got in a row tonight has had to double over sick on this street at
some time in his Career

& then I walk as straight & proud as possible away from the
noise & lights of Dawson & climb careful up the gangplank &
down to my bunk in the empty hold

I collapse with my boots on, dizzy   & dream of fights &
feathers   & Clare's tongue running up & down the length
of a blonde girl without a stitch on & with the little dents of pox
scars forming constellations all over her heaving Bosoms

him licking out Formations
joining star to star

—Eva, don't be playing with that please
—with what
—you know with what, girl   what's that in your hands
—your kit from Alaska
—my kit   that's correct
—but it's just up there in the attic, doing nothing
—don't be poking around up there, it's not for children   you
could fall through if you don't walk right
—I know how to do it
—I'm sure, Jam Tart, but I said don't go up there, now don't sauce
me back
—I'm sorry, Sir
—does your mother need a hand with supper?   leave that
here

she has got my rucksack down, has it open   my Rabbit Fur
Coat in a pile now on the floor, dirty, damp & smelling none
too dainty   that silly strap of sock across the front that
I added that first winter, to protect my face from the wind
          later, instead of removing it, I embellished it with a fur
lining to be softer on my skin   who cares about Looks in
the Alaskan Interior, eh boy   Survival was the thing

my stitching not as poor as I had featured, having held up these fifteen years   I could patent the design perhaps, give us something to fall back on when my body is too broken up to Work

truth be told I do not know how soon that day will come, having already the Rhumatax in the cold weather & the wet   I always been one of the Delicate Sort, susceptible to Colds, Recurring Aches & Pains & General Malaise

    M—, Your Effects do Linger on in Us
    Despite Your Physical Disappearance
    & Though My Years are not too Few
    I still Wonder if You Missed Us?

(Yes, that kind of thinking do not Quit you no matter how Old you gets & how many things you been through)   we all got these Glaciers on the inside, or Icebergs   massive, ancient, frozen Hurts that even the hottest, wildest type of Living cannot fully melt away from us   we all have them   for some of us we takes it different than for some others

(I do not suppose I makes much sense now, but this is the Lightly Lubricated Mind of Duke   near Suppertime   A Few Fingers In)

I hold the coat to my face, feel its softness, cradle it like a Barn Cat that is tamed enough to come inside & eat off the floor of the kitchen   the coat like a Pelt that I have shed in past warm seasons   this used to be a part of me

It Do Not Stop

& though we reinvent ourselves with each breath, still that Glacier do come with us   it keeps us company, holds our hand in hours of need, it is our One True Companion in this Walk through Life, & the One to Comfort Us as We Shed our Corporeal Self & Exit into Ether to be sorted Good & Bad & sent to our appropriate Resting Place on High or in Hell

    where shall I go?

& will I know some others there with me?

(my Berg got some echoes of M— & Father & some Baby Arthur mixed in, maybe some other things as well, which I have not yet rightly identified   for though I have done my share of Living, Thinking & Working o'er the years, still I do not Know all Corners of Myself

Perhaps we can never fully Know Ourselves
Unless in Death this is somehow realized: The Glacier Melts & at its Heart There is that Final, Missing, Shining Part of You That You Didn't Know of, Previously, But Had Suspected Might Possibly Be There
All the Time You Were Alive)

Eva trots back out into the hall   she's got me vexed today, she's at that age where she wants to know where the firm lines are which she must not cross & thus is testing me regularly to find out my limits   this trick with my kit is not the only incident of late   she stayed out in the woods past dark on Thursday, her mother nearly needed salts, she was beside

herself   Eva came waltzing back in blithe as can be at a
quarter to ten as though there is no harm in it   her supper
a wizened mess inside the warmer   her mother's tears
having made swollen pouches of her eyelids

—I have blackberries!
—Child   you are forbidden out after dark   you know
that
—I'm sorry, Ma'am   (silence)   it wasn't dark when
I left   (silence)   I walked out far & then forgot what
time it was   but I started back as soon as it was getting
dark, it was just far away where I was   (silence)   I got
so many berries though, two buckets
—you must have been over near Bonavista, if it took you till ten
o'clock to get back to us
—I'm sorry, Ma'am

Her Mother called me in from where I had been hiding in the
Parlour, reading the Daily News & trying not to make a sound

Wife smiled at me with her face quite tight   —Eva has a
lesson to learn   (& I Must Teach It)

I took my belt off   I had made sure earlier to change it to
the softest one I own, but still do not relish this aspect of my
position as Father of this Household

Wife watching with an Eagle Eye   Eva bent over my
knee, trying not to breathe, her ribs thin as fish bones

the belt doubled & coming down on her backside, not on bare
skin mind you, but I must not spare force with her or risk

getting my own Punishment from Wifey, later
after fifteen whacks or so I sensed it was acceptable to stop
    Eva wasn't crying, she had her jaw clenched:
           The trademark Stubbornness is exhibited early
           in this specimen
           of the Genus Tilley Sapiens!

—I am sorry
—go to your room, Girl   we will not repeat this event

my daughter's small jaw was clamped tight & the muscles of
her chin were working to keep it that way, lest she shed a tear
        she is too Proud already   she stamped her foot
slightly as she turned to leave, although her head was bowed

—Goodnight
—Goodnight Father   Goodnight Mother
—don't forget your Prayers   & a special one tonight to be
    forgiven for what you've done
—Yes Ma'am

I put my belt back on & sunk into the rocking chair opposite my
wife

the anticipation was worse than the act of hitting her, for us
both, I am sure   (Poor Eva, what will this Life bring her
to Endure?)

In the morning we start for White Horse & when the boat leaves shore many of the men, though seasoned hands, are sick overboard   even our Clare seems pale & grey & there ain't much whistling out of him either, though he do not hesitate to tell me that Bess was fully satisfied several times last night

—lost sight of you there, Dukey   hope you got yourself a bit of Oyster too
—let's say I had sweet dreams & leave it at that   & I gives him a wink   (let him think what he wants, no skin off my nose!)

we start following in the wake of the steamer White-Horse, the flagship of the N.C.&C.CO. & our sister ship   she'd left five hours ahead of us with the mail   we're burning wood, two cords per hour, while the White-Horse is burning coal from the mines up on the Yukon   this morning in the boiler room the Drink is sweating out of me, & last night's Adventures perfume the air ˎ   I am a sorry sort of Lad   silently counting down the minutes till Slop   then the word passes down that the Captain has decided A Race is in order   we will try & catch the White-Horse & steal the mail

A Race will bring us back to life again, when we feel so tired &
sickly, is his thinking, & I suppose he may be right, though at
first I do not want to Raise my Energies

two hours into the trip we come to the first wood yard &
wouldn't you know but word of The Race has spread   the
passengers line up on deck to help us load our wood on
          men in shirtsleeves throwing the junks upwards
& I recognize a gent or two from our time at Five Finger
& think how only Circumstance & Collared Shirts separate us

we all want the mail first   if Jennie or Father or even Daisy
has written me then the extra push to win will be worth it
          though I would just as soon slump down into my bunk
for the afternoon to soothe away this Headache

whenever the smoke from the White-Horse is spotted they start
yelling up above   —more steam! more speed! we will soon
see her!   & then it's us Boiler Men what got to step the
work up   it's hot as Hell down here   seems like since
I've left N. F. L. D. it's been nothing but jobs in which you sweats
all day long, like when I worked in the blasted Plastic Factory
          Ernest saying —you'll love it, Duke   easy work,
steady pay   Plastics are Future

down in that factory, working the same machine every day,
taking the same green plastic combs & attaching them to the
same cards with the same small pieces of wire   the same
green combs over & over & no woman's hair to put them in
          stripped down to my overhauls by noon, it were that hot,
Ernest laughing at me when I'd come home half-dead   but
he doesn't know, he works in the store not in assembly, he don't

know what the repetition can do to your mind, it's all I would see when I closed my eyes, combs & combs & combs & all of them Imitation Tortoiseshell, which you can only tell if you hold them up sideways to see the faint line where the two sides of the mold join, otherwise you might mistake them for The Real Article

—before you can sell, you have to sound like a proper American, not some salt-soaked bumpkin from Newfoundland   said Ern
—what do you mean? I said
—whaddaya meen   he laughed through his nose   —no one will buy from you, Dukey, if you sound like that

he has a New England accent so thick now you'd never know we were related   on my last night in Leominster I brought him up to my room for a drink of Nan's Gin, & I finally come around to asking for money for Father
—why should I care if the store goes or stays, I'm never going back to Elliston anyhow, he said, & held his glass out   & that was more or less the end of that

Ernest would perish, were he to work the boiler   all that keeps me standing upright on days like today is the Tilly Stubbornness   handy in times of physical exhaustion but perhaps not so good for issues of Compromise

with my Stubbornness I make it through the day & all the way to dinner time, despite the Salvation Army drum going off inside my head   twice we manage to pull up beside the White-Horse & capture the mail, when she has to stop to clean the coal fires, & twice she gets it back from us   each time, the Crewmen & the Passengers all crowding the deck & cheering & yelling friendly insults back & forth between them

it is A Wonderful Race & the day grows dark before we stop our efforts for A Feed of Salmon & Potatoes   Cook even gets A Pudding going, which is fortunate, as The Race has Worked Our Bellies up   it is The Best Meal we've had on board for at least 2 weeks & my plate is Shining when I hand it back

we continue on into the morning & 'tis us the S.S. Dawson that has the mail & pulls in first to White Horse, though when we dock the other ship blows her whistle not half a mile downstream from us, so it isn't much to brag about

as soon as we pull in, the Mail Bag is opened & the first mate hands the Mail out to us on board & to the people who've come down to shore to see what the merriment is about
      there is a Note from Father regarding the selling of the sheep & directing me to send money soon   I have sent him everything I have, apart from what's saved for my kit & five dollars which I had to lend Kate   (though I cannot tell Father that)

there is also a Postcard from Jennie, with 'Elliston' done out in cursive & little violets in the corner

      To William Marmaduke Tilly
      From Jennie Chants
      Best wishes for your
      23 birthday

she were nine months too early, but I suppose she didn't know how long it would be until the mail arrived, especially as I got

no regular digs to direct the Post to   Bob had written
once that it could be fifteen or more weeks, depending on the
season, & that's if they're sending to a fixed address, not to
Boiler Man on Steamers, always hopping

I turn the Card over twice in my hands   checking
I suppose for other writing   maybe a tiny purple
message written into the side of the flowers   but there
is nothing   not surprising, seeing that it's Jennie, what
learned to read from newspapers she would nick off Father, &
who has to go through him, too, in order to mail anything out

message or not it does me good to run my fingers over the
letters she'd printed out, writing my name in green ink which
I recognize as the kind we sold in the store

I tuck both the letter & card into my jacket pocket & think to
spend a few cents on A Small Oilskin Bag to put my Mail in,
the next time I am handy to a Shop

FISHING!
DON'T HAVE IT IN ME!

do that make me a bad example of a young N. F. L. D. lad?

in St. John's they say so, when I go to sell or buy for Father

they say those of us out in The Bays ought all to fish   what
a Pleasure & a Privilege, they think, to go Out In Boat whenever
the Spirit moves you

(none of em ever spent a morning on the splitting table with
your skin raw as if you washed with sandpaper, or out on the
water on a choppy day with the rain spitting back up off the
waves, eating straight Salt Pork to stay warm)

IT'S NOT FOR ME! I am more like Mother than Father as I would
rather ~~practice my piano~~ read a book or help around the house
than go out on boat   & don't really like the snaring or the
hunting that we do, THE SKINNING IS TOO BLOODY

(though I do like the bang of the rifle when you sets it off
It is Terrific)

on the outside Father seems as though he prizes Culture first, what with him being Shopkeeper & Church Founder & man with whom the Minister stays when he comes to our Town   but these things are not the centre of him   in the centre he is out on the Land, speaking to no one

FATHER IS STRONG, HE IS STRONG AS ANYTHING

Ernest told us about The Wreck   Father will not talk about it   he do not like to parade his accomplishments   he do not like to say 'I did this brave thing' even if he did

Ernest told me all about it, he were a child of seven but even still he remembers it clear as anything, as I suppose you would if your father saved so many souls from shipwreck in the dead of night   Ernest had a nursemaid, Rhoda, at the time (—imagine that! your very own maid! I says) & she took him down to see the bits & bobs afloat upon the water from where that boat got stuck on a rock in the Neck, between the Cow & Calf

    It was called the S. S. Eric
    It were A Sealer

Father & two others found her crashed in the winter storm, stuck out on the rocks & they got every man up & alive
    they all had to jump the pans in a heavy sea   if they fell they would get ground to death among the pans before they drowned   & one who had lost use of his legs with frostbite got them smashed to bits when they hove him up the cliff by a rope, but even so he would have lost them legs anyway they thought, & in the end he DID LIVE, WHICH IS THE MAIN THING!   Father sent word back to Mother to

ready a brigade's worth of Soup & Hot Buns, her & Grandmother & any other woman they could muster, so that those forty-odd men what nearly drowned could get warm again as quick as possible   & everyone knows for that you got to start Inside the Body & work your way back Out   Blankets only got so much Purchase

Four came to our house & Ernest says he was in charge of stripping all the quilts off the beds to wrap the men in & then he was allowed to sit with them in the kitchen even though it was nighttime   & though he wanted to hear what it had been like to be shipwrecked, they did not speak much but just ate their meals & then lay down where they were with the blankets on them

later they gave Father a medal & there were a special service in his honour at Church

when I did not believe this story (as Ernest has been known to flannel me from time to time), he snuck into Father's wardrobe & produced the Evidence, a medal sure enough, with embossed letters saying Royal Humane Society of London, with a figure of a man in a sheet on it & a blue-striped ribbon to hang it round your neck

Father knew just what to do that night, he did not waver, & by the time the news spread & other folks showed up to help, all hands were already up the cliffside & safe, & Father had set to work on the old man's legs, cutting back his trousers & getting him in makeshift splints till they could bring him inside & fetch the doctor from Bonavista

he is the same now   he would still be the first to sight an
accident, the first to respond   the strong one others
look to as their Captain in times of Danger   he would
have the most ability to combat natural disaster because Nature
is His Home, he knows how to find his way in Her, how to be
comfortable in the most undesirable of conditions

when he's indoors I can see he is resentful of the walls, the still,
stale air   we must all make sure to keep our voices low &
tread carefully so as not to vex him

I study my arithmetic as best I can, for I think he features me
his legacy in the store, the one with the head to Work Accounts
        & though I don't got much stock in that, I do what I can &
strain against my natural inclinations as he has had to do
        (as must all men in some capacity, it is a mark of what
makes us unique among the Species)

Bob is more Nature than Culture, but most of the rest of us is the
other way around

I likes it Outdoors good enough but should not like to Live There
        har har

Baby Arthur is so small still that it's hard to tell with him
        (though he does like the wind on his face, when Mother
lets me take him on little strolls)   right now it's hard
to tell which way he will turn, but soon he too will Settle
        maybe Father gave him his own first name in the hopes
that Baby Arthur will take after him, & be a Hero   most
at home all alone by hisself, in the heart of the Deep Dark
Forest

(Mother told us the Little People live there   & also a Witch with a Candy House who boils up Naughty Children for her Dinner, but I DO NOT BELIEVE HER)

I look like I never worked boat before due to my pallor this
morning

—don't get sick on your way down the river, my son
        shouts our man Clare from dockside
—if I do it's on your head, you know, you & your constant
carousing
—take care, Dukey, write me sometimes
—& yourself, you rascal   say hello to Bessie for me
—I'll give her a squeeze for you, my boy, & a few other things
—I should think you will!
—watch out for wolves up there   especially if you're
travelling solo
—how motherly! I didn't think you cared!

he blows me kisses from shore, which makes me laugh, rather
than feel sorry to leave him, though I dare say that sentiment
shall creep in rather quickly in the coming days

there's a mite of difference being on a steamer when you're
travelling Passenger instead of as a Working Man

this ship's older & also larger than my Dawson
            the Ida May is known by all as the best boat to catch
downstream to St. Michaels, especially at the end of the season
            despite her age, she's built swift & solid & can crack
her way through ice, if pressed

there's four hundred of us Passengers & fifty Deckhands   &
after working boat for months I feel more at home with the
latter   though to tell the truth there isn't much difference
between us, this go-round   most of us Passengers got to
find a place on deck to put our blankets & that's all you can do
            she's stuffed to the gills & if you want passage at all there's
no sense complaining   meals are about the same, though
there's Pork sometimes   the problem is there aren't many
tables in the dining hall & if you don't get in there quick the
ones ahead eats all the food & there's nothing but Buns & Gravy
to console you with   I don't mind so much, having slept
bunkside & worked the boiler for ten hours a day most of the
summer with not much but Slop for Grub, most days
            having learned if not to Enjoy, at least to Tolerate my
Present Conditions   besides, the Passengers gets to go
to the Saloon & who cares if there's naught but Buns for Dinner
once you've had your dose of Decent Scotch Whisky

it isn't much fun sleeping on deck, though, once the frost begins
to form   & I wish I could go down & work the Boiler for
a while, just to keep warm out of it

when we tie up at Eagle City the mate next to me gives me a
nudge   —hope you brought your bankroll, because now
we're in Alaska   Life moves a Hell of a lot faster from
here on in

though Gambling is outlawed down in Dawson & in White
Horse, on this side of the line it is Industry   & you know
some men came up here just for that, you can see it in their
eyes, what look like Shiny American Nickels   no laws here
in The District of Alaska, or not yet, so the Eagle City folks are
eager to clean up on the boats coming up the river   there's
only one Saloon in town but it's a big one with plenty of card
tables & plenty of liquor   though to my disappointment no
Dancing Girls with feathers, & few Ladies at all   just some
of the commoner types of Whores, leaning on the staircase or
sitting on the laps of the card players   everybody ready to
take all the Fun they can from the evening

the big games begin at nine o'clock, but I'm not playing
          I can't spare the money, though I'm itching to double my
lot as I see some mates do   to send something home
early to Father

but I know I have no Luck in me & it is best to shy away from
games of that sort   & besides I am distracted by the Fairer
Sex in all its states of Shamelessness, & though the sight is not
so dazzling as down in Dawson, it is still Welcome

I am having a fine enough time without betting a cent & the
Gazes are free as well, so it is only my Whisky & Grub what
costs me   by ten o'clock I am soused & so it seems is
everybody   one gent by the door knocks the card table
over onto his competitors   —this game is rigged! I knew
you Alaskan rats was crooked   give me my money or
you'll get my fists down on you & I can't be responsible for what
happens after that

this shouted over top of the din of the Saloon, which is so big that they set up two gramophones, one at either end, the first playing Over the Waves & the other, In the Sweet Bye-&-Bye, buddy yelling bloody murder on top of these two tunes meeting each other in the middle where the tables is & it is quite the racket   though I notice this only makes for more Business for the Ladies   seems the more Ruckus gets kicked up the more we Crave to Satisfy our Urge to Repopulate

around midnight things really get out of hand & of course there's no Mounties to come & put the lid on it, now that we've crossed the border   a fist fight begins & that is all right for a start till all hands joins in & you can see the teeth flying   then a gambler pulls a gun from out of the drawer under his card table, a hard-looking sort I had marked before as one not to stare at too long, lest he take offence & deck me —everyone settle!   & the gunshot puts the lamp out (my heart jumping right into my mouth at the sound)   the gun goes off again, more & more shots   BANG! BANG!   till all the lights are out & we are in complete darkness with everything being cleaned out & smashed   the men just letting their Natures out, hitting at whoever might be near them in the Black

the shrieks of Ladies everywhere in the dark & I let out a gasp when one finds my arm & clings to me, the feel of her half-clothed Bosoms pressed up into my back, soft & warm   I dare not breathe till a few minutes later when I leave her safe under a table & head right quick out the back way with wobbly legs & hands

(I had taken care to mark my exits earlier, having learned that lesson down in Dawson)

I stop in the back lane to get my bearings, glad to be clear of the fracas, but some of it has spilled out of the bar so I have to keep walking & end up sleeping in the church, which is a better place than most of the rest found tonight, I'll bet

by the time dawn breaks the town is transformed with the sleeping bodies of drunken Passengers everywhere   some have all their money gone from Gambling, Whoring or Getting Robbed, though many can't remember which has happened to them   I awaken on the front pew of the Anglican church & the Minister lends me some paper to write to Father & let him know I am well & have reached Alaska & have found a House of God, though not the sort to rightly suit him   (at least it is not Catholic!)

my mate Simms is sleeping there, too, so we go to the Post Office together & then back towards the Saloon to see how bad the damage looks

some men are still curled up in the frosty thoroughfare, passed out around stolen bottles, which they had nicked as the lights went out   some who woke early are trying to pry the Painkiller out of their mates' frozen, sleeping fingers, desperate for a swallow to rid them of their chills

we walk by the remains of the two gramophone horns
          both smashed to bits & rolled down the bank of the river
I suppose somebody did not enjoy the Medley

those horns look powerfully sad lying there busted up on the
bank like that   it cannot help but put me in mind of M— &
those operas she had sent over to her from the British relations,
with German or French names in curly script on the front of the
casings   You never heard such Sounds!

when we get to the Saloon it looks like it has been attacked by
the Kaiser   all the windows are smashed out & the
verandah is tore off & half of the wood already stole, I guess by
Locals   there are no bottles on the shelves inside & bodies
are lying everywhere, though when folks begin to stir it is clear
there were no Deaths, despite the Chaos   men & women
alike are just knocked out or out cold from drink or plain asleep
on the floor of the bar where they'd hidden the night before
          tis a Miracle

I find the table in the corner where I'd left the girl last night, &
there she is, curled up & happy as a cat, about eighteen & on the
stout side but with a pretty face, at least while she is sleeping

I leave her a nickel, although she done nothing for me except
press into me a little in her panic   (at least now I can say
that one time I paid a Working Woman, when I'm old & they
ask me about My Travels!)

to be Frank, I do grow tired of this   I cannot wait till I gets
to The Back Country where Bob is & we have no more Saloons
about   & no more Women, no Cards or Drink taunting us
in our Weakness

Tormenting the Worst Aspects of Our Natures
Till We Become the Poorest Versions of Ourselves

I get to my forest place & lay down my vest for a bed on top of
the squish of moss & needles under a little cave made of an old
fallen tree with the circle of its roots now tipped up out of the
ground   the moss is orange & drier than the green moss,
better for napping or just lounging around

this do be at the cliff's edge & at the edge of the woods too
              where the two do meet   so I get the sea breeze for
the flies & the shade of branches too, which is important when
you're one of The Driven, prone to crisping up in sunshine like
the rind on Jennie's Sunday Ham

this is my lonesome spot, what sets my heart right when it is off
kilter   no one else would come here as it's nothing but a
moose trail & the way is muddy & steep & the view not as good
as Beach or Island & there is no Berry here to speak of at all

but to me it is Heaven, & Heaven feels like having a Secret Spot
where there is no separation between you & the moss & ferns &
sea & sky & sap on trees & the partridge thumping now & again
not too far away from where I lie

(Father would call that Dinner
so I will not tell him about it!
  HE DO NOT NEED
  TO KNOW ALL!)

The Captain has the crew up at the crack to get the lashings off
the wheel & let the engines warm up   I can hear them
starting their work from my blanket up on deck, the familiar
clang, the voices grown stiff overnight, calling out their good
mornings & their dirty salutations   they are working fast
          that slush is packing tight now   we can smell
Winter closing in

I get up to watch them at their work   it is better than just
lying out with a scum of frost on me   it is warmer by the
hatch down to the furnace   a few others found this out too
& we all crouches round & someone hands the tea down the line

today is not the same though
when I opened my eyes this morning I knew today was Marked
I had The Shiver, as Mabel would call it
& sure enough:
soon after we are underway, the current of the river snaps one
of the frozen Eccentric Rods, 20 feet long & 3 inches thick, just
like it was a matchstick
& by this point we're gone much past Eagle City but not halfway
near Tanana

& our Food is scarce & of poor quality
& our Whisky stores are sorely depleted
& we have our fair share of souls on board so we know we're
doomed if we can't fix it but we only have a small hand forge to
work with

I say We although now I am A Passenger & not even supposed
to help   luckily the coal is plentiful & with several Stokers
on the shovel the Chief begins his work

they shovel full tilt into the firebox, & I watch from the side of
the hatch, itching to join in & help the struggle to get the fire
hot enough   the Chief jumps the rod together, the sparks
flying out this way & that from the white hot in the middle & we
are cheering him on   the Eccentric Rod looks solid,
though a tad lumpen   & we Passenger Men help hoist it
up the hole when it's cool enough & put it in place, but in the
freezing weather the thing immediately busts again

the Passengers are really shaken when they see this, for word is
out that we've Limited Stores, most of which are Mouldy
          & no one wants to Die stuck halfway up the Yukon River,
or Survive by Feasting on your Neighbour   such thoughts
don't make no one too Cheerful!

the Chief is swearing & kicking at the Eccentric Rod   —I'm
damned if I can fix this   useless Yukon Steel   he kicks
the rod again & stubs his toe   —I need a drink! do we have
any Blacksmiths, travelling Blacksmiths here among us?

Buddy steps up what slept two bodies down from me last night
          Mike Piercey   & of course wouldn't you know but

he's a Newfoundlander   from his voice I can tell straight
off that he's from somewhere up the Cape Shore

Mike Piercey, travelling up a ways to start a smithy   there's
probably good money in it & I have always admired the skill, so
I crowd in further to see this N.F.L.D. Blacksmith do his work
        & though he's but a small man, he swings that hammer
something fierce down on the molten shape of the rod with
more precision & more feeling than our man Chief Engineer
        a few of us Passengers descends to help & I do not mind
being back in the Boiler Room at all   some go to
hoisting the rod there in the slings & I set to the bellows to get
the fire hotted   it feels good to help in time of crisis
instead of being relegated to the sidelines   Piercey
punching it together quickly while we all struggle to keep his
fire raised

he pronounces it done & orders us bring it up on deck   &
when it has cooled he picks up a sledge & pounds it down onto
the join with a hearty Clang

—go ahead, Chief, & let us get started   I guarantee it'll
break any other place before it breaks there again

& Clare's voice in my head says   —See, Dukey, boy
        the Newfoundlander is always there with the goods,
when he's needed
& I join in with the cheering for Mike Piercey the Blacksmith, &
when he passes by I clap him on the arm
—nice work, Piercey, is it?
—you from Bonavist'?
—out Bird Island Cove way, but close enough   Duke Tilly,

brother to Bob what works up here   how long you been
over on this side of the World?

we start to walk together back to the passenger deck, pressing
through the throngs of The Curious

—this is my first trip up   I hope to start a smithy in
Fairbanks & send for the wife in a year or two, if things get
civilized
—lots of work for a smith out here, I reckon   my brother's a
Sourdough & I plan to meet him at his camp & go partners
          he wrote he was on to a promising prospect & couldn't
keep up with the work   truth be told he don't know I'm
coming but I aim to surprise him
—& stay how long
—as long as I got the strength I suppose   I got to make
some serious money before I fix to go back Outside
          though with some luck it won't be long between us till
we strike a fat seam
—well, good luck to you   look me up whenever you're in
Fairbanks   I figure I'll be easy to find
—yes, we'll have a drop of Whisky   & if I need my
Eccentric Rod fixed, well I'll know where to go
—or horses shod   rocker boxes   an axe   you
dream it up   write me in advance & send the message in
          I can have your gear made for you by the time you
reaches town

we clap arms again & I crawl under my blanket on the freezing
cold deck to avoid a chill, what's easy to catch after working up
a sweat & then sitting around in below zero temperatures in the
open air on the Yukon River, on days this late in the year

Today I seen
    1 frog in bog on road
    1 robin with worm
    8 humpbacks surrounded by 2000 gulls & about 450 puffins
    3 squirrel & a mink behind the chickens
    1 eagle
    many cormorants   80?
    2 cats (wild)
    Mr Power's flock of sheep   35?
    & Lightning, but I do not count him for he is more a Brother
than a Horse to me, & I believe I love him more than anyone
I know

        His Eyes are More Kind
        His Nature More Trustworthy

Jennie is not the same when she goes over to Picnic Island
Jennie's eyes are no longer kind there, & I did not know how
much I would feel sickened, now that her way has turned so
sharply   she is a different person over on the Island, sitting
on a blanket with Gar Penney & Petey Hiscock & a few other
rough ones who don't give us so much as a smile, we are Too
Good for it, I suppose

Jennie has made her choice   she has crossed the meadow
over to them & sat down on their dirty blanket, laughing hard in
that way that makes her mean, leaning back on her elbow with
the sun bringing out the red in her hair

she's taking sips of Rum off Petey & he's saying something that
must be Comic Genius because she got her head tipped back
so far from laughter I fear her neck cannot bear the weight

SNAP! JENNIE'S NECK!

& WE ARE TRAPPED ON THIS ISLAND WITH NO WAY
TO GET OFF EXCEPT BY PULLEY CHAIR & NO ONE IS IN
SHOUTING DISTANCE TO HELP US! JENNIE HAS A
SPASM & BLOOD IS IN HER NOSTRILS!   IT IS OVER
SO QUICKLY!   ALAS SHE IS NOW DEAD!
& THERE IS NOTHING ANY MAN CAN DO ABOUT IT!

(we would call the picnic off, of course, & head back to land in the
chair, two-by-two, pulling ourselves on the cable strung across
the bay   squeaking in slowly like guilty laundry, me sitting
with Dead Jennie & pulling for us both with my magically
enlarged arm muscles, as in the funnies

& at her Funeral no one would cry but me & she would not have
a Head Stone, having none of her own money & Father thinking
it a frivolous expense for a Hired Girl & her own family having
shut the door to her, all save her sister, who don't believe in
cemeteries, or Churches, or Father & his Authority, or much else
that I can figure   & who some do call names, which I will
not utter they are so Foul

I would plant some Boys Love on the bare plot of Jennie's grave
to give her fragrance through all time, & Sweetest Dreamings
          & around the spot I'd put a living fence of blackberry, of
raspberry & hawthorn, which would overgrow her altogether,
over the years, & give me permission, therefore, To Forget

& life would go on as usual but we'd cook for ourselves &
Jennie's chores would get divvied up among the girls

& everything would be much the same   & we would clear
out her room   & could even take a boarder if the need for
it arose)

I sit on the blanket with Kate & James & Genie & Billy Rex &
Mary Lawrence & a few others & we are only twenty feet from
her but it's like she don't see us or if she do, she wishes she
couldn't   like it is US who shame HER, not the other
way around

it is HER what works for Father   HER what is
paid in room & board & one new dress or pair of boots per year
or a new coat, she must choose

she's got last year's rough green washing dress on & should not
look so brazen like she's the Queen of Maberly, but her crown
of daisies & clover flower turns that ugly dress into a natural
part of the meadow & Jennie's now a Good Person, not a Real
Person at all   & Gar & all the others are Charmed

the light catches her different than the rest of us
marks her out as one to be wary of
(she may well Bewitch you, if you are not Most Careful)

Kate pinches my side & passes me the pail of crab legs
        I fish out four that I lay in front of me, all lined up neat
on M— 's old rose & robin tablecloth   she's got lemonade
mixed strongly with Grandmother's Gin in a stout bottle &
I nick it from her for a swallow
—don't be gawking over there, Dukey   she whispers
—over where
—I got my eye on you
—what for, Katie
—I'm not stunned   I got eyes & ears
—you do?
—I am aware of what is happening
—Let's see: a picnic, crab legs, you're half-soused, I'm bored,
Clare is hard on her & said he's going to jump in the south side
without any clothes

this last distracts her   I knew it was bound to, Kate being
set on our Cousin Clare since she was a baby & he would sing
to her in his high boy's voice & gently comb out the knots in
her hair   gentler than M— & much more so than Alice,
who didn't have the patience   Kate sucks on her second
crab leg & doesn't speak, a little too interested in its contents,
having never been one to relish shellfish
(Another Rhyme!)

(I note my rhymes down sometimes
for M—, in the hopes She is Watching Over Me
& from On High she reads these Verses
Copied out neat in a Ledger Book
Which I took from the Store
but I will admit as I grow older I knows this to be Soft Thinking
        & once written down my rhymes don't seem so grand at all

& I think they are a foolish pastime for a grown man of twenty
years like myself
& M— would not like em anyway, she would see their Poverty
& so I have torn most of them up
& have taken Vows to desist in their Creation

For Tis a Sin to Waste
So Much Good Paper)

I spare Jennie one more glance as I suck the sweet crab out of
its brittle case

she's let Petey put his head in her lap now

& though her fingers are not in his hair
& she is looking at the sea, not down at him
it is but Cold Comfort

—I'm going to go find Clare & see if he needs rescuing   who
wants to join me?

James gets up & so do Billy with two crab legs each for the
journey, we three spitting bits of shell into the grass & sharing a
bottle between us   & me grinning to myself as I watch
Kate's colour rise at the thought of following us & how she
daren't try it, although she longs to see Clare out there in his
Nature more, I think, than anyone else, even his present
sweetheart, Ethel Baker, or Annie Baker before her (Elder Sister
& now Bitter Rival), or Maggie Butt, who I know would don a
certain dress for him & tie her hair back in a pressed white
ribbon, when she saw him in the distance, heading up the shore

October 19, 1906

We get to Tanana at two o'clock in the morning & this far into
Alaska that's not too late for much of the carousing   the
sky full bursting with blues & greens & yellows in a pulsing
dance that makes me dizzy   especially when coupled
with all the noise & music coming from the town

everybody is anxious to get to shore in anticipation of a good
meal, & a spell near a woodstove, & other things, depending on
their Natures   the Saloons are flooded with Gamblers &
the Perverse as well as the Plain Hungry & I tell myself I'll go in
but only long enough to eat my meal & then back out again & to
the nearest Church to catch forty winks & then write home to
Father   I hope twill set his mind at ease to know I'm
come this far & am close to Bob & to making some money
          just got to find out the route & buy the rest of my kit &
then I am off in search of him   so surely one last hour in a
Saloon is not too Sinful

there's seven to choose from & I take a gander at all of them,
poking my nose in long enough to view the scenery & smell the
perfume of Booze, Smoke, Lamp Oil, Women & Blood, varying
from hall to hall only in terms of Proportion of Ingredients

I settle on the last place   out of indifference, mainly
          the folks here seem to have come at their card games
late in the night so they aren't as worked up to the point of
potential riot if a misdeal might be called

big games running in every saloon with the Card Sharps
cleaning up on the last boat up the river till spring   the
Passengers throwing away their money quick as they can
because there's no more saloons after Tanana & the Temptation
is too great, they cannot Help It   the Sharps laying back
in their seats, the winning's too easy

I watch this happen from the corner of the seventh saloon,
tipping back the Whisky   taking my time searching out
the curves   full, round & sweet   my eyes
lingering on choice round lines   warm as Fresh
Bread & just as Nourishing———————————Jennie————Jennie
————~~I do miss you & I miss dead baby Arthur~~————————
~~Jennie I am sorry for what we did when we were young~~————
————~~Jennie I long to do things I daren't even think about~~————
~~it's only Whisky what keeps me from it, anchoring me here on~~
~~this stool so that I don't jump up & act like Clare, taking one of~~
~~these girls by the hips & holding her against the wall with my~~
~~Manhood pressed into her, my head in her bodice, glorying in~~
~~the taste of her Nipples while the whole bar is free to watch~~————
————————~~the stares making me all the more dedicated as I root at~~
~~her Flesh~~———————————~~attempting to bury myself alive in a~~
~~Cathouse Girl's Bosoms~~

Whisky, Drown Me!
DROWN THESE THOUGHTS
Curses to Clare

For Rousing Up Things
I Thought Dead & Lost!

I tell the Barkeep to hurry with my Bully Beef & Potatoes as I must
leave here quick before the Devil catches me up
—Alaska makes the spirit Wild & it's like your Virtues wash away
till you're nothing but a skeleton clothed in Vices, each one
Sourer than the last   —you're right about that one, Chum

the Beef arrives & I chow it down fast, my gorge rising but I can't
help but cram it in   Nothing but Stomach   I ask
the Barkeep do he know Bob, as is my want to do with all new
faces since crossing into the District   & he near causes
my heart to seize up when he says sure, Bob been a customer,
off & on, since '98, when he's in town, but he works at his camp
upriver, most of the year

I got no breath while he's talking Bob   Bob lost to me since
I was a boy, though I can still feature his jawline & brow in my
mind if I work at it   Bob what used to terrorize me with his
fists if I said I'd tell about the girls he'd have his hands into
          Bob what used to fish in the morning then work the
land all afternoon & once evening came went just as hard &
dedicated at his Pleasures   Bob the Provider & Bob the
Curse & Bob the Bear of a Man who in my mind is two times the
size of me with hands like hamhocks   this bell starts
ringing down the street & I think maybe someone caught
Bonanza Fever but then remember about the wedding

there was this young one on ship named Ella Jane   she
was not a Scarlet or a Hall Girl either but a Society Lady   &
she was due to be married on arrival to some big Muckamuck &

sure enough in they come straight from the church, she with
flowers in her hair   the owner of the saloon orders his girls
upstairs to get respectable as we's to host the wedding party
            the groom shouts to the grumbling gamblers what are
being displaced   —don't worry chaps   all seven bars
are open on the house!   for seven days!   go elsewhere
tonight   you got a week of drink on me & don't say Sam
Tate ain't generous

that changes the general mood of the establishment & next
thing you know the piano starts up   it turns out one of the
Working Girls, the one with black hair in two long braids, is
also very Musical   I want to say to the Barkeep to tell me
all he knows of Bob but that poor soul has enough work for ten
men now what with the flow of liquor ordained by Sam Tate
            so I sit & watch the black haired girl who looks much finer
when engaged in her playing   & I wish to listen to her play
until the morning comes, but am grabbed by a Passenger Lady
& drawn into the dancing   she is bold for a Woman of
Character!   I assign it to her seniority   a full ten years
older than me or more with a modest dress buttoned to her
chin as well as gloves, but smiling just as open as the Whores
                placing my hand upon her waist, making me lead
her around the saloon floor!   under the thick serge
of her dress I can feel the warmth & the bone & the flesh of her
                her hair smells of lilac water

the room whirling round us & coming apart in the sides of my
vision as this stranger's eyes are fixed on mine & we are dancing
into the other laughing & unlikely couples

the Working Girls watch longingly from the stairwell

(they love to dance, but at weddings they're not allowed out on the floor)

& I'll admit it, Jennie   that night under the church pew I go to sleep with my hands Upon Myself   thinking not of you, & not of anyone in particular, more a kaleidoscope picture, turning & fragmenting, of the varied shapes of Womanhood folding one into another   bits & bobs of women lacing together in a dizzy array

Me with my Hands Working
Thinking on that Lilac Smell

Guilty & Happy
As I Sink into Sleep
From Whose Depths
I Shall Carry Back Nothing

Though I had planned to start looking for Bob in the morning
I stay in Tanana for a week with the wedding party, drinking
until I am that soused I can't speak & dancing is impossible
          it's hard to resist a week's drunk from someone else's
pocket & I am in plentiful company   falling down each
night in a corner with a group of other men in similar states,
one of whom is bound to have a bottle   all of us toasting
to Sam Tate's health & to that of his wife with our arms around
each other, newfound friends with bonds between us forged
from a full week's soak in Whisky

& though we do not know each other's names, there's real love
there
& I can't bear to leave these folks & head on out to look for Bob,
not before it's Necessary
& then on Day Six my mood turns sour
& I question the Purpose of My Existence
& on Day Seven I am that tired of being stagger-drunk I quits at
noon, a full twelve hours before the end of Sam Tate's Generosity
& by 4 o'clock I feels almost Sober

I goes up to the Post Office, which got a line around the perimeter of folks waiting to get in & find their news out   it looks pretty plain, a log building like the rest, but when you step through the door she's like a church, with shafts of light coming through the smooth panes of glass & lighting up the neat edges of holy white paper in their spotless, varnished pigeon-holes   shiny men in shirtcuffs with waxed whiskers gingerly lift the envelopes out of the cubbies as though the Mail were Poke

& I suppose sure enough them Letters are good as Gold round here, they take so long to make it to this Territory   all the men hungry for a bit of News from Home, be it Portugal, the United States of America, England, Russia, Italy   or N. F. L. D.

I buy a few postcards   one for Father one for Jennie 'I have reached Tanana. Heading for Bob as soon as possible. Give Lightning his oats for me. Your loving son, Duke'   'When the leaves fall from the trees, oh Jennie, do you think of me? Your Friend, Duke'   I hope Father allows her to see it (I find it hard to be formal, & did my best at least to be brief)

her postcard has a snap of my steamer S. S. Dawson
          Father's has one of Tanana's mission (C of E), to show him I'm committed to My Betterment

I ask the postal clerk with perfect walrus moustaches who takes my coins for postcards do he know if Bob Tilly has mail here as I am his brother & plan to set out for him straight   he says he can see the resemblance round the eyes   I always thought I looked more like James than anybody, or M— perhaps

the clerk asks me am I going to the Homestead, then
& that's the first I heard of it

—two miles out of town's where he keeps his Wife & Kids but
like as not he's upriver in the country his own self

he tells me the way to get to Bob's kin   I tell him thank you,
& take the few articles addressed to them, tucked into my waist-
coat for safekeeping

Bob got a Wife
& Bob got Children!

though he's always kept his news to himself, I never figured he
would keep from us that he had A Family

I got Nephews maybe Nieces I never met   & I got a woman
foreign to me what's now a Sister, by Marriage   this is
Strange   & I think it's Welcome

I have Kin   someone to anchor me here, where nothing is
quite Homely

—Mrs Tilly would be the one to give you proper directions up to
the camp   it's a fair ways out but if you start soon I would
say you'll catch him before the winter really hits   & give
him my regards, Willis Keeping at the Tanana Postal Office, if
you please

that night I goes back to the church to get some winks in
         though it is not the right denomination to suit Father,
the rector there is a good sort what will give out paper to write

your letters on & share his bread with you as well   I am
sore tempted to open Bob's mail & wish I had one addressed to
me   he has one there from Daisy & one from Alice &
I can already guess the kind of nonsense they have put down
about their easy life in the State of Massachusetts & how they
won a prize for preserves or how they have put lilies in the
garden   a kind of life that seems impossible now that I am
in this place, not that I feel any sort of longing for that gossipy
town or Ernest's thumb or that factory   I sets down my
kit, such as it is, at the foot of the back pew & stretch myself upon
it   though it is but hard plank it feels like an embrace
to this sad body   my spine clicking back into a straight
shape with the coax of the board, drawing itself back into its full
length, what was beginning to curl up like an orange peel from
Nonstop Adventure in the Alaskan Territory

We go up the path half soaked in Rum & Gin, we three arm in arm like Musketeers   James starts up a song so's to hear Clare answer him   they are like two birds with their singing out, doing call & answer on The Darby Ram   James's lower voice echoing off the rocks into Clare's tenor

I wonder if Kate can hear this back at the picnic field, & if her face have turned beet red yet

that one is in a fix, she is so smitten   Father has made it clear that while other souls on the Shore may permit it, he do not allow his family to marry inwards, not even Second & Third Cousins, it is as bad as courting below your Station   so Kate's designs on Clare have been marked a sin against Christian Thinking   & though he will pal around with her & may well goad her on with the ease of his flattery he is like that with everyone & I do not think Clare has ever had intentions toward her   & Kate's badly hidden feelings, therefore, make me sore & tender with Brotherly Love, but I also like to tease her with it as she thinks that no one may guess Her Secret Thoughts   & yet any talk of himself do get her jumping like she has fire ants nesting in her skirts

I tease her more than I should, perhaps, but it helps me to distract myself

James calls out & Clare answers, sounding closer than before
        he has gone down the Gulch I think, which is hard to climb back up again, but there is a large rock standing up out of the water there & it is an ideal place from which to sail into the ocean without no skivvies on

Clare is on the rock bowing to the onlookers, who are all men of course   he's already stripped down to the waist & James is singing a bit of jaunty reel to encourage the show & we let out a round of cheers as Clare gets down to his skin & shows his milk white arse to us before hollering like a Savage as he drops into the sea & the water turns to foam

10 seconds when I fear the worst, Clare always been so reckless

& then up he pops with a screech & shivering something fierce, like to chip his teeth from it

—come on in, boys, the water is divine
—you're off your head, James shouts back
—come on, Jim boy, you're as bad as a woman   someone's got to come down here & join me   who got the guts
        not Dukey, I know   how about Gerald?
will you take up the challenge?

Gerald don't answer, he's laughing strangely at something happening over on his side of the bluff   he steps back to let a mate pass by & then I sees what he got to laugh about

Down onto the Rock climbs Mabel!
Dressed only in her Petticoat
With her Hair loose all around her!

Mabel, from over in Maberly!
& no one takes a Breath or Drink
For what must be One Minute!

after she surfaces & with her hair flat to her head she don't look
so much like Jennie, but in the everyday you can see that they
are sisters   though Mabel is darker & elder & a mite taller
& one might say she also has a stronger frame meant to better
Withstand Life's Torments Without Buckling   but the eyes,
their mouths, their laugh, the way they flick their long braids
like Ponies, these things are the same & so Mabel seems more
familiar to me than the sum of our acquaintance should warrant
          & I can predict sometimes her Look or Action as though
she has been more great a presence in my life than mere sister
to our Working Girl

but Mabel WET is a Brand New Mabel, she got a shape to her
which is a sight to gaze on & one day I would like a stereoscope
like James's & a card of this vision, Mabel in Bird Island Gulch
In her Petticoat, Dripping Wet, Standing On a Rock Beside My
Dashing, Dripping Cousin

& don't Clare look miserable, shivering there forgotten as Mabel
starts climbing up the side

no one goes to help her & the cloth is slicked down on her like
whitewash so I can see even her Navel, & certain other Parts,
beside

some of the boys are running back up the path now, as though she'll charm them (& tis true she do resemble a Mermaid, as much as Human Woman at High Tide) & others like myself are as perfectly frozen as the victims of a Medusa, doomed to stand before her as statues & gaze on her forevermore with the love-beams in our eyes

there is a power in that soaking petticoat & I do not know if she knows it to be so, but Mabel could at this moment order us about with obtuse whims & we would gladly walk to Bonavista to get her some particular thread or button, we would build a boat for her or slaughter our cow just so she might drink a cup of its blood, we would swear never to love any but herself even if she should scorn us in future   Mabel on the Rocks is so powerful that we cannot help her climb them, though she has bare feet & between the rock itself & the nettles we know she'll be tore up

it do not matter
we cannot touch her
she is now a sort of Religious Figure
& No Mortal Girl

I am dizzy with drinking & I squat down as my vision gets filled with blood spots   I lie on the path & let my eye bring into focus the variety of tiny organisms living here in the constant brunt of the wind   some Animal & some Vegetable, desperately latched onto the Mineral   I will be fine & overcome this & all will be well if I DO NOT DRINK MORE & also EAT NO MORE CRAB LEGS   those actions will undo me (like one or another of the Chants girls

I can see it now:

THEY WILL BE YOUR UNDOING!
BEWARE CHANTS OF ALL SORTS!

a Prophecy written in dark red splotches, covering everything, floating above the lichen, hovering in front of me no matter where I looks

I do not wish to heed it, & drive my palms into my eyes with forcefulness sufficient to make the letters swim   & break apart)

The road to the homestead is made of mud   a semi-frozen
ooze with a skin of snow   with stones & the odd patch of
horse dung worked into it   & I suppose if anything I got
to say Thank You Lord that I am not walking it in Mosquito
Season   I got holes in my boots & make a determination to
save my money from draining out the small end of the bottle, as
I must clothe myself more proper to suit this situation if I want to
remain whole for long enough to rescue Father from the weight
Templeman is exerting on his head

the road is but two miles   but two miles in the snow &
mud is not a short distance

puts me in mind of Lightning & our saunters up the shore in
the summer, once both our work was done for the day & the cart
unhooked   he did so like to go for a ride & though he never
quite was broken he was a good horse, & I could take his antics
without falling

I do dream about him

what I wouldn't do for a sit on Lightning's back at the moment
& a canter to carry me where I am headed instead of relying on

my own short paces   slopping up this road on my sorry
legs, gone down to nothing but the sticks from lack of eating
this past while

there's a scattered place or two along the way but they are spread
out thin, closed in by trees, good places to live if you wants to
keep your secrets   & some of them I pass by don't got
anything in the window holes or else there's no window holes at
all, just solid wood & no light getting in to their interiors   &
some are grander with real glass panes & gardens hemmed in
with fences, though most things are long since pulled up   &
I think about the root cellars at home & how if he don't got
one I will build a cellar, for Bob & me to keep our taties in

I keeps on walking because that's my directions from Willis
Keeping though it seems about ten miles not two & I am dumb
with hunger   he said there's a path off the road & you won't
see the cabin right away but there's a yellow rag tied round a
tree at the turning & you can't miss it   —as long as the
ravens didn't come down picking the rag away, he said with a
smile   & I could not parse the odds of that possibility

late afternoon I spies the rag, waving Hello in the wind   a
bit dirty, what with hanging out in the weather, but definitely
yellow as per Keeping's description   & I wonder is it the
colour of Mrs. Bob's hair   I wonder if either of their
children is named after me   or named for Baby Arthur,
what was named after Father   though thinking on it Bob
never met Babby before he Passed Over & suddenly I am sick
to my heart with fear, though of what exactly I cannot say,
except to meet these new faces of the Family   I got faces
enough that need something from me, no matter how many

miles I travel into how many different countries   & also
I got a lump in my throat that longs to see a Woman again
          a creature not of the dance halls but a Woman like
the ones from home what keeps good house & teaches their
daughters how to sew & write & starch their sheets, darn socks,
make duff & figgy pudding

my feet proceed down the yellow rag path at a slower pace &
I fish for the letters in my coat   I will hand them over
first thing, in case my speech deserts me

as I come upon it I see it is a cabin like many of the others
          waxed flour sacks for windows   they let the light
inside but give you no view to speak of   & though not
tiny it is not big   there is a small patch of field that has
been fought from the trees with rows tilled in & stones forming
its outline, & right close to the house I think there may even be
the remains of roses, the thorny twigs stiff & leafless   I can
feature what colour they must add in summer to this place
          the wife must have planted them as Bob never had
much heart for it   he always said why waste my time
on flowers when I could be eating what I sow   (the
opposite of James, who went ape for the showiest colours &
would often cut a few blooms in the morning to pin to his shirt
front, which made some girls go mad for him & others think
him Soft)   but maybe Bob's a changed man since
entering the wild territory, wanting something to civilize it,
roses doing the trick with their velvety petals pink as a
Maiden's Blush

there is a thin curl of smoke coming out of the roof-hole
there is not A Chimney

I can smell stew of some kind & I know I won't ask for it but perhaps some would be offered, as I am a Relation

my heart racing, my feet moving, my hand stuck in front of me with them letters glued onto it & a crazed smile frozen on my face   be calm, Duke's Heart, don't betray me in a faint
          & I don't know why I got myself in such a state, but I feel like to die from Palpitations of Nervosity

when I knock on the door I can hear movement inside but no one comes to answer

I cough loud & knock again & there are voices in there of children & a woman's voice too hushing them, though I cannot make out the words

a pause ten breaths long   this feels an hour   I can feel my courage leaking out but I surmise a woman with kids alone out here in Nowhereland, Alaskan Territory got more to fear than I do, so I decide to make myself plain

I knock again & call out   —I am BOB'S BROTHER come to find him   DUKE TILLY from N. F. L. D.   BOB'S YOUNGER BROTHER   it's been a few years now but I hope he's mentioned me   I arrived in town a week past & only yesterday found out how to find you   please, I'D LIKE TO TALK TO YOU   to meet the CHILDREN   I am fixing to MEET UP WITH BOB & I HOPE TO WORK WITH HIM   I brought your mail with me & Willis Keeping at the postal office said he could SEE THE FAMILY RESEMBLANCE ROUND MY EYES   I WILL NOT CHEAT NOR HARM YOU, MISS

the door comes open just a crack   enough to stick a
musket barrel out

I raise my hands up to show I am unarmed & drop the post
          I bend down to retrieve the letters & the shot goes over
my head   the echo of it shaking the branches & I stay
crouched down, pick the letters up, my heart hammering hard
into the front of my chest, coming up my gorge like bile

—please, don't kill me   I come here as Family
bearing Letters   I have no gun on me   Please,
I'm kin to you   I just want to talk   I just need
directions to Bob   I got no intentions toward you
I don't mean to harm or scare you & am deeply sorry if I have

the door opens up a crack more & I dare not look up   a
hand plucks the mail from my shaking fingers & a moccasin
kicks hard at my side   I keep my eyes shut & lie a minute
in the snow & the muck   & after several seconds I feel
fingers on me, not rough or nothing, small fingers touching
curiously

a boy with black hair & skin like brown bread is touching my
face with little pats of his fingertips   he doesn't smile
but he looks in my eyes & then backs off quickly with some
words I don't understand from the woman, still standing in the
threshold, still aiming at me   this Indian woman with
her settler-style apron & smock & her braided hair & beaded
moccasins like a Native   half in & out of dress of each &
I am kneeling now with my forehead in the mud & overpowered,
mighty Dizzy

—please Miss, I fear I made a mistake here   I got directions
at the post office as to Bob Tilly's homestead & it was his Wife
I was hoping for   please Miss I will not keep you & did
not wish to startle you & if you would just return the post to
me I will be on my way & sorry for your trouble   Pardon
Miss I do not even know if you speaks English or not

she says my name in full & it sounds different in her mouth
          I nod my head & dare to look her in the eyes
                    she says my name again   again I nod

she lowers her gun   the boy grabs my hand & helps me up
          she steps aside to let me in

—Bob never said his Brother was coming
—He doesn't know a thing about it   it's a Surprise

Even when the other boys remove their shirts for piddly sticks
I dare not for I am Fair as the Driven, Mother says, & will not go
brown but will turn red & then my skin will start to come off in
thin white pieces like milk that is spilled & forgotten until it
dries into a sheet on the tabletop

—You're Fair as the Driven
—The Driven What?
—The Driven Snow, my love

Mother puts her hair in a braid then she coils it into a perfect
bun & tucks the end in & she doesn't need a pin to keep it in
place   she does this every morning so the only time I ever
touched her loose hair was when I had croup & she sat on my
bed late at night & put a cloth on me & her hair hung to her
waist & it was shiny, straight & brown & when she leaned
forward with the cloth it was like a curtain around the two of us,
shutting the World out & a bit of it in my fingers felt like rabbits

—you're Fair as the Driven too
—you get it from me, William, & your mouth too, I think
          & your Genius, of course!

—Genius!

—yes   I believe it   everyone is a genius at something

—they are?

—if conditions are right & they dare risk the safety of their
 everyday life to chase after it

—like your piano?

—no   my piano could have been my genius   if
 conditions were right

—they're not right now?

—they are not

—but you play at Church & teach us & no one on the Shore can
 play as good as you

—I know, but that is not all of what I might be able, had I risked
          let's start on the potatoes   go get the bucket & put
 your muck clothes on

—I love your piano, it's my favourite thing that I can think of

—that's enough, we're on to potatoes   don't make me
 cross today

—yes, Mother   but what's my Genius, then? I do not know
 it

—being the best son, better than the others   you are The
 Good Child

—but is that all I have

—that's enough   I have a headache   when you're
 grown there may be other things   now, My Good Son, do
 as I say & get the tools out   & tell me how many is four
 times eighteen plus eleven minus six plus two

—can we do one & then the other please?   I don't like doing
 them at once

—you can think while you farm, boy   you have brains
 enough for both

I go to put my muck clothes on
& when I come back she has for me
a piece of dark fruitcake tied up in a napkin
& a glass of cold water, just drawn from the well

October 30, 1906

Sin has rotted my teeth under my gums, God has done it as punishment   my back teeth on one side gone to mush, decomposing, & isn't that a funny situation

the sides of my face no longer symmetrical so I resemble a victim of hornet sting, my left cheek stuck out a full inch bigger & so tender when the Doctor touches it I can't help but yowl like a stuck cat   no way I can start out to Bob's camp like this & have stayed on extra in Tanana to get them excised & have lain in my room in the hotel in agony & absolute fear for three days straight with a vision of my own Death in the Doctor's chair looming over me   like M— I have the delicate blood & I know how much these things can affect me, I have had the spasms before just from the thought of the Doctor drawing near
        Positive Thinking is Daisy's motto so I take a page from her book & try & think of the things coming out of me, finally, not EXCISED but EXORCISED, gone from their throbbing cradles of flesh, gone & with them gone from me my Sin

    I am Repentant!
    God Forgive Me!
    Let No Breast Break Unto My Consciousness!

I Do Not Welcome You! I Shut the Windows
Of My Soul to Bosoms Forevermore!
I Shall Shun the Fleshly Dreams of Old
As Long As This Pain Will Quit (up the side of my head
into my eye like a black stabbing rod, crowned with little
bursts of white pitch)!

the Doctor is sweating like he's off his drink & he's asking me to
grip tight so I know sweet Christ it's going to hurt a treat

—a glass of Whisky if you have it, Doc

& although he is hesitant to give it me, I am glad for the burn
        the tooth coming out in a gush of blood   & under
the slash-agony of Doc chopping into my gums with not
inconsiderable gusto I can feel another pain   the soft,
rotted roots pulling free   did I do something in particular
to merit this Hellish Life or is it merely the Sum of my Faults,
Accumulated

—GOD DAMN MY NAME!
—one more coming, sir
—GOD IN HEAVEN! STOP! NO MORE! PLEASE!
—now, sir, it'll rot to infection much worse
—I CANNOT ENDURE IT!

the ends of the chair gone scrappy where I dug my nails in &
I am crying out like a birthing woman & cursing him   &
M—, & Father   & Bob for living here

WHY DIDN'T THE DOC HAVE MORE WHISKY READY
ONE GLASS OF WHISKY IS NOT ENOUGH

—all right, Mr. Tilly   the extraction is through

I got that many sobs in my throat I can't talk anymore & the
blood is gunking up my mouth so I lean over & let the drips run
out   Doc throws out his washwater & puts the bowl on the
floor between my feet & I bend over & watch my drops slishing
into the centre & spattering out into fine red bursts on the wet
porcelain

—thank you Doctor
—the bleeding should stop in a half hour but you needn't stay
here
—I don't mind sitting a spell
—that's all very well but I have another in a quarter of an hour
—a few minutes with the bowl then, & I'll quit you
—you'll be fine by Monday if you stay off the drink
—what about the pain, Doc?
—the pain will pass & you can't risk infection of the gums
            it's six days
—all right Doctor, thank you, but isn't alcohol a sterilizing liquid
—I am quite serious, sir
—yes, thank you Doctor, I believe I catch your meaning

& I close my eyes   think positive like Daisy   six days
        six days   6 DAYS with my damned swole head
gashed & slashed & kicking quite the stink up

three days & He Rose Again

God strike me down for comparing my Dental Agony to the
Pain of the Saviour who Died for Us, but even so, Six Days is an
infernal stretch

Doc puts them evil teeth on the table by my side on a bit of
cloth to look at   the roots are long & they got a slime to
them & around the sides they're gone black tinged with brown
& a hint of green   I got splotches rising in my vision just
from seeing them & thinking how they lived inside me & now
they're out   & how sick & poisoned they look   & how
that is due to my poisoned thoughts & my sickened-up insides
          sat down in that slop no wonder them teeth got slick &
dark like that

churchgoing got no real dominion over my soul anymore, not
like when we were small, in Bird Island Cove & God Was Always
Watching   I say I'm a Good Man & a Christian but I know
my thoughts are not Correct   come Judgement Day
there's no real hope I'm going Up for a Rest with Baby Arthur
on a Cloud with Harps Playing, like I thought would be my Lot,
when I was A Lad

the blood is going in smaller drops now & Doc wants me out of
there
—more teeth, is it, next?   I put his money on the table
—one with a dead toe that's got to come off   you can
count your blessings
—I suppose I can

our man with the dead toe walks in like a cockeyed duck,
waddling into the furniture, & you know he hasn't been half on
the drink & sure I can't blame him   my swole cheek making
little wells of hot blood in the back of my mouth so I ask Doc to
shake that cloth out that the teeth are on   he asks do I want
them for a Remembrance & I tell him to burn them or keep them
for his records but as far as I'm concerned I don't want nothing

more to do with them & sure don't need nothing to remember the events of the morning by

our toe man asks for the Whisky & the Doc got none left   sorry Fellow, that one is on account of me & I suppose that's one more thing I got to get off my slate as it can't be far from a Sin to take all the Painkiller for your teeth when there's our man what has to get his TOE off presently   I put the rag up to my mouth to spit in & get out of there quick   if I had money to spare I would buy him a bottle & bring it back for I do not envy him his next few hours & would want someone to do the same if I was in a like situation   but as it is, the teeth have cost me this week's journey up to Bob where I can get some money made & the rest of the time I have been spending it not taking it in & though I have stayed off the tables with discipline, there are other ways to watch your coins trickle out of your pockets   the hotel meals are decent but eating & drinking both are costly & if I don't start out Monday it's going to be tight

so I go out into the street & don't get no drink for the dead toed man or anything else   I go to my room & lie down   I already spent my supper money   though I dare say I couldn't eat anything, with my face in the state it's in

poor sod with no Whisky now probably screeching or out cold under Doc's knife or tearing the life out of the armrests more than I done   & here I am with my last drop of my own bottle curled up on the bed with no supper but the Poor Man's Soup or Liquid Painkiller or Most Faithful Sweetheart, whatever you want to call it, taking a big swig & out with more cat sounds, it hurts like Fuck & that's not something I'd state ordinarily, that type of phrase being below what Father would term My Station

liquor stinging into the new tender craters back there in my butchered jaw & I got tears leaking out & the Doc said not to do it but who could blame me when I have a pain this bad & the Whisky is here to save me   each swallow has a measure of guilt tipped in from promising the Doc to stay off & going right back to it but he never had no teeth pulled today & consequently doesn't know how keeping off my drink right now might finish me   I slug at my bottle more slowly, braced for the pain

all night I lie on the bed clutching the bolster, sorry for myself as a jilted bride & crying just as fearsome, the cloth tucked up around me like a baby's outfit to catch the bloody drips

— HER ADOLESCENCE —

Eva is tired, she's been tired since she woke up, she's been tired since before that, since last year, and who knows, maybe even since before then. She has dark circles under her eyes, which, when she catches a sidelong glance of herself in the mirror, she thinks make her look dead, already. A spook. She feels dead. Although supposedly once you pass over, there's some rest.

Eva doesn't rest anymore, she barely remembers the sensation. She is in constant motion, even in sleep. Mabel's strange sentences swirl through her dreams, often to the tune of *There Is Power In The Blood,* or one of the other hymns they used to sing in school. She tosses and turns with her jaw clenched tight, fighting off the words all night, waking with a headache that starts in the fibrous knotty muscles in her jaw, spreading upwards through her ears into her temples. Coming awake with the words still faintly there, in the background, wafting away on faint tendrils of imagined music: *there's wonderful power in the Blood.* This morning when she woke she had to pull at her jaw to get it open, massaging around the lump of muscle in her cheek, clenched so tight it felt like bone. For several seconds there was nothing but the cool morning air on her bare feet, and the circular motion of her fingers on her jaw, and the sound of Mary, still asleep, and the view out the window, the wind lapping up peaks of water into frothy white mountaintops, and the gulls dipping in and out of the valleys, fishing for their breakfasts. For a minute or so she was content, trying to remember the words from her dream, content to stand and strain her mind toward remembering, as though there was nothing more to life than that. Then the last traces of music left her, and she was once again forced to acknowledge that this was not simply a sunny morning with a nip in the air, but that her mother was ill, she was very ill, she was getting worse daily, and it fell to Eva to replace her. Eva's shoulders dropped a little, and she clenched her jaw tighter. She held her spine straight and prepared to get through the obligatory morning chores. This was her life; it was a life of service.

She drinks her requisite two glasses of water from the bedside pitcher, and dresses in her work skirt and blouse with the elbows nearly gone. It is a chilly morning with a premonition of fall, so she puts her woollen stockings on, and pins her hair back as tightly as she can, which is not very tightly, as she has never worn her hair any way but loose and long or in a braid, until last year, when she turned thirteen. Now Eva always wears her hair in a knot, with any stray strands secured with small metal pins. Her mother told her how to do this and then made her write it all down in her notebook, as Mrs. Tilley was the schoolteacher and used to giving dictation. Now that she is ill, she is determined to continue in this fashion, leaving behind a record of necessary information that Eva can look to when she is in need of guidance, afterwards.

River water is most impure and still water is unfit for dishwashing or cooking. Still water always causes fever. Every healthy person requires 2 to 4 pints daily. Bathing is the most important thing in life. Do not Bathe an hour before or after any meal.

The proper way to wash dishes is: first you collect all the dishes. Cups first, then saucers, then spoons, then knives and forks, and small plates, lastly large plates, all in separate heaps. Then get a clean cloth and a pan of hot soapy water. Wash cups and saucers first, knives and forks next, then small plates, lastly all your large plates. Then get another pan of hot water and rinse them all in the same order then dry with a clean towel or leave them on a rack to dry.

Of course Eva already knows how to do dishes, although left to her own she would not have executed the task in such a scientific manner. In the past year she has dedicated most of her time to caring for four things: her mother, the young ones, the house and Duke. She has taken down nearly a full notebook's worth of dictations from her mother, about ninety pages; a few notebook entries are occupied with other, secretive thoughts: about Walter, or else occult in nature, or else her draft letter to the girl in the Yukon, Miss Flora E. Middlecoff Mayo, whose father knew Duke when he was a young man out in the wide world, up in the wild country he sometimes gives talks at church about. *Life on the Alaskan Frontier.* Eva tilts the book away from her mother as she writes. She has learned how to perform all household chores with efficiency on a strict weekly, daily, or hourly schedule—the schedule is written out so she doesn't forget. She has disinfected, dressed, washed and massaged her mother. She has combed her mother's hair and washed it. She has helped her void her bowels, she has cut her toenails and tended to her sores. She has given her a cleaning with lukewarm water every day, using a flannel sheet to cover all but the part being softly washed with a cloth and quickly patted dry. The sheet, the cloth, the bowl, all boiled in carbolic acid when she's done, as are the numerous rags. Eva has had to cut up two whole bedsheets for rags, as her mother's cough has grown worse in recent weeks. There are two bowls, one for clean rags and one for bloody, and last thing at night Eva boils down the bloody ones, her smock and mask still on. Then her sickroom clothes are washed in acid and hung over the woodstove.

For Duke, she's just cooked, washed and kept quiet. He's at home as little as possible. He's got work to do and is caught up with the new political man, or is at least using that as an excuse to come home long past suppertime, on most evenings. Eva remembers way back to when she was Bob's age and Duke would let her ride him around the yard like a pony while she helped him pick potatoes. Now she absents herself as much as possible when he's around. When they eat together, they barely say anything. Eva has learned to read Duke's hand gestures for "fetch more bread" or "pass the salt." She has the babies eat in the kitchen as Duke can't tolerate their voices, and they are too small to stop their chatter when it's prudent. They can't read the storm clouds gathering behind their father's eyes, not like Eva can. He seems to be growing his whiskers out longer these days. The children at school used to call him Mad Man Tilley. They said he was half insane and if he caught you on his property he'd skin you and tan you and make himself a coat— or a vest, if you were on the scrawny side.

Mustard poultice for adults. 1 part mustard to 4 parts Flour. Make into paste with lukewarm water. Hot water if used will destroy the quality of mustard. Spread over half cloth then turn other half over. Fold corners. Do not keep on for longer than 15 or 20 minutes.

Now that her mother is too sick to teach, there is no school. For the first four months of her illness, Mrs. Tilley had continued to grade assignments and set lesson plans. Now she doesn't have the energy, and has abandoned the school altogether. Mrs. Tilley knows she will not recover, she can feel the illness inside her lungs, wet and spongy, glutting itself on the oxygen she struggles to drag inside. She doesn't tell Eva this, nor does she request a visit with her other children. She keeps her opinions on her imminent death to herself and continues to maintain her teacherly demeanour, even as her eldest daughter tends to her as you would a newborn. Mrs. Tilley dictates the rules for tooth-brushing, bed-making, for the cleaning of sores. How to make baked apples, and coffee for Duke, and rhubarb water with lemon, and cream toast where you toast bread and dunk it in warm milk with salt. Eva sits in the sickroom chair and writes down all she can, as her mother spells out the ways in which a woman is supposed to keep a house together, keep everyone nourished, and clean, and comfortable, how a woman has to work very specifically, on behalf of all those in her care, to fight grime, vitamin deficiency and sloth.

For her mother's birthday, Eva makes a feast, consisting of all the recipes she'd been dictated so far.

5 dishes. Mutton broth, fruit jelly, milk pudding, hot water toast and hot drink.

She has never made milk pudding before and burns it, but her mother eats some anyway, and says it is a good first try, although not a passing grade. Eva is stung by this, but knows her mother would never grade her higher than what she deserves. She is a strict teacher with high standards for all of her students, but because she expects so much, her praise, when won, warms you through to the bones. Today she tastes everything and even has a half a bowl of the broth, which Eva thinks is a bit too fresh, but her mother says that in recent weeks she's had an aversion to salt and it is perfect. When taking the leftover food out, Eva disobeys her mother's very first rule about caring for a sick patient and does not discard the remainder lest someone else be contaminated. No, she does the opposite, the dangerous. She drinks the broth—the perfect broth!—from the bottom of her mother's bowl, tries to feel it in her mouth as it would have felt in her mother's mouth, soothing her, pleasing her, giving her a minute of contentment amid the long, strained days and weeks and months that she's been in the sickroom.

Long journey. Lady fading. Sad lady wastes in grey. Up high in the air. We see her disappear. No starlight and no lamplight for thirty days.

In a way, Eva wants to contract the illness too, as she doesn't want to think about what it will be like later, once the inevitable happens and it is just her and Duke and Bert and the little ones here, and Duke really taking to the role of Mad Man Tilley, setting fires in the woods and never changing his clothes, forgetting to eat or to bathe. Drinking himself to sleep out in the root cellar, slung over the turnips. Mary and Bob clinging to her legs like burrs, wailing with grief. Hungry, dirty. In need of her.

BOOK TWO

THE CAMP

November 3, 1906

Sixty miles to the claim, sixty miles   Bob wrote the
number 60 in giant script in that first letter he sent us way back
        I thought nothing of it, his handwriting being uneven at
the best of times, but now that I'm started out a few hours I'm
thinking about how big he wrote them numbers in that letter:

I wish my boots fit better!   I wish I had a horse!
I wish I didn't have a hammer-pain in my ankle that still has my
foot stiffened up all these months since!   after walking
on it this long today I got a list to me almost as bad as Dead
Toe Man!   I wish I'd put some food into myself before I left
Tanana Town!

I wish I had a Drop to Drink!
I wish I had a Drop to Drink!

I even momentarily wish not to have sent all my pay to Father from them weeks coming up from Vancouver raising the fire with Clare, who looks about made for it, big arms on him & not minding the smoke in his lungs if he can step out into a different outpost every night & make acquaintance with all those who have ended up there looking to form those sorts of Alliances
those kinds of people, those people who populate the Rush Towns, those Men who live for a Laugh & a Risk, who spend all they have in pursuit of Dreams, & also those of the Weaker Sex who, for various reasons, must look to their own Interests   I'd kill someone before I'd see the girls go at it & although Father did once call M— the appropriate title for one engaged in such a profession I am sure it was emotion speaking & not proof of action at all   M— being A Mother & a Grieving One, what's more

anyway if brief bouts of Friendship with Women yanks your crank then I suppose the steamships are straight from Heaven as a means of working, if you're strong & you don't mind them cramped ship's quarters with the hammocks swinging & the men stacked one on the other for want of space & all of them sweating & smoking & drinking & boiling tea up & all them smells heating up together in the closed-in quarters & turning into a thick hot blanket of complicated stench like a gone-off kettle of stew   find a place to put your gear & say nothing, don't draw no attention to yourself, for fear of robbery once you drift off   (unless you're Clare   unless you're like him & you naturally become that man the others circle around, protect & dare I say it LOVE   even though he don't do anything special for anyone & is just his normal, cheery, saucy self   for Clare I see how it suits, as he was always the most sociable among us, & not very keen of the nose neither)

O cousin Clare, I could do with you now, for company
     for your singing voice!
O cousin Clare, my feet are nearly froze off!
O Clare how many miles how many more miles!

I need a drink   or a horse & cart   or a concussion,
with some Savages to drag me to Bob's camp on their dog sleigh
          or a quick death, like the judge at Tanana said was
my likely fate, for there is no Law to protect you in these parts

when I asked him, Judge said the rule was to get the other feller
before he got you   this is none too comforting & any sound
I hears I thinks might be a Criminal set to Kill Me for the sake
of my Outfit   (Soapy Smith! Sure, he been dead now a few
years but don't tell me the whole Bunco Brotherhood is up &
Disappeared!)

I cannot do this
I am not Strong Enough
I am the Weak Brother
The Good Son but the Weak One
~~The One Before the Dead One~~
The One Partway Shrivelled
The One Half Wounded
The One of Sins & Sorrows
The Last One Banished
The Only One Banished, really, the Others having, in effect,
Banished Themselves

O Cousin Clare fly to me, deliver me!
I could Curse myself for thinking I was fit for this
Hard kind of Life!

I hang my head against the blare of sunshine & watch my feet continue stubbornly on, sense the trees going by & feel the throb of my absent teeth, hear the sounds of little unseen animals (probably rabbits) that I think about stopping & trapping, I'm that starved   but I got no trap & no kit to make one & I have to keep walking & the night comes down fast like someone sliding their hand over my eyes & the shift is total with new sounds & everything, new howls & whimpers that weren't there before

I want to lie down & go to sleep by the side of the river or maybe just lie down & perish & let the wolves eat me, God's choice, but instead I keep walking by snow-light for many hours as I know I am not far from collapse anyway & an extra day out here with just tobacco & water with my head half tore up & freshly off the drink might cause me to pass over, finally, to Baby Arthur's side

I reckon it is twelve o'clock by the time I stop   I have to make a fire to keep myself alive & safe from wolves & cold & then I have to somehow stay awake, although I am not sure it's possible   good thing I spent my last money on this Rabbit Coat I got in Tanana   the Outfit Man did his job on the selling: Waterproof, Windproof & Suitable for Outdoor Slumber!   Saved More than One Man from Death on the Alaskan Frontier!   The Only Thing the Indians Wear Themselves, so you know it's the Real Rig-Out!   Bound to Last for Years!

hood up, the fur lining against the back of my neck, warm & soft, just about saving me, how gentle & good that fur feels   its

softness is allowing me to maintain my Human Comportment
in the face of Trying Circumstances which are threatening to
turn me Savage   I tuck into a ball by the fire, thinking
about the value of a Rabbit Skin Coat on the Alaskan Frontier
                    my raw red hands hove into the clefts of my armpits
send an arrow of ice up my spine   I must let a beard
grow in to help with heat retention   for tonight I work up
a kind of scarf from my spare socks, knotted onto the legs of
my extra overhauls   it is not too pretty but does its job
          I make a mental note to put a flap across the front of my
hood with a hasp on the side for when it's extra cold out
          make a secondary mental note to see if Bob has a needle
& thread or if he needs to send to his wife for one   & as for
the hasp I am thinking I can fashion something out of bone,
having made buttons for M— that way before   third
mental note to catch rabbit to obtain fur to stitch across &
also I wouldn't mind a chomp out of his haunches neither

fourth note: acquire paper so as not to have to keep remembering
everything!

I put my hands into the circle of heat from the fire   turn
them slowly like roasting meat on spits & think momentarily of
eating them

this is a serious thought but after a minute I can find a reason
to laugh at it

the howls of the wolves coming from some distance through
the trees make me feel not quite so lonely as before   Hello
Wolves, I'm out here with you   & hungry, very hungry

when I wake at sunrise there is a crow on the branch nearest my head, but when I grab a rock to kill it with it flies away

I drink some water & smoke a pipe
        that's all I have to call breakfast, & neither item wants to make it past my numb lips, what feel like flaps of flesh no longer attached to my Nervous System

I walk closer to the bank of the river & keep my eye out
        when once I sees a boat coming it seems unlikely it is real, but I got my coat off & tied to a sapling in case it is no illusion   SOS my fellows, take pity on this soft N.F.L.D.er what never featured how long 60 Miles could be when you're half-starved, stunned as a bum & don't know the Lay of the Land

The worst Sob Story in the world is the Boy who watches his
Old Man Pickle Himself
        & then the Boy grows up & turns out just the same, &
every day is Quitting Day, he vows, as he looks his children in
the eye at breakfast, but by noon he's already sneaking sips out
of a bottle in the barn, hidden behind the buckets & cursing
himself

(the self-loathing keeps him belting it back in secret all afternoon,
coming out with the bottle in full view on the table, at
suppertime)

& although I can sense how it poisons me, I keep on pouring it in
        it is the one thing I suppose we did still have in common,
as no Church & no State would e'er part Father & his Drink

No one but Jesus, Come the Reckoning

I do ruminate on Him a lot, these past months, since Kate had
her dead baby that give us such a scare & made her sadder than
I ever seen anyone, even M—, even a Camp Intruder, caught in
a snare

& no amount of good booze is going to wipe away the memory
of both of those faces, or of Kate's   their worlds of sadness
that make them untouchable & unknowable to the rest of us

    I never want Eva to feel that way
    I want her protected from
    Life's Extremities, Its Opposites

    How things can mirror-flip
    As quick as you draw breath—

    There is no predicting it

I want the boring, safe, humdrum life for her that she will not
want to lead, she being the sort to play at Robbers, Pirates &
Soldiers rather than Lady of the Manor

& she do be fascinated by my Adventures Up North & Tales of
the Indians & Grumpy Uncle Bob & she swears she will go up
there, one day, herself, pushing her glasses up her nose to
squint at me   a sign of how serious she is

& I think the right man would do well with my Eva, in a few
years, if he's the sort who don't mind a woman with Ideas
    & plenty of Energy & Brains to outwit her Mister

She would keep you on your toes, all right
& twould never be A Boring Life, that's sure

She will grow up Pretty, in a Plain way, like her Poor Mother,
though I can see my own brow & something of Ernest & Daisy
in her mouth   & somehow with all those faces there
making up her own, Eva also is quite Herself, already, at 12

I'll drink to that, I'll toast to my daughter's Self-ness, & try not to
let my eyes go too teary, or bleary, or both

there's only so much longer that I have her here, under my
protection & my care
admiring me & finding my life thrilling

there is still a spell left before she sees me in a new light:
A Failure, A Coward, Slave to the Sauce   ~~Though Bert
is a fine lad & Mary & Bob are both good Children it is Eva I feel
on my Heart~~

Sorrowful Knave was the thing Mabel always said when she did
my Leaves, ~~that & the other, secret thing that made me cry, that
message from him, from Little Baby Arthur, which I have never
told anyone, not even Mabel, after she would come to out of it &
ask me what she'd said~~

~~That is Our Secret~~
~~Mine & His, my little brother~~

~~I can feel his grip around my left index finger still   &
though it is hard with the rhumatiz to bear the pain, it keeps
him here with me, all these years since   I can remember
his big eyes   his soft white skin   his ever-
changing expression like clouds passing by   & his tiny
fingers tight around mine possessing such amazing strength~~

~~that memory is the purest joy I know & also the sharpest pain~~

(Whisky do help dull both ends of Feeling)

November 5, 1906

THERE IS NO GOLD
Nary a Speck
There is no Hope of it neither
(Except for the shiny caps on two of Brother Bob's teeth)

Got here this A.M.
Half-starved
Had no food since Wed.
Nor no Drink
& sure what kept me going since Monday Morn was thought of cozy cabin, Bro Bob Happy to see me, a Swell Old Family Reunion

Reality: Boys take me in their boat up river a few miles & let me off on a clear patch with instructions to walk for an hour, which turns to a few more (it seems everything takes longer for me here than is proper)   I finally catch sight of smoke through trees, my eyes tear up & I rub the tears away with numb fingers lest Bro see how soft I am (he oft did taunt me for it when I was a child: —Why must you have So Many Feelings)

No cabin, boy, just some stitched-together old lean-to
just some sticks with flour sacks & branches over top
& an open fire at the mouth
a pillar of smoke like a curtain drawn closed

me thinking I must be mistaken as to Brother Bob's coordinates

man under boughs looks up through smoke with gruff eyes
sunk into purpled hairy face, beard like fancy lacework & with
long black lace eyebrows & he do look as though he half thinks
I am a mirage or something, appearing in the wave of heat off
the fire   a squint at me like —how dare you
& —who are you   —this is MY land, boy   —I have a
mind to snuff you out as much as shake your hand, it would be
easy, look at my Size

Bear of Man with ice blue eyes
I am Afraid
& more so when I recognize the look in them
it hits me like a draught of river water poured down the neck of
my coat   there's no mistake

this is my brother

Brother the Elder with the True Tilly Gaze

& there is no Camp, no Cabin

& it do sink in that I am no Bear of Man myself
(Muskrat maybe? Titmouse? Lapdog? Trout?)

& there is a chance that I Will Not Survive This

I must make myself known to Bob quick, for he got a rifle & he do not know me, ain't seen me since my boyhood & I suppose I changed some & sure why would you expect your long-lost sibling to appear out of the woods full-grown & without warning at your digs in Nowheresville, Alaska when you ain't written them in years?

—Bob! It's me! It's William!

he sits with rifle cocked & do not say nothing   his breath like the growl of a dog set on dying before the night is out
—it's Dukey, Bob! your brother?
—Well   Fuck Me
—hey now, old man, that any proper kind of greeting?
—what are you doing here?
—oh, I was out having a stroll & thought I'd stop in for a cup
        (he does not find me Clever)   I came to find you
is what   to help you with your claim   with the 2 of
us we'll nose it out faster

Bob laughs this sick, oily laugh that makes my bile rise to a sour taste on the back of my tongue that I must work to swallow down again

—my claim   go home
—& that I shan't   I just got here!
—my claim   he spits dark globs into the snow beside him
        it ain't worth a dead whore's cunt, that's what
—you wrote before
—what else was I to say   Dear Old Man, I am indeed A
Failure?
—he sent me here   he wanted me to find you   to work
the claim the two of us

—that so
—he's got big debts now   the Crash was bad   the
others are not helping & he's in as tight a spot as I've ever seen,
he had to give over the shop to Templeman for this year at least
& maybe longer if we don't fix him   & Templeman hired
Uncle Robert to run his affairs, so you can imagine, now, how
turnt Father is, with not so much as a By Your Leave about it

Bob laughs at this & that sets him into coughing & spitting
more black stuff out onto the snow

—is there no Gold at all, Bob?

he is not used to talking, I guess, for his voice is creaky
          —not for you or I   this land's used up already &
the few who made their money are long gone   (he laughs)
just like you to head up after the action's gone out of her
          (he sighs) Fuck me

I stand a while & stare at the trees while letting his words settle
          Bob is still having a good chuckle at my ridiculous notion:
Me & Him, Chancing On Some Colour
—it can't be true   what will I do
—I advise you to head home again   give the Old Man my
regards & say me to Mother
—you do not know the news then   Bob, do you not write to
Him at all? It's been years now (he do not speak)   she left
us, back in '95, in the summer, went down to Boston somewhere,
who knows why   I was 11, no one said much of it to me,
you know what Father's like, No Questions   he just started
up this game of pretending she never existed in the first place &
we didn't say her name or anything   then by '97 she was
back again, real brief   real brief because then she passed,

I hate to tell you   about three weeks after she came back
crying at the door for him to forgive her, she loved him & us &
did not wish to be away from us anymore   it was bad,
worse than if she'd stayed wherever she ran off to, but she didn't,
she did not want to die alone, I suppose   Father don't speak
her name anymore   (Bob's face like stone, unmoving)
          the last baby died in '95   she'd never recovered,
too many of them, three dead is too many & this wasn't like the
others, he was not a new thing dead that we didn't even know, &
barely had a name yet   I suppose you heard tell of him,
though? Of Baby Arthur?

(he nods yes at this but his eyes tell me otherwise   maybe
Father never told him about Babby at all)

—please may I come & sit under there? I been walking near 3
days to find you

he shoves over on the pelts (wolf?) he got lining the floor of the
lean-to & we sit shoulder to shoulder with our faces turned to
the smoking wet mess of the fire

the heat don't reach me straight away   the outer layer of
my flesh is too cold   when it thaws it hurts like the ache
of a muscle that's not used to working anymore
& it is not yet proper Winter

—my lily-faced baby brother come to find me   well, stick
me in my deadeye   now that is Rich!   I'd as soon
have featured old Alice making the journey as you, boy
—I was stoker with Clare on the Dawson all summer   I can
work   the two of us together, right, well maybe your claim
is not all hopeless

—my claim   you muff   (he goes to putting another
bit of wood on the fire)

& then I understand how deep his lie went
& how he never had a claim to begin with
& how Father got us all caught up somehow
& even Bob the Bear is not impervious
& I am lost, there is no hope
& shall probably die here without no money to send Outside to
show for the end to my sorry Existence

Brother Bob puts a Huge Hand on my Shoulder   & when
he says Whisky I know he means he's sorry for dragging me
here, through 3 Countries & a Territory, One Ocean to the Other,
by telling lies I could believe in

& he don't say nothing much after that but we two sit in fairly
companionable silence, staring into the flames, each with our
own misery that don't need no more voicing, & we polish off the
last of his Painkiller as the wolves in the woods around us set in
with their nightly howls

Shoo Fly Don't Bother Me
Don't Put Your Tiny Feet On Me
Don't Do Your Poo & Pee On Me
You! Fly! Don't Bother Me!

(Mother if you read this don't be Vexed!
I mean for no Human Eye to See it,
These are my PRIVATE THOUGHTS
Which is why I hide them
In the crack under the Stairs)

I have 42 bites incl black fly & nipper + 2 horse fly
Dolly has as many

Dolly is with a Baby & it is due to arrive very soon & Father said
this time I would help him as I am now 10 & grown enough to
understand it

I know there is to be a mess as he had me outfit the barn with
        Buckets of Water
        Soap

Rags
Fresh Carrots
Blankets & New Hay

I go brush Dolly daily
 (Sounds like the start of a Nursery Rhyme!
 I'll finish it for Baby Arthur, when I have the time!)

today we have been in the barn since noon   she has been
panting & restless & Father is waiting & smoking his pipe by the
door   he says it will happen today so I do not want to leave
him but this waiting is a Chore   I busy myself with lessons,
& muck out the stalls again though I already did so this morning

I load up on more Oats
Dolly likes Oats the best of all Foods

& the start is so quick by the time I goes from Barn to Cellar &
back again there is a change & Dolly is heaving, she got a scared
cast to her big horsey eye & there's a small hoof on a small leg
that's jutting out from her rump like a tiny extra limb, like that
nightmare I had where there was an extra head coming out of
my chest & it was talking to me in some kind of language I never
even heard before

Father is soaping up, his sleeves to elbows & jacket off
I do the same

—how do I help?
—for now you calm her, keep her attention   from the
looks of it I'm going to need to help her   she doesn't
have it the right way inside

he puts his hands inside of Dolly, with a wet & squishy sound
from one end of her & a fierce neigh of protest from the other
   I have her head held tight & am cooing to her   she
wants to bolt but cannot for Father have tied her on good

she can kick though & kick she do! I never heard him
make that kind of sound before, so loud & surprised
—OOOOOOOMMMMPPOHHHHHH   AHHH
   he doubles over but do not let go of her

—are you all right?
—come here   Come Now, Boy   take the leg
 there's another about to come   you are to pull strong &
steady, nothing sudden & I will guide the rest of the foal out

his hands inside Dolly, the little legs like tree branches sticking
out

Pull, Pull, Pull it's hard work, for the legs is wet & slippery
& very thin

I do not wish to break Baby's ankles before he has a chance to
caper in the Field!

—pull, Duke
—Pull!
—& Pull
—Pull!
—one more big one
—Pull!
—one more
—Pull!

& we feel the give & turn of the foal & the weight of him come quick towards me

as soon as he starts to move in there, he comes out very fast & strong & in no time at all he is standing right beside me
        this wobble-creature   long legs thin as fishing poles with big eyes in his little skinny horse face, his sides heaving with his first breaths, greedy for all the air he can gulp down, so strong for one so flimsy-seeming & new to this world, standing right away & walking, not like Baby Arthur, who is just now learning how to stand himself up

Father & I wash him down, for Dolly is too tired
        she lays & watches as we clean him with rags & warm water & I give him a drink in my hand, Father gentling him with his fingers & speaking sweet & soft

—what is his name, Duke?
—I can choose?
—if you're quick about it
—well, for the way he came out so fast, I should like to call him Lightning
Father smiles   —he also has a white streak on his nose
        has that nothing to do with it?
—no sir, for when I first saw him, he were covered in blood

(& then Father thinks to check his leg, where Dolly kicked him in her panic, before our Lightning was born)

she got him good   right in the shin   Father tears his trouser leg up along the seam   —your Mother shall not like that   he says   —now clean & wrap it tightly, Son

Red of Horse & Human Blood the same & both as tricky to remove
from the skin beneath your fingernails   with a bucket of
cold water, in the privy

   Lest Mother Be Upsot To See
   The Evidence Of Our Savagery

Been a few weeks now that I been with Bob up to the wood camp & though there is no Gold that do not mean we cannot Prosper   there are plentiful wild meats to catch with the .22   you can get yourself a Grouse (what we calls Chicken here) without too much Exertion   & for trade we can trap fur-bearers but must wait a bit till it gets colder & their thick winter coats have grown to their prime   & for money we can cut for the steamers & we got our own dock down on the river with the logs all trimmed & stacked in 4 foot lengths as is the rule 50 feet from the bank, ready for the boys to carry them on when they're wooding up   though no other boats shall pass up this year as the river has now froze over   the S. S. Ella was the last boat up & that was on the 15th of the month & she only took 8 cords as she would not be going back down till thaw & just needed enough to get her an hour or two more up river to where they banks her till breakup   for now, we chop more & stack it up & wait till thaw to sell it   we got 30 cords now but we have room for five or six hundred & that's good money when it comes   we got to wait, which is just as well as I don't fancy the 60 mile stroll to town to post money to Father in this weather, what is setting in quite cold already & is sure to be much worse come the middle of December (we got our bottles lined up in the Alaska way outside the cabin: Quicksilver   Coal Oil   Jamaica Ginger   Whisky (though that is drained)   St. Jacob's Oil   each one freezes at a lower temperature than the rest so when you looks you can tell by the ice in the bottles how bitter it is & thus if it's fine enough for trapping or too cold to leave bunk   we are only at Quicksilver today but I think we may reach Coal in a week or two   Bob says that's not likely & calls me Weak & Soft & Womanish for minding the weather already what to him feels like the Balm of Summer I suppose)

the last time Bob went to Tanana I sent some mail with him for Father & for Jennie to explain the situation

money do not flow in winter but like the river seizes up this time of year then starts its course again late April early May & that is how we are fixed & there isn't anything I may do to change it so he must sit tight like I am & practice Patience
      I know Father will be vexed with this as I did hope to send him more already, but he is going to have to eat his Pride & let Templeman have the store this year & it is not all bad, as Father could still work there for Uncle Robert & Templeman & make a living   but it is the thought of working for another at his own enterprise that have him turnt   & his own Brother beside what he haven't spoke to for at least ten years   but there is a time when Pride is an Impediment & must be pushed aside for Pure Survival so I hope he don't stick to his word to let Templeman starve him out   he got more than himself to think about with Jennie there & Grandma & Aunt Sus needing help too   they got no men at their place to look after them   & Lightning needs some oats or he will wither, though I know Father thinks him worthless, especially

now that he isn't allowed to haul wood from our land
      Lightning may starve if Father is pushed to it
I am not there to see to his survival

I do not want to get the letter back that tells me of Father's disappointment in my earnings, so I am happy to stay here in our new cabin whose construction have occupied us in the weeks since I been here   Bob was comfortable enough with a lean-to for himself but it is cramped in there at night with your grown brother sleeping next to you   the cabin is small but she do seem roomy as a Prince's Quarters after those first few evenings   14 × 16 as I measured with my boot lengths, which is a far enough cry from Father's House   but we've enough space for 2 bunks above each other & a little stove with pipe through roof & a table with 2 chairs & a daybed what Bob hacked right quick out of some of our timber (he always had a good hand for that kind of work)   you don't want it no bigger, small like this keeps all the heat in close not spread out so you got to burn twice as much of your money (lumber)

we got the walls up right quick   there were some folks come by & helped us   Fellas that lives nearby a few miles: Anderson & Hedy & Mr. Coleman, Mayo & some Indians: Little Charlie   William   Luke   Peter & Big John

Bob knows all the men who lives around here & it seems it is custom to walk to another's Camp when you are lonesome or you needs something like axe, hammer, paper, rope, tea or sugar, Neck Oil, lard   & these things do travel man to man so you do not need the full outfit to yourself if you can trace each item   we got hammer from Hedy & axe from Chief Henry & all brought a tipple of Neck Oil in their flask

& they helped us raise the walls in a few hours only
it is Fast Work if there are More Bodies

the roof took a while though, for at this time of year it is tedious
to fill it in with the moss what is already frozen in the ground &
so much harder to cut out & it must be at least a foot thick to do
the trick & keep us warm in winter   & then over the
moss you have to put sand or clay of course for ballast & that is
a trick too as it's all frozen over & we had to build fires on the
bank to thaw it out then cut at it with knives & picks to get
enough to spread & I knew if we did not finish soon we would
be lost to snowfall   but the Indians came through that
time as well & they did help us drag the clay from the bank &
spread it on the roof in exchange for Flour, Butter & some Coffee
          at first it give me a start to hear Bob talking in their
tongue & they in ours mixing words from both & putting them
together in their mouths like it was normal   but I suppose
that is the way of this place & sure Bob needs to know Indian
anyhow to be married to his Missus, whose family is from upriver
          (Little Charlie is her younger brother   he is only
a lad still about fourteen but he does the work of men the same
as the others & is the kind of lad Father would want in his fields
          he don't complain none)

I imagine in a few months I will not find it strange to hear their
words in Brother's mouth or to see him in the Moccasins he has
taken to wearing rather than his Real Boots, what are left like a
monument by the stove without no feet in them   it is A
Real Stove   we are most lucky to have traded with old Jerzy
who was leaving for Outside & selling off his digs   Jerzy's
stove is a proper iron one drug in by horse & it makes this cabin
a Home   or so I thinks now, after being here a while

One can get used to any Circumstance, given time to Settle

Bob is gone now down to Hedy's for he was feeling Poorly &
needed Whisky as he do loathe St. Jacob's Oil & likewise Jake
Ginger   we did not have a thing to trade except two
Chickens which anyone can get themself but Bob said it's no
account because we will just Owe Him   I don't like that
thought as it brings me right back to Father & Templeman but
I got to learn the way things are in Alaska   they are not
like at Home   here everyone do Owe something to their
Neighbour & they do not write it down in Copybooks or Ledgers

I saved a bit of moss to chink up the door what we made from a
few proper boards we found down on the sandbar, must have
come loose off some steamers at one point & there were just
enough to cobble together for our doorway, but they have gaps
between that let the wind in & I do not feature standing for that
come winter   moss might work if mixed with something
sticky, maybe sap, but that is frozen now under the bark of the
trees & hard to pick out   I tried it a few minutes this morning

I am here thinking of ways like that to fix the cracks
          maybe candle grease like we did with the flour sacks to
make our windows (you dips them in the grease & when it dries
that makes the cloth translucent & you can see shadows through
them   & sunlight   & when a man comes to the
door you see the outline of his head & shoulders like them
silhouettes the tin pan man would cut when he came through
town, for 2 pennies, back in Leominster   I remember
Daisy got one of herself & Ernest joked that the man was kinder
on the contours of her chin than he should have been, when she
was out of earshot)

we don't got enough candles at present to fix the door up &
I should not burn them all & waste them anyway, especially as
I am none too sure it would work, so I contents myself with
stuffing the moss in straight to see if it will hold there just with
the force of my Willpower

I am squat down at my Fools Errand & Big John the Indian
comes & says Peter's child is sick do we have Painkiller & I says
no just Jacob Oil & Ginger (which the Indians don't truck with)

I tell him Bob is gone to Hedy's to get some for he's poorly too

he takes instead a slab of bacon & gives me for trade Tobacco,
which I am glad for   we have had none for two days now
& that is not right, it is our constant friend out here where there
are so few Pleasures, save Pipe & Whisky   he don't want
to stay for tea, though I presses him

a few weeks ago I would have been quivering in my boots if an
Indian come to see me but now I looks forward to it, for it is
better to talk to an Indian than to nobody   & they are
good help to us when we needs it

—I will send Bob up with Whisky when he gets back or I will
come myself if he's too soused to make it   say me to Peter
& his boy

& Big John who is Proud is also Grateful
He Tips his Native Cap to me while he is leaving

(Father, you could learn a thing or two
If you were Neighbour to some Indians)

THINGS I DO IN MY FOREST PLACE
I lie down & look at: Number 1 the clouds   or the
birds 2   or the water 3
4 eat a bit of lunch that I sometimes pack up in a flour sack
          Hard Tack Apple Ham etc
5 read a bit of verse or write a rhyme for someone SPECIAL
          I keep some books here, tied up in a piece of oilcloth &
in a secret spot where none can find them   Book of
Hymns   Book of Psalms   The Pilgrim's Progress
6 think about my life & things I want to do later on & things
I would do different another time & other things I love to do but
which I know I SHOULD NOT DO & YET I DO ANYWAY!

this place is special, like a small world inside the world that
makes me more myself   here I am fully alone & can
believe that no one knows of my existence & my deeds cannot
hurt others & I need not do anything but sit & listen to the buzz
of the horseflies around my ears & try not to move   they
rarely land

here I can feel things that are not permitted inside the House,
on our Land, in this Bay, in My Real Existence

Here I can daydream about What Could Be
If my Life were that of Someone Else
With none to mock my verses or condemn me
~~Should they catch me thinking of Her~~
~~With my hand upon Myself!~~

December 25, 1906

Merry Christmas to Me, What Feels like Dying!

We walked in from the wood camp two days ago & my legs do still be shaking, muscles knotted up in pain from 60 miles in moccasins which feel like a few pairs of socks out on the ice with the knobs that stick up pure white so you can't see them & you stubs your toe & thinks you broke it & limps along just hoping for it to go numb, which it do in a few minutes so you don't care till you finds another tricky piece of ice sticking up & repeats the operation   shuffling along like you're in your stocking feet, though it's better than wearing our Factory Boots, what make the walk more slippery

Bob seemed not to mind walking 10 am till 8:30 in the night not speaking to each other with just one quick stop for lunch what was Cold Meat & frozen hunks of Bread that we chewed standing up on the trail with a swallow of Whisky to moisten the journey down our gullets   one time we seen smoke up ahead & Bob got out the rifle for we did not know if these be Good Men or Bad   but they were good enough & gave us Hot Coffee I suppose around six o'clock in the evening which did us some good & stood us well to get through the last few hours

I tried hard not to show how tired I was & how my feet were numb to the knees & my fingers to the elbows for Brother Bob did not seem to even feel the cold (though his beard was turned to ice like an Ogre in a Fairy Story)

& sure when we arrived I could barely move   I thought my legs were going to be seized up for good they were aching so bad   even worse when we got indoors next to the fire

Mrs. Bob gave me tea straight away when she saw how shaked up I was with the walk & every minute or two one of the kids came back with the kettle to thaw out my cup again   it was at least 45 below & indoors there was frost on the table

Bob went back to work early the next morning with strong legs & no pains in his Bear Feet   out chopping wood for Missus over on the Island with the dogs dragging it across on the sledge   we got a few more pups that Missus was keeping for us & that should make our trip back the easier for we shall not have to cart all the provisions ourselves   though our sledge will not bear our weight plus the food   the pups are still young so we will not get a ride but will still walk it

Bob was at it all day & I joined him past noon though it did hurt me to walk around with the pains in my legs

& I fear I will not heal from this   but will carry it like my others

my Hammer Ankle, teeth-holes (still oozy) & the rest

anyway I grinned & bore it for I would not like for Brother to see me too weak to work beside him, as that is what I promised I would do while I am here   & besides I had to do my part to pay for all the good grub that Missus had prepared for us

we have eat well every day we've been here, & even had a Ham
          Boiled Potatoes   Gravy   Bacon
Biscuits   & Pie with native berries for Christmas Supper
          I was that happy with my stomach full I laughed out loud
& felt like I had drunk many more drams than what I did tip in
          which made the Chillians laugh too, they are warming up
to me, especially the boy Isaac   & Brother said to his wife
—Eva, maid, were I not here I believe Duke would propose
marriage just on account of the pie   & she smacked his
arm but there were a mite of a twinkle in her eye

once we were done on the island last night it was time to head
to the Indian Village outside of town 1 mile   they have
built some cabins & a church all for themselves & at Christmas
there do be at least 500 of them brought together from all places
up the Yukon & Tanana River shores   we could go too last
night to the Potlach which is a big kind of party for the Indians
where they dance & sing with drummers & the people all must
bring gifts which are paraded around the room with great
ceremony to a special song & everyone has a look at what's on
offer   all kinds of food & rifles, blankets, axe, nails, beads,
mittens, all things a man would need to live

we brought with us a great slab of bacon & a pair of moccasins
beaded by Missus with rabbit fur trim that were very nice & a
harness set for dogs that would fit 6   Bob thought it not
enough so I scrounged through my kit & got a notebook to add
in that only had one page used up, which I tore out (Provisions
List)   Bob said it was a good present but I don't know
who wanted it, the book was left pretty near the end after the
first few rounds of choosing were through   & then they
came after the Whites with the blanket, & oh my son!

they put you in the middle of the blanket & all the men take up
a piece of the edge & they tosses you straight up into the sky
the aim is to see how long you can stand it & to laugh
even when your guts are churned with flying through the air &
if you cries out they just tosses higher   some begged
for it to stop & I will not say I didn't do the same   when
I was in there it seemed they were trying to fling me right up to
the Lights & that them Lights didn't want me & were throwing
me back down to the Men who were laughing as they could see
how my mind was scrambled with the tossing that felt like it
was fifty feet if it was only ten

—please stop! Please!

my good dinner from Bob's Eva threatening to rise up & expel
itself onto the Indians who were laughing at my begging
        I was not good in the blanket though did fare better
than some like Hedy who afterwards was so mad he punched at
several of the Indians & got a good shiner for his work   some
other men did try that tack too & they all got the same result for
there were lots of Indians to help out the mate who got swung
at by those angry, dizzy Whites   & custom is not to hit out
after but to give a gift, as thanks for Blessed Release from the
Tossing   Bob did not tell me that beforehand so I searched
in my coat & gave them my only pen & inkpot

        —to go with the book of paper, so you can write things
(I shall have to get another in Town)

the pen was a puzzling gift to some but I know a few of the
young women there were happy with it, they sat together in a
corner later & tried it out   & when I went over to them

they showed me their drawings in the book: geese & fox & their
kind of tents with skins on them & a bear that took up a whole
page   so I suppose they were decent gifts to bring after
all, if not customary to the Potlach   & if I am here next
Christmas I shall know better & bring more meat & flour & maybe
my White Man Boots now that I got the moccasins
lots of the Indians love to get White Clothes & they wears it
with great Pride

All Hands went home with something   I got a Cap that
one of the ladies made with fur from foxes on the inside to keep
my noggin from freezing up   it is real nice, & as welcome
to me as anything else I could conjure   now I am a real
Alaska Boy with dress half White half Indian, such as used to
startle me when I was new to this Territory

it is queer how quick new things do become Ordinary & then
when you reflects on where you used to live it is that place which
seems Exotic & Strange   Father's Store & his Garden with
the Dahlias seem like a Dream World where I never really been,
just visited in Sleep

& there is nothing more real or normal now than getting
chucked in a blanket right up to the stars with the sound of
men laughing & drums going in the background & you are
seeing strange blurs of faces & the changing colours of the
Northern Lights, one & the other, lights & faces, lights & faces,
over & over, till they mixes together & all the people are made
of light & there is nothing but sparkly faces lining the night sky

The boys I am bunked with think St. John's is the true centre of
the world   all of us come in by boat or buggy or train
from the small towns   I am more worldly about it,
myself, as there've been a time or two in my younger years
when Father did take me down with him, him then a Captain of
his own rig with a crew to answer to him & great piles of salt
fish for us to sell or trade   & everyone knows a child of
five is old enough to hawk fish down St. John's harbour, if he's
sensible

so yes I know a bit about the place & can tell the other lads
where to find things though some things have changed
considerably, there having been a fire or two since my boyhood
days & the whole city started over from scratch, in an
approximation of the way I remember it
          & I knew it would be a change from the Bay, where
Bonavista seems a Metropolis   but all the same the
bustle of the streets did take my breath away the first time or two
I stepped out into them
          I feel rough as a hobnail compared to some of the boys
you see here, in their tailor-made coats   & all the ladies that
buy the fabric for their dresses from the British importers with
flowers in the windows of their shops   & wouldn't

I like to get a bolt of kelly-green with sprigs of white for Katey
& maybe lilac silk for Jennie   for once I would like to see
her light as a lilybud   (light enough to float!)
          but I know it is too dear   Father would take the
price of it out of them in other ways which would scarce be
worth the cloth

this time in Town I have no fish to sell & not much money either
          but I am not Proud & am happy to do any work from
which I can get a coin or two to get me down to Leominster

I have addresses for Daisy, Alice, James & Ernest, writ out on the
cards from last Xmas
& so am sure to find them
& if they are not happy to see me or if there be no work then
I shall carry on, as far as I can, to some big city where one can
get lost, change one's name, start over
& in two years when I've cash enough to help him, Father shall
forgive me my trespasses
& I shall voyage back home, like looking down the wrong end of
a telescope to see the world shrinking, becoming familiar again
& that's when I'll shed my tears over this, My Banishment
& not before then   not one Tear, not for One Minute

This I do Solemnly Promise Myself

April 17, 1907

April is soft as Hell   we are hard pressed to Work for the
snow is on Death's Door & you sinks right through it to your
waist in spots

we can go 1 man at a time to get some logs with the snowshoes
that Bob paid 7 dollars for from Charlie ~~the Indian~~ (at the time
I thought that was a pretty dear price but now I see their true
Worth)

First Mosquito Today

Bob says I will be longing for Winter once that Mosquito finds
his Mate & produces Several Thousand God-Damned Youngsters
to bite us on any part we are stunned enough to expose

they say the Mosquitoes up here are so big & fierce they do
not bite so much as take a chunk from you   I always
been attractive to Nippers so I suppose I'll be et alive come
Summertime   yes it's getting warm & now the river is on
its way to breaking & there is water over top of the ice in places
which means soon the steamers will sail up & we can sell some
cords, what we've been labouring over for months

the cabin roof is leaking from the top dressing of snow that now is melting in the fine temperatures   I got all our pots & buckets out around the heavy drips to catch the water lest it turn the floor back into mud (I think this summer I shall haul some river boards in and lay them down, as they drift up on the shore & I can salvage them)

Good Day for a Haircut, I thought this morning, first thing
          I have not touched my mop all winter, it being insulating, to a point   but now the hair touching the back of my neck do itch at me & make me sweat so I asked the dago would he mind having a go at it this afternoon when he come up with Hedy for coffee   I always admired his hair which is glossy black neat & combed to one side & kept short at the back even in winter, right Civilized

Bob joked I should look like a dago too when he was done with me   I shot back twould be better than to look like you, drug up from a Sourdough's grave, what died back in '98 sometime
          that is our type of talk together when Folk is about there is knives under the words even if the crowd is laughing

Bob went then on the snowshoes to try & haul out a few of our traps as the snow is too soft now to support them   I sat down in the doorway & the dago went to work on me with my little pair of sewing scissors that Missus Bob gifted me along with some thread & other truck when she saw the work I was after trying, sewing the face-flap (wool sock!) on my rabbit coat, without a proper needle, just a slip of wire bent over on one end to put the thread through   the dago sharpened the little scissor blades on our whetstone & Hedy started boiling coffee   that man is mad for it   he drinks more

coffee than is fit   no wonder he has a Short Fuse & do be
hopping around in his talk & body both like there's electric
current running through his blood (though he works fast too
          he can pull out more than I can in an hour with one
hand behind his back)

the dago is young   he got few words of English but we gets
on well enough   he came over here from Spain to get money
from The Colour & like me his timing was off   I think at
home he used to be a Farmer but do not know for sure   at
any rate I joked to him that he could open a barbershop in
Tanana when he is sick of bunking at Hedy's   if he
understood me I don't know, as most times he just gives a soft,
quiet kind of laugh to whatever we are saying & this time was
the same as the rest

he got a light touch with the scissors & when he was done I used
the kettle as a second mirror so I could see the back of my head
& sure enough he done a fine job, neat & straight (though my
newly exposed neck looked Womanish, too pale & soft to belong
to one what just spent the cold season hauling logs and killing
things)

I gave him a chaw or two of Tobacco for his troubles & he
hugged me tight to him so I could smell his Odour (which is no
different than any other man after living in the woods all winter
          Smoke, Sweat, Dirty Wool, Bacon Grease & Painkiller
for those who wonder what a dago do smell like)

I do not tell Father in my letters that I am friendly with These
Types of People as I know he would not like it (sure even Hedy
do be Foreign   Swedish?   but he been here long

enough to speak good English & is Fair of Hair & Complexion beside) & I do not blame Bob either for omitting certain details of Wife & Chillians when he writes Home

I think they are Fine Persons but it is too bad you got to live here a while first to know that & do find it hard to accept straight off

WE HAS A SPECIAL TYPE OF EDUCATION HERE IN TAKING EACH MAN FOR HIMSELF

Hedy & the dago left after their coffee, taking more coffee back with them to their camp & I do not doubt but they stopped halfway there to boil another pot up   I got busy on the sledge I been building this past week as now we have pups enough to run it proper come next winter when they'll be big enough & strong   I had a good look at the sled Anderson got for himself that he bought in Fairbanks & took note of its dimension & kept that in my head while I started but I suppose the result don't look much like that one what was all polished & fine with special-made fittings   ours is plain but solid & will do the trick, I think   though the runners do not slide good yet   that is why I traded Big John some molasses yesterday for extra stovepipe to put on the bottoms   he laughed at me as I suppose he pictured I was to stretch our chimney another 10 feet into the sky   it is no easy trick to cut it though   we don't have the right gear   I think of Mike Piercey the Smith from N. F. L. D. as I know he would trim it to the right length faster than draw breath   I tries a few things such as axe & skinning knife that are no good for the job, & now am set to saw it down lengthways   I must admit it would be better if Bob were here for this as he could steady it &

make my cut straight but I got nothing else to do today & don't want to just sit & admire how the breeze reaches the back of my neck for the first time in months

Idle Hands are of the Devil & do lead to naught but Blackened Thinking

balance pipe upright   stand on top of sawhorse to reach the top of it but the pipe is still taller than me & I got to just prop it diagonal & brace it with one hand, this is a stupid way to do things, the sawhorse not meant to stand on, the angle for cutting (one-handed!) is nearly impossible, there is a terrible screech as saw teeth attempt to cut into the metal, SCREECH, SCREECH, the noise is awful, this is not going to work, I am quite a Rube about things, SCREECH, slip a little on the sawhorse, pipe wobbles, saw connects us, now saw wobbles too, we all wobble together & then we fall & I clutch out at saw & pipe as though they may save me from the crash but they got a Fierce Bite instead   I falls with em both onto the yard & the sawhorse is on top of us   SAW BURIED RIGHT INTO THE MEAT OF MY PALM   MY RIGHT PALM   IT IS MY FAULT FOR CLUTCHING IT TIGHT TO ME LIKE THAT   & MY FAULT TOO THAT THE PIPE, THE SHARP EDGE OF THE PIPE IS PRESSED TIGHT INTO MY SKULL & LETTING MY RED OUT   howling like Fitz in heat, no one here to help me, the dago long gone & Hedy too, no Indian come down the trail, my blood on the soft puddles of melting snow beneath me, my eyes going funny from it, I am always too Womanish for real things, it's nothing serious, I should not panic, stars in front of my eyes although the sun is out, world goes black, maybe I am crying, the world goes black & closes up on itself

when I wakes up there's Bob with water flicking on my face
        —can I not leave you without a nursemaid, Duke?
he got a cloth tore up to bind my wounds but first dabs on the
St. Jacob's Oil to clean them   I try not to howl out, fearful
stinging, dogs barking, I am full up with shame

—it were an accident
—always trying more than you should
—I know
—if you waited half an hour we could have fixed it together
            you won't be good for nothing now but eating up our
fucking food   I suppose that'll satisfy you   have
me do all the work while you laze about?

he throws a packet at me, letters from the post office

—here you are, Nancy   you got seven this time, I just got
the one

Jennie had her hand in mine & that is how I knew I was AWAKE
    her nails digging into the back of my hand, hurting me

AWAKE

Awake with Visions, swimming visions, dance-dance-dancing
across my Sight

What Were You Doing, in the Corner of the Cellar? What Did We
See, When We Went in for Potatoes?

What Was it You Were Doing In There?

~~I think I know what it was but I never before thought it to myself~~

I am not sure what it was
But I saw your Faces, & that was Proof
That it were A Thing to be Guilty About

Jennie & me ran, we ran & ran away, we ran as fast as ever we
could up the road & I did not care if Mother should be cross

later for there was no possibility of us staying at Home once we
Seen Them Things

the force of what we seen sending us running
running running running

over to Sandy Cove, down to the beach & into our Stage
          the familiar stench of fish always makes me gag on first
breath, even on a day like today when Stage is shut & no men
are there performing their fishy operations   Father
says I have to learn to Like It if I am to take his place one day
& What One Cannot Like, One Must Learn to Stomach

I asked once why it would be me, & not one of the others
—why not Bob?   he could come back & do it
          or Ernest? why not Jim? he knows his sums
—Don't Question me, Boy, I am the Authority
—Yessir   (& that was the end of it)

Once we are safe in the stage, Jennie puts her hand in mine
again

We both need Comfort

—what were they doing in there?   I ask
—I'm not sure   are you afraid?
—a little
—me too
—when you're grown up, do things seem Different?
—how should I know?
—you're older than me
—I'm thirteen   don't feel too Grown, though I suppose

(she sighs) I've had a share of living, haven't I?

(Rule #1: Never Remind Jennie of Her Baby, Her Lost Baby What
is now her 'Nephew' Ned)

—you're just a kid like me, though?
—yes sir   that's how I feel   who wants to be grown
—but what age do you turn into a grown-up then?
—I don't know   I don't think it's sudden
—probably different for everyone
—I guess it happened for them, though   do you think
they're adults now?
—they don't act like it most days   I can't stop thinking
on it
—I know   me too
—I thought Clare was sweet on your sister   I say
—I thought he was sweet on yours!
—on the World itself, it seems!

the sun is starting to set & we are in Sandy Cove without potatoes
         Mother asked an hour ago   we know we'll both
get the Strap
—let's take some fish back   Jim's getting the spuds, he said
as much to us, isn't that so?   & I give her a wink   —at
least now we have a secret, me & you

& we shake Spit Hands for a Promise

we take our fish & leave   we hear the gulls, see the puffins,
then the whales   capelin nearly rolling   we stop on
the beach & get our bottoms wet from sitting on the sand, which
means an extra lashing, but you have to watch the whales going

about their business when they come right in like that
    Jennie agrees

the sea of silver fish, a tide of living bodies   the clownish
birds with stumps of wings & roughly painted faces   the
whale's tail flipping up out of the water, a rude gesture made to
drum up laughs, for I have a sense that whales enjoy a joke or
two   & when they blow their spume then rear right up
into the air to plummet down with a mighty smack of spray
that echoes off the harbour like a thunderclap they do not do so
to be Majestic or fill us with Awe & they don't even do it for the
capelin, who are up closer to the surface than warrants such
deep diving   this leaping up & slapping down with wave
of tail is naught but THE WHALES LAUGHING AT US!

(WE CANNOT SWIM
AWAY FROM HERE!

WE ARE NOT FREE TO GO
WHERE WATER TAKES US!)

on the way back home the tide begins to come in & we flirt with
ruining our boots by daring the waves to catch us, which they
never can

we do not run home but walk it slowly
(why hurry a beating?)

the road is mostly dead for all are tucked into their suppers
save us & (of course) Norm Chaytor & Petey Badcock
        they come out with their rocks for me like they always
do when I dare to pass by the bit of road they feel they Owns

Norm spitting in the dirt & glaring at me with his pudgy face the uglier for the meanness in it

—It's Little Lord Tilly!
—The Duke of the Kingdom! (Petey)   Oh, isn't he a Pretty little Lord?

I try to hurry past them but Jennie stops in the road
—Hey there, Norm! How's your mother?

He doesn't answer straight away   Petey puts his rock hand in his pocket

—good   on the mend   getting up & about now,
   Norm says
—keeping her food down?
—soup anyway, soup & tea & a scattered bit of bread
—I'll tell Mrs. Tilly, she'll be glad to hear it   we could send her up a drop of something, when I do the supper for tomorrow

Norm's rock-pitching arm hangs limp at his side

—thanks, Jennie   none of us can cook too good
—you're all boys up there   what do you expect?
Goodbye! See you tomorrow, I'll be up with it before suppertime

once they waved at her, it were all over, they had no fight left & pelted nothing after us as we walked on down the road

I turned & called out —Good Evening! to them, in a Rare & Reckless Mood   Norm & Petey said nothing, did nothing, like two paper cutouts of themselves

I Got to Laugh,
Made Bold by Mysterious Acts
Which I had never Featured
Till I Witnessed Them!

~~What Were You Doing, Brother Jim?~~
~~& Cousin Clare?~~
~~What Were You Doing To Each Other with Such Fury~~
~~In The Damp, Dark Corner of our Cellar?~~

~~Was it for Play, or Serious?~~
~~& Is it Your Own Private Ritual~~
~~Or Something That Happens to All Boys~~
~~Once a Certain Day Comes~~
~~& They Ripens to Grown Men?~~

July 10, 1907

First time I seen Bob in a week

we do be partners still but who wants to live with your brother
now that we got the two camps going (me) (not He)

I get on his Every Nerve   he thinks me soft & addle-minded
& I know he is right on BOTH ACCOUNTS but I do not love
his manner & how soused he do get & then how mean (he often
Hits Out)   nonetheless I finds the weeks I spends alone
goes by real slow although I got my tasks lined up:
Smokehouse   Boat   Salmon Net   I progress
through each of them good enough, on Fine Days

sometimes I longs for his fists, if only for the change they bring
to this routine

we got hopes of a contract for 300 cords with N. C. & C. Co.
        we bought out Johnson for the land up above ours as all
our big trees are already cut & waiting

we got acres of stumps & saplings & cannot sit idle & wait for those to get ripe enough to fell

when I first came here I found the trees to be Majestic, so tall & straight   & now they are to me just Dollar Bills in waiting & I feel nothing for them when they topple over, nothing but desire for the work to be quicker, easier, not to make my back ache so   tis a hard life if you are no Bear of a Man
          & esp. if your Bear Bro would rather live in a tent 10 miles up than have to see you every day

I know he loves me though   he brings me moose meat when he has it & drops my letters to me on his trips from Wife to Tent & back again (got to keep the Youngsters coming & even I, Who Am Not Worldly, knows you can't do that without a trip to the Homestead now & again)

wish I had a Missus   sure I would not keep her in a cabin 60 miles hence   no, I would want to see my Missus daily
          I am sure Bob got some soft talk to him somewhere, else how do he have a Wife at all, Squaw or no?   it do not make sense

his Missus is handsome enough   Eva is kind & a good hand at all manner of work   Sewing   Cooking
          Curing Hides   Raising Dogs & Kids & Planting in the Garden   & sure I would keep her Company as good as Bob or Better

if he do Die I could take his Place

she'd be handier for a Wife than a Schoolteacher
or Father's Live-In Help

I've given up on Jennie anyhow   she have not written in
eight months   she is gone from my Heart & I feels Nothing
for her   her ratty skirts & hands sore from lye

Nothing   Nothing

ENTER BOB TO THE WOOD YARD

I know he is here before I sees him from the change in the air
          (what once felt loose is tight)

he don't say nothing   just nods at me   drops a
lynx & two geese down in the sawdust by the chopping stump
I never seen another Man take such pleasure from Trapping
Animals (To Him, It is True Sport)

—Good Day   I says

he don't reply, just heads over to check out the Smokehouse I got
done since he come through last   it is big enough for a
nice few Salmon at a time & a chunk or two of Moose beside but
it barely fits Bob, who is too Large for Life   I can hear him
grunting to himself, squat in the doorway, which is none too
wide

next he inspects the Boat   it is not done yet but the ribs
are pretty fair   he pats it on the side   I think this
is a sign of approval but am dying for a Word   say it is to
your Liking say I am not a Useless Sod say I can do something
to contribute to Our Life

he got me drove, so I heads inside for the Whisky   I gets a
word for this at least

—Cheers
—Cheers, Brother   say, will I cook up a duck?
he shakes his head   —heading back up now   come
along   too much to haul out myself

I put some buns in my pocket for the journey & we heads out
just like that with no more words between us

hot day with a cloud of Mosquitoes on our tail & a few Rabbits on
the way up   we do not even bother going for them,
Rabbits are Maggoty around here these days

stops only for a Bun & a Swallow at the Scree & it is while
relieving myself over the bank that I sees it   —Bob!
          he comes over we leans out together & then I starts to
Pray

Poor Bugger don't got much of a face left   looks like it
been smashed   that is a sight I never seen before, A Man
Dead of Violence

—you stay here, Bob says   —if you goes down you're
like to faint away

he's right & that shames me but I cannot change my Nature

I watch him climb down & at the bottom Strong Bob starts
Retching & that is a novel sight   must be powerful bad to
bring him to it   he finishes that Task & then gets some

boughs down & throws them on the man & heads back up the
bank

—that were no Accidental Death, you can see he was stabbed a
time or two before he tumbled down there   forget the
camp, now

we turn around on the path & head back down the river toward
the wood yard again   all I can see is the man with black
& red paste for a face what would not be known as a man at all,
were it not for his arms & his legs

—what shall we do, Bob   will you stay at the Cabin tonight?
—no boy, what for?   I got to get off to Tanana for the
Judge   I'd send you to do it but we got to be quick, that
body won't stay there too much longer as it is before the critters
get into it   Poor Fuck
—I can be quick
—quicker than Wednesday, I'm saying

he grabs the Flask from my coat pocket as we walk, & my
handkerchief too   he loves to scoff at that hanky (my
Airs), but today he has found a use for it   dousing it in
Painkiller & wiping clean his ashen face

August 9, 1895

THINGS I CAN SMELL FROM HERE
   1 sap
   2 salt water
   3 fir needles
   4 rocks (they do got a smell you know)
   5 mud
   6 wild roses
   7 moose plops
   8 ham
   9 apples
   10 my own sweat
   11 a whiff of rum though I ate the apple last to hide it
   12 mint I found by the river & am crushing with my teeth
to rid me of my Rum Breath & my Stomach Upset, both
(though it's probably just the ham gone off that's giving
me this feeling, I could well be Consumptive, A Witherer,
being always one with ailments, ever since babyhood
Like ~~Mother~~
Like ~~M~~——
Just like M—
Too much like M— for my own Good)

now I feel I may bring up my lunch & decorate my forest spot
with particles of Ham which have been half-digested
        Ham & Apple & Mint & Father's Drink

Today's Sins Are Threefold:

Stealing   +   Gluttony   +   Sloth

My Fate is to sicken from the inside until I rot into an empty shell
& someone can prick me with a needle & let the air out & I will
take up no room at all & Jennie can fold me up put me in a box
& send me to Boston or wherever M— sent herself

& I will know her as a Wholly Realized Musical Genius & she
will know me as her Perfect Genius Son

    Come Back! Come Back!
    I cannot bear this Despair!
    Alack! Alack!
    I have torn out my hair
    & now shall wear Black
    For at least a full year!
    Come Back, M—, Come Back!

I shall lie here another hour as I know where Jennie's going, this
time of day   it is Our Ritual

but I shall not do it & I will not do it anymore   it is Bad
Luck & besides Four Sins in one day is Too Many

she's at the trap, pulling down the ladder, headed up into the
Attic   you can see her legs with her skirt hiked between

them in her fist   she has no stockings on   on her left
calf she has 5 nipper bites equidistant from each other like the
corners of a pentagram, bright red on white with tiny fine hairs
you can only see when the light is just right & you are really
close to her   as you might happen to be, if you were
following her

    Up the Ladder,
    Up into the Attic,
    Where I Shall
    No Longer Go.
    Not I. No!
    Never, never, never.

July 21, 1907

Bob sent word from his Homestead that they have a man in
custody for the Murder at the Scree & he will be tried next week
          Bob will stay in town to see it   also he heard from
Father who said to tell me that The Hired Girl had run off

& I do forecast by Father's writing Bob about it (to whom he
never writes, save at Christmas) he somehow figures me to
blame

perhaps she'll write me once she's settled somewhere & it will be
something other than the standard greeting scrawled on a
postcard: We are well   Wish you were here
(what else is she to write, Father is Postmaster too & reads the
household mail before he divvies it   it is his Privilege)

now the letter containing her real thoughts, the letter without
filter of Father, now the letter from her heart will arrive & perhaps
I could send for her & she could live with me here by the river
          she would get on well with Mrs. Bob & is hardy enough
for the Alaskan Territory

Jennie be strong as a mare

So if she Writes me within the Year it's Settled:
Jennie Chants & William Marmaduke Tilly

We Shall Not Return
& We Will be Quite Happy Together,
Though it would Boil Father's Blood
To see his Youngest Living Son
Shack up (in a Bona Fide Shack!)
With His Housekeeper

& if she do NOT write me I have other Prospects to ruminate
on, who are Fine Persons whom I would Do Well With & should
be Grateful for Being Matched With In This Life

& sure twould not be the death of me to return to Bird Island
Cove, & in many ways so much easier than keeping on here
            though I have grown used to this life in my own way &
think I would miss it a fair bit if settling Outside, at Home, with
Miss E. Pearce

Jennie should be struck from my mind for good   why do
I continue to pine for her?   we were once close, but she
do not write me, Emily do   Em writes good letters, she
has nice script & good grammar   she is a Schoolteacher
so this is natural to her & I take extra care in composing my
letters back

Jennie's probably had a dozen Beaus by now & me out here with
no one but the Squaws & Doves   she's probably run off to
marry, or she is with child again & run off to have it   she's
probably keeping house for someone else with a softer hand
than Father (& a fatter, looser purse   ~~are they Lovebirds?~~)

I must be a daftie to think she'd wait this long, she who always
had a handful of suitors knocking softly late in the eve at the
kitchen door   why should she stick with Father? how
lonesome must she be, bearing the brunt of Him?

it's been two years since I left, nearly eight months since I have
heard from her   I must be soft in my brain all right, to
feature Jennie Chants still thinks of me at all

But still I will wait out the Year
Just this One Year, & no more
Then I will Quit—for one can't blow any longer
          than they got breath—
& if no word come July 21st of next, there's Emily
& there's many worse than she to Settle For

William Marmaduke Tilly

Hell & Sin

These Words I Vow NEVER TO FORGET
These Words Are MY TRUE MOTTO

Hell & Sin

Hell & Sin

It is all I have to Think On, For My Future

Walter Chaulk & wife Katie Murphy
James Baker Crew & Miss E. Symard
Robert Pearce to Miss Rebecca Hobbs
Thomas Pearce to the old juniper
All to be married by the first of May 1906

Ellen Eugenie Tilly to Gordon Hicks of
Catalina the oldest son of the late Capt. R. Hicks

~~Kate oh Kate~~
~~my little grief~~

Job Baker to Ethel Gover, Trinity

There are others I am sure that I don't know about
It is likely that I will not see their Weddings

Home home sweet home there is no friend like Jesus
There is no place like Home
It is Our True Station

William Marmaduke Tilly
Bird Island Cove
Age 21 years
Heavy snowfall on the 15th of November 1905
He got ready to start for the States on the 18th of November

William Marmaduke Tilly

Hell & Sin

Hell & Sin

Hell & Sin

I Shall Not Return till it is Washed From Me
& Forever Shall ~~Regret~~ Repent My Trespasses

January 29, 1916

I am so sick it feels like all of me has been expelled from Mouth & Anus simultaneously so that I am doubly empty & every muscle is sore from the contractions related to these efforts

I am No One, &
Even my Guts are now Deserting me

I find it hard to tell when I am Angry (I think instead that I am Sad) & I feel this is, as in the Greeks, my Tragic Flaw

realizing this feels like falling down a well   down & down forever   I am Sick now to realize how often I have taken my Anger & turned it inward   Scared to think I know nothing about myself, who is my Only Staunch Companion in this Desert of a Life

I do not know My Self   (& if I do not, WHO DO?)

Father sending men for the bed frame & the chest of drawers tomorrow & I would not DOUBT but my Emmy's shoes & stockings as well, as he gifted them to her, Before

On Tuesday night, when we did hear the door bolt shut & we did feel the fingers of the wind reach into our collars, I carried the baby inside my coat & Em clung onto my side so that we three all were as one person deforming hisself into hunchbacked Paroxysms in the presence of the Winter Wind

as one, we cringed & shuddered & staggered up the road to any place fit to take us   to them who we figured have fixed Father in a sour light   & many of those still would not take us due to the Church, or their Accounts, or His Reputation
           though Mrs. Ladd did give us Hot Tea on the doorstep & sent us on with a napkin full of Buns & Lard   the little one crying   its bawling Drowned Out in the Storm

& we walked all the way to Maberly, past all the doors that would not open to us, even though we were with a Baby & no proper clothes

& I understood then that Father had the Ear even of his Enemies & I knew that I had nothing in this world, save the two other heartbeats huddled close to mine
           (now I can thank Father
for bringing us together like
that   if only for A Brief Time)

he brought us, really, to Mabel   to Mabel's house
           what do not go to Church & what do not truck with Father
           what showed me all the best spots for blackberries when we were children   & brought the bread for my pockets
I always claimed I had forgot

& who I haven't laid eyes on since I was twenty-one, before I lit out

she has A Reputation, folk darken not her door, but at that point we had been walking for hours & no one would let us in & I saw the lamp lit in the window

Mabel took Em's hand before she said anything, Em who she never met before

& I cried then from my Deepest Place & stumbled o'er the threshold into the heat of a fire not yet bedded down for the evening   & I fell to my knees, laying baby on warm hearth stones where there it ceased its bawling

we lay on the floor before the fire awhile & Mabel came with blankets & Hot Toddys

I introduced her to my wife as Mrs. Chants, sister of Jennie what used to work for Father   & then I fell asleep as they were talking, waking some hours later when the baby fussed to find myself wrapped in Mabel's quilt with the soft squares of red velvet, which I recognized as salvaged from a dress she'd worn, when younger

& I knew myself the complete King of Men
FORTUNATE BEYOND ALL OTHERS

August 1, 1907

Left Hand Writing
Please Excuse It

Dear Father

I wrote you several times since April though you say I didn't
        I don't know why you do not get my letters when I send
one or more every time we go to Town   we sent $32 by
money order on July the 6 you should get that soon we can't
send more now we have much wood stacked on the bank but
can't sell it yet   Bob don't get many letters from you & I get
only one every few months so do not say we are being hard to
you for not writing when it is the same here & I got only one
more from N. F. L. D. this time & one from Bob Hobbs in BC &
one from Jule Chandler that is all for getting news none of the
rest do write not Ernest James Alice Dais Genie or even Kate
        I do not know what I done for them to forget about me

why did you not say me directly that Jennie is gone   I do
not know why you write to Bob about it but do not tell me in
your letters   do you think I do not care to know   sorry

to see that she was such a Bad Girl but she will find that this world is a hard one when she got to work for her living & keep on the move   she will soon want to come back again when that life tires her out so don't worry about it   she will find this world is a hard one to get through if you don't tow the mark

if you know where she went tell me in your next letter so I may write to her & try & talk some sense for there is no better place for her than Elliston   when have you done her wrong?
not at all in my memory & I suppose I do remember most goings on   more than Bob   he was up here before she was with us so I wish you would tell me about this not him for you must know he do not part with news too easy   it took about a week for him to let that slip at all & by then we were back from Tanana & I could not write you direct about it but had to wait   I am glad to know Daisy came home to see to you so you are not alone to fix for yourself   she is a good hand & maybe better for cooking than Jennie   though I did always like Jennie's way with pudding but she was not so good at Fish, or Roast   I am getting a fair hand with the cooking myself

you spoke of us giving you a little extra money to start a fish business   you would have had it long ago if I could have done it but I couldn't   don't be cross with me about it   all our wood is on the bank but we expect to sell it pretty soon & we got a chance of a four hundred cord contract too but if that happens we got to buy the man out that's cutting above us on the river which will cost to start but then we might be able to get you a few hundred dollars this fall   as soon as we get the money you are sure of the most of it   Bob is satisfied to go in on shares or any how you wish when we can

get the money   how much more would it take   let
me know the number in your next letter so we can start our
plan to save it but we do not spend much anyhow   we
got enough salmon & white fish in the nets & more beside to
feast on & feed the dogs   so much fish you got to throw
some back or give it to your neighbour   the rest of what
we needs we trades around & only pays for letters   &
like I said if we buys the man out that will cost but it is a good
chance for us to make more   once that happens we will
have four landings to ourselves, the only ones on this stretch of
the river so the cords will be sold quick & we shall likely need to
take on a man or two to help us

it would be a good chance to make a start better than how we
do now   (though we do not fare worse than any other
it have just been a hard summer   the strike at Fairbanks
have stung on the bum but business is starting up again)

now I hope you got that order for $32 Bob & me sent to you
          it was mailed from Bob but we both put in the money as
we are full partners so whatever name is on the orders know
it is from us both at once   his name was on it for
he goes to town more often than I do to see his Wife & the
children   they say to you their greetings   you
might meet them sometime if he ever goes Home

I would like to see you & have a good feed of Fish & Salt Pork
          I am that sick of Salmon now it don't taste good
anymore

I hope if everything goes well to see Elliston again   please
God

you must excuse my writing I got no other pen so this is scratchy but I do not wish to spend for another also I got to use Left Hand ~~had a small accident a while back~~ Right Hand not so good for writing now but serviceable for most things just not small work like writing or sewing, which I have mastered in a fashion   you would laugh to see it   me stitching up the holes in our socks by the cozy glow of the fire while Brother Bob has a snore

give love to all & say me to Aunt Sus Daisy Lightning
        I am glad you did not kill him but now where do he go since you did violence to the old barn?   tell me all in your next letter   do not leave out the news no matter if you think it small

I will see you again, God Willing   know that we are working for your money as fast as we can

Good Bye   It is Dark

I am your ever-loving son
Duke

Moccasins going through the snow soft like in bare feet
        tis new fallen snow fell all this morning so there's no
hard lumps for my toes to nose out yet   pretty snow
what's only been here the week, the first trace of winter Sept the
2 when there were 1/4 inch of ice in the top of the water bucket
upon my rising   & I thought well now there's a Change &
a Change is as good as a Rest

we don't have too much time for resting in these parts & I would
not want to anyway for that is when the Black Thoughts come

I cannot help our luck this summer, I told him as much in every
letter I sent but still he is cross about it   there was the
strike at the N.C.&C.Co. & it went on long & now they are
sending more coal steamers up than wood, I suppose it is more
Economical & what are we to do when I got at least 200 cords
here & Bob got another 300 up at his camp & we sold only 12
the whole summer?   & now the river will be freezing in a
short time & then we will sell nothing at all but still Bob keeps
on cutting   he tells me to keep on too   our luck will
turn, he is sure, & we will sell our 500 by the end of next Spring
        as it is we sent what we had Bob $32 in July & me another

$30 in August but that is not good enough for Father's purpose
            he is fishing now   he wants a bigger boat so
he can do it proper & he writes his arm is bad so he has to hire on
men more than he wants & see the money go that way

well I know that feeling   (that your Body is keeping you
from your Cash)   but there is nothing else to do
I spend little   I did send $30 to town with Anderson for
food but that is a necessity as I was scraping by here with no
Tea, Sugar, Butter, Flour, for weeks just getting by on Salmon,
White Fish, Rice & Berries with the last of the Coffee portioned
out small & watery   he must think we are cheaping him
& Living Large with all the best of everything but if he saw the
cabin he would have a start as it is half as small as Jennie's
pantry & that don't compare to Bob's place where he be living
in an Indian house that is just skins stretched over branches,
when you get down to Brass Tacks   though it suits Bob
fine, Father would have the fits if he had to spend a night in
there on the boughs, him used to his proper bed frame with
feather mattress & sheets you can wash regular because there
are two sets of them to alternate while the one set's drying out

(Sheets!   I do remember them

here we got just the hay-stuffed flour-sacks & the rough wool
blanket to pull against our skin but you know we are right
grateful for it & after the first few nights it do not seem too
rough no more)

the wood yard been making me Stir Crazy lately   I do not
feel like chopping when we sell nothing   I would rather
spend my time on other Occupations that will see some result

Am out for Rabbits today & did not feel like traps
          I took the rifle & set out to walking   the further
I get the happier my step   I am glad to be clear of the
stumps that mark our reach back from the crumbling riverbank
into the Land, glad to get past that to the place where the trees
still grow tall, straight & majestic   even more so now that
they got their caps of snow back for Winter   snow has
the power to make everything new

I suppose we all thinks this come September & then by mid-
November is back to hating it   for now I will accept the
Peace it brings & hope I was right when I wrote to Father I would
be Outside in 2 years, Bob too   that is the agreement we
are working toward though it depends on enough cords sold
          Bob says we can do it & he knows better than me, he been
living here long enough

Fresh tracks!

a rabbit or two going away from my usual route

I am craving Meat like nothing else   I am that sick of
Fish I could forego it forever were it not the thing that been
sustaining me these past months   I am not fool enough to
waste it, though with the wheel you wastes some anyway: it
scoops up the fish then dumps em in a box & by the time you
collects em there could be 500 in there, 300 dead so they are
wasted & 200 good ones that are fit to smoke or salt or eat fresh
or to freeze now that it's cold enough (that's the four flavours of
Salmon) & there's White Fish, many hundreds, & a supply of Dog
Fish for Fitz, Murph & the rest to keep em through the winter
          my smokehouse going full tilt all the time that I can

manage it   the smell of fish permanent on me as I suppose
it is on Father   out on boat like he never would before,
not once he took on the Store from Grandfather

that marks the distance Templeman got him drove & he only
got Cousin Harry there to help him (though he's as tough a lad
as they makes, same as his Bro Clare, & would be a good hand
to have aside you)   it must hurt Father's Pride to go
back to it at all   he was never easy around Water, he
Mistrusts it, & has bedroom in back of house, facing Road, as a
result

I drew a crude rendering of a salmon wheel for him in my June
letter & told of how many fish gets wasted & he wrote me an
idea for a salmon trap using lobster pots which we do not have
here on the river but which I am sure I could fashion without
too much trouble

it seems a good plan to me, many less would be lost   he is
clever like that & has a good head for figuring improvements
          me, I just keep on the way I first learned & do not think
to fix it (save socky flap on front of coat, that I did discover & it
has brought me Comfort these Winters since, though I cannot
convince my Fellow Bush Men to Adopt it)

yes, We Will get Home in 2 years   Father will come off the
Water   We will have a start   We will get the store back
     We will all work the land & there shall be
     Good Will Among Us

Rabbit gone fair deep into the woods, snow falling   hush of
Nothing spread wide around me   sound of just my breathing

It's been 2 years since I left home & it feels like the more I try & keep the faces clear in my mind the more they melt away

        I recite the features to myself but the memories get dimmer   & that's with the Living, the Dead are harder still

for a few I got photographs   I got one of myself sat with Kate & Genie in Leo before I left   a Posed Portrait in Our Finery   I keep it hidden on account of the things Bob says about it, about my looks   clean, soft, pale, shaved & combed, in a suit with a boutonniere, I seem a much different Duke to the bearded, ragged face I can make out in the shine of the kettle, now   I keep the picture under my mattress & hauls it out sometimes to look at the girls, my sisters with their smiles, looking right into the lens of the camera, identical smiles, the same as mine would have been, too, if I'd actually been smiling & not just sitting with rigid hands clutching one another in the lap of my fine trousers, betraying my Nerves

nevertheless I cherish said photograph for its ability to keep K. & G. close to me, in memory

how can a Mind be so soft that it can lose the features of a Family?   it do seem Strange

there are some others for whom I have no photograph (E. P.) & who, as modestly-recompensed schoolteachers in Bonavista Bay, have not the means to acquire such a thing, not now

        (it is not a Priority   she is building up her Trousseau against my Return, as apparently All Brides Must have their Dozen Doilies & their Teapot Cozies & other Giddy Truck)

Emily now is just an outline   just the memory of her slight
weight in my arms that time at the dance, that first time that I laid
eyes on her, & how she would look across the aisle in Church
after (she started coming up to Elliston for service, so I knew she
took me seriously)   her mocking smile when she laughed
at my fresh haircut that first night   & how I got to know
her since, from the postal cards she picks out, with glittery pink
paste edging the flowers (they seem rich & foreign as diamonds
to me, holding them in my logger's hand amid the stumps, fish
& dogshit)   I have come to know her from the way she
makes her handwriting, neat & square & all lined up as I can never
do, especially after a drop or two of Whisky or Jamaica Ginger
(I take it regular now for my Neuralgia, Bad Ankle, for Headaches
& for Rhumatiz   & Not Always in Medicinal Doses:
Add to My List O'Sins, SVP)

Emily, I am hardened now, I am not the one you met at that
dance in Catalina
I am not a Bear of a Man & no Clean Young Lad neither
I got Calluses
I got Scars
Dirt ground deep into my Skin
My Teeth do ache
So do my Bones
The Stoop has begun at the base of my Neck
I have a Headache more times than not
& A Lasting Melancholy

you say you love me   you say we will get married   but
what kind of girl waits so long for one she barely knows, save
through his letters, which I take care to make as pleasant
(therefore as False) as possible?   it is a Hard kind of life

here & any Nicety I had at Home has now been stripped from me   would you be proud to see me out here in the woods, my gun in hand & dressed in Rabbit Fur, hunting more Rabbits, like some kind of figure in a joke of Clare's telling? I cannot see you living here   I cannot feature you fitting in beside me   & I hope to God when I get home this Life will melt away from me & leave no Stain, & I will look at ease in my Flannel Suit again, as if it fits me   if not, you shall think me Too Changed & Too Rough & I fear ye shall not want me for Husband & then all—ALL—will have been for Nothing

RABBIT RABBIT I want you to show yourself now   am tired of wandering, been gone at least 6 miles more than I reckoned & will have to double back on that to get home
        snow falling thicker   mind unravelling like the crazy looped path my rabbit's after making   I should just turn back but do not want to face the empty wood yard anyway with no man for company   the dimming prospect of catching myself a Fluffy Lunch is better than that

RABBIT RABBIT come out wherever you are   come dance in the sights of my rifle   I will feel sorry for you but it will be LYNX or BEAR or COUGAR maybe HAWK for you soon enough if it is not Me, & when I has my shot I am gentler than they are with their claws & teeth & beaks

snow falling hard now   my tracks are nearly covered
        light is going

I start back on my way out & cannot find it   tracks of rabbit & of Duke alike been filled with snow   I am a FOOL who do not know his Bearings, a FOOL to think myself fit for solo Rabbit Hunt, I AM NOT MY BROTHER

too much thinking on postcards   Mooning, as Bob would
say   I did not stop to take stock of my position but let my
mind wander   Bob has said before that this would be my
Downfall

I AM TOO DREAMY

RABBIT RABBIT, you got me, you are far more Clever than this
Homo Sapiens!   I am turned around with only a shred of
Smoked Salmon in my pocket for my dinner   turned right
around & might as well face it I will not make it home tonight,
not once night falls   good thing I am wearing the fur of
your Family, Mr. Rabbit, it is the best protection against cold & the
best Friend I could have out here tonight, where I suppose I must
sleep cuddled up against the stars, snug as a bug in a snowbank

I WILL NOT TELL BOB ABOUT THIS, he will think me less a
man than ever
I WILL TELL NO ONE

I WILL NOT WRITE OF THIS TO FATHER, EM, CLARE
OR TO ANY ONE AT ALL, SO HELP ME

THERE'S A KIND OF THOUGHT
A MAN SHOULD KEEP TIGHT
TO HISSELF, I HAVE LEARNT
EVEN IF YOU'RE DYING TO DIVULGE IT

--- HER ADOLESCENCE ---

Eva wants to be close to her mother, closer than her mother's rules allow. The caregiver is not to have excessive physical contact with the patient or to breathe too closely to the patient's face. She has special gloves she has to wear. She keeps them in the pocket of her sickroom smock, which hangs outside the sickroom door, and is long enough to cover all of her clothes. She also has a cloth mask to put over her mouth. It makes her feel like she is hiding, and in a way she's glad her mother can never see her full expression. Eva doesn't think the smock or mask have much effect as a barrier, but her mother is very strict about maintaining as much of a quarantine situation as possible. Duke and the children are not allowed inside the room, as it is important to maintain consistency: one person with the utmost standards of hygiene should be the sole caregiver of the patient, and Duke is a fisherman, a farmer, a trapper and a logger, so hygiene is not on the top of his priority list. He has work to do and food to be procuring for Eva's rudimentary preparations, and besides which, he's become strained and awkward with Mrs. Tilley since her illness started, as though he doesn't recognize his own wife anymore. He's never been one for making talk with strangers.

So, throughout the spring and now the summer new rhythms are established, which, strange and topsy-turvy at first, soon transform into the unacknowledged everyday motion of their lives. Eva leaves off everything she used to do for herself, which wasn't too much. Her Sunday group. Practicing piano. Walking in the woods with Walter. Stealing up to Bird Island Cove to see Mabel, against her mother's say-so.

She'd been foolish for Walter, recently even, foolish for that eerie feeling on the back of her neck. Ever since she had turned thirteen in April they'd been going up back of the farm together. He'd touched her bubs before they'd even started to show, and hadn't let on any disappointment. That wasn't long ago. They had been picking raspberries. They had a secret spot they liked to go, out back of the farm where the land was still the same as when people had first arrived here. The raspberry bushes went up past your eyes and were full of vicious thorns, but Eva knew a spot where there was a bush you could push through into a little clearing, almost perfectly round, with berries on all sides. About big enough for two people, if they were friendly with one another. Duke had showed it to her long ago, he called it a Charmed Circle. Supposedly if you stayed in there too long, the Little People would catch you in their snares. It was a story his father had told him when he was her age. Duke knew all the secrets about the family land. When Eva was a girl, they would pick berries together and he'd dare her to go pick by herself in the circle, and she never would, because she always half believed his stories. He had a serious expression when he spoke.

That day with Walter, back in July, the bucket was not very full, and what was there was carelessly picked, as they were only half paying attention, more intent on nuzzling each other. His breath was hot and sweet and his tongue was stained with berry juice. They had been kissing for weeks now, but this was the first day she felt his hands on her, burrowing their way into her clothes.

> I wish I were an old boot
> and you a piece of leather
> and some kind friend would come along
> and nail us both together

> If my heart were a head of cabbage
> That grew and split in two
> The leaves I'd give to others
> But the heart I'd keep for you

She'd written those before the notebook had been taken over with her mother's instructions. There were a lot more poems than that, at least ten pages worth, at the front of the book. Near the back were her notes from the visits to Mabel. *Sad at heart. Red bastard. No words but the lips will betray you. Some girl but she looks like a sheep. White cream girl. Him hands like wasp stingers.* That day, after he'd touched her and she'd backed away in shock and then relented and kissed him on the mouth, she'd let Walter see the front of the notebook, to make up for things. He'd laughed at her, but there was something shy in his eyes too. And then maybe some fear as she took out her pencil, turned to a new page, and wrote out her own set of instructions.

Ten Commandments of Love

1. *Remember thy beloved sweetheart*
2. *Thou shalt not make goo-goo eyes at any other girl*
3. *Thou shalt not wink at any other girl*
4. *Thou shalt not love to kiss but kiss to love*
5. *Thou shalt not be to thy sweetheart a penalty*
6. *Thou shalt not do anything in private that thou would not do in public*
7. *Thou shalt not love two when one will do*
8. *Thou shalt not ask for a kiss but take one*
9. *Always kiss a girl when she refuses for she does not like to say yes*
10. *Whosoever reads the ten commandments of love must pay the penalty asked. If he refuses, take him away from me.*

Walter said Eva was contradicting herself with these so-called rules. Eva said that she regretted letting him touch her there, and didn't think it was proper, as she was only thirteen, after all. Walter said that was hypocritical as she'd just shown him her love poems, hadn't she? Eva wanted to know why love always had to be about the body. Why couldn't he just love her in the way she wanted him to? He asked for a kiss and she refused so he forced one from her, as per commandments 8 and 9. She protested more and he kissed her harder. He touched her on the bubs and she said no, don't do that, and he said back that he knew that she wanted him to. They spilled the bucket of berries when he pushed her down onto the grass and she kicked out in surprise at his weight on top of her. What's the penalty I must pay for having read your rules? said Walter. Then Eva began to cry and he felt very sorry. He pushed out through the thorns and got water from the brook to wash her face with, and picked up her glasses and wiped them before giving them back. Walter told her that he loved her and that although they were very young he was sure this was forever. If she wanted it, he would ask her father about proper courtship, even though he did think Mr. Tilley was a dirty Smallwood man. She said she liked the secret of being with him, and that it was their special thing here in the circle. He joked about the Good Folk bewitching them some night, leading them astray into the Good Kingdom, until they lost their minds and turned into animals, naked on all fours in amongst the trees. Eva meowed like a cat and Walter pounced on her, and kissed her, and she said no, don't, so he did it some more. She pried herself out from under him and got up, scrubbing at the raspberry stains which were blooming all over her skirt. Walter seemed unable to stand.

You always disappoint me.

What does that mean, Walter? I showed you my book, I told you things, you kissed me, and now I have to go as Mother needs her tea.

You always pick your mother over me, Eva.

What an evil thing to say, you bastard boy.

I don't care if it's evil, it's the truth.

Don't be a sook. She bent and kissed him and said she loved him but couldn't he understand? Her mother was sick, she couldn't fix her own tea anymore, she couldn't do anything, she needed help to sit up, to do her toilet, she couldn't do anything anymore, you understand? Walter said he understood, but Eva didn't believe him, and ever since then they'd only gone picking once and he hadn't tried anything much, and had avoided her eyes, looking like someone had kicked him.

When you're ready to be sweet you come and find me.

Thinking of Walter makes Eva think of berry picking, which makes her think of the blueberries up in the meadow, which are ripe, which makes her think of her mother, who loves blueberry buckle more than any other dessert. Mrs. Tilley used to talk all summer about making the first pan of it, walking up to the back of the land every morning to check for early ripe ones once August hit and the berries started going from white-green to pink to blue. Eva has the recipe, although she hasn't tried it yet. As she washes the young one's clothes and wipes the floors, she thinks of her mother's face, pleased and proud. Even if she cannot eat it, the smell alone will do her good. After reading, and sums, and lunch, she sends the babies across the road to play and heads up to the back of the land with her bucket. Her mother is sleeping well, and won't need her till at least four o'clock. Eva swings the bucket happily. She starts up past the raspberry patch, and then she stops. There is a sound. At first she thinks it's a partridge. Rustling. Then there's a kind of moan. She heads straight into the raspberry circle with her bucket in front of her, a shield for the thorns.

They look like a painting, having frozen in place when they heard her charging in on top of them. For a second no one speaks. Nothing moves save the blackflies. Eva feels herself grow flushed. She had been warned. *White as cream. Red hand boy. Fragile girl is turning to marble.* There in their spot, in her charmed circle, where he had kissed her neck and felt underneath her clothes and said he wanted to marry her. It is Duke's property. It is a place only she goes to, or Duke himself, and Walter knows that, and has chosen the place purposefully, maybe hoping for Eva to interrupt them, or else Duke, who knows. When she crashes through the bush on top of him and Gertie Hancock, Walter's face doesn't look any redder than usual. His hands do, though. Seems once a boy turns fourteen he cannot live for a week without grabbing hold of some girl's bubbies. Gertie Hancock's flabby bubs. She'd been the most well-developed girl in school, back when they had school. Gertie had lumps at nine, and a womanly shelf at eleven. Eva always thought it was embarrassing, but obviously Walter thought otherwise. He didn't look sorry at all.

You bastard, bastard boy.

Eva, girl, you drove me to it. No satisfaction for a month.

Gertie starts crying, scrambling to do up the front of her dress, wiping her face with her hem, trying to stand. Don't tell my father, will ya?

You can both fly to hell. *Hands you know on strange snow. Thorny bush all around the circle.* Eva throws her empty bucket, and though she means to hit Walter it glances off Gertie's shoulder and she starts crying even louder.

Sorry Gertie. Walter, you can burn to blazes for all I care. Get off my father's land before I call him up here.

Eva leaves the bucket, pushes roughly through the bush and walks back toward the house, stopping at the cellar to pull out a few potatoes to boil with milk toast, for supper. There would be no dessert. She has scratches starting to sprout bright beads of blood on her arms and neck from her quick retreat through the thorns. She'll never pick in the circle again. The raspberries could rot off their branches, she wouldn't care about the waste. The berries could all ferment into wine, get the foxes drunk, she'd leave them for the Good Folk. Her blood gone cold, and slow. She drops the potatoes into her pockets then thinks better of going inside. Her mother doesn't expect her for an hour, and Mary and Bob are still across the road. There's an acid fire inside of her, the shape and size of bastard Walter's bastard hands. She feels numb. She might cry. A walk will help. If she goes quickly she can get up to Maberly and back again before starting supper.

She sets off up the road, half-skipping, the potatoes thudding heavily into her thighs.

Mabel, are you sat down to the table or what? Eva knocks on the door off the kitchen. Mabel is rarely found anywhere else.

Get yourself inside, I just made jam.

If it's raspberry, no thanks.

Mabel comes to the door, her face red from the stove. Don't tell me it already happened.

Gertie Hancock.

Gertie Hancock. And what happened to your arms, my girl?

Mabel is wearing work trousers, like Duke's, and Eva knows this is part of the reason why her mother does not approve of her. Well, there are other reasons, too, but Eva privately disagrees with Mrs. Tilley on those. Mabel knows things, Mabel sees things. Tea leaves, cards. Once, down on the beach, Eva saw her receive the voices straight. Mabel. Her hair long and grey, parted sharply in the middle, combed straight and left unbound, like a gloomy waterfall right down to the seat of her trousers. Mabel told her two months ago that she foresaw infidelity, another woman, she even pinpointed the location: Berry bush circle. Hidden private yours. That's the kind of speech she has when she's reading leaves. Who and when had been a mystery. Mabel spoons some warm blueberry jam onto a thick slice of bread for Eva, gets her a cloth to wash her scratches, and puts the kettle on. Mabel's jam has won prizes at the Bird Island Cove Fair, and perhaps this is another reason why Eva's mother doesn't like her very much.

The cup she reads from is an ordinary one, a white teacup, like the plain kind Eva's family uses when there's no company in. It's not the cup. Eva is glad for her daily dictations, as she can easily copy everything down. When Mabel starts to speak the leaves, she doesn't stop. It all comes pouring out.

Long journey. Cross water. A long dress and a pair of high heeled shoes. See a flag half masted. See a strange fellow walk with him. On top of cup good luck. Get my wish. Long long journey. See flag half masted. Visitor. Box. A long, long way from home, removal past wonderful. Grey lady turns to dust. Boat. Strange message. Good prospects. Journey across water. I walk with strange man in new shoes. Man unpacking bottles. Lady is air now and lady will vanish. Dishes. Book. Give me journey. See flag half masted. Play the church organ. All the flowers cut down they go into the hole. Get wish. Lady floating into lights. Laughing on a boat. The flowers in the hole are dying. I am laughing the babies are crying. So much noise. I am going across water big laughing big breathing no one who knows me is there. Time going still again like playing at going to sleep.

Eva stands abruptly and puts her hand over the cup. Stop. Stop, please, that's enough.

Mabel blinks. She's back in the room. Anything?

The same as before, a journey and a book. Me getting my wish.

Well, that's good.

Eva puts on her coat. I'm going to be late. She darts out the door before Mabel can see the guilty tears starting to form in the corners of her eyes, as she allows herself, for once, to luxuriate in the forbidden thought of her mother's death, and to long for it.

Nursemaid Death, sitting on her mother's shoulder, lips to her lips, sucking the last bit of colour away.

Mother cold, gone, in the ground.

A boat, a journey, a place where she's a stranger.

The children taken in by relatives.

Eva wipes her eyes and begins to run, pounding dust up in a long trail down the road towards home. There are sheets to soak in carbolic, rag bowls to empty, poultices to change. She is grateful for the coat, for once—the scratches on her arms are hidden from sight. The mask smells clean and scrubbed, she finds it comforts her to put it on, to close off as much of herself as possible under sterilized cloth, boiled in acid until nothing can live on it. She enters the sickroom. The remains of her mother's face look up at her, sinking further and further back into the starched pillows, cheeks turning in on themselves, hollow pits, grey and moist. She's barely moving now, and will not take more than a mouthful or two of cream toast for supper tonight, Eva is sure. She clenches her jaw behind her mask and gently brushes her mother's hair. She softly strokes her mother's face with a warm damp cloth; Mrs. Tilley doesn't want a full bath tonight, she doesn't have the energy.

Eva wipes down her pencil and the covers of her notebook in carbolic solution before opening it. She sits, ready to copy down any instructions her mother might be able to impart before six o'clock, when she generally grows too tired to give dictation and asks that her daughter please read to her. Soon afterward it will be time for Eva to gather the young ones outside the sickroom door, to call in their goodnights and sing one of the old hymns Mrs. Tilley taught all the children of Elliston to sing, gathered around the church piano, a long time ago, in the golden days when she was a schoolteacher.

BOOK THREE

THE SLIDE

November 26, 1907

The blank pages still before me in this book are too numerous

I do not wish to be here long enough to fill them up

only a quarter do be marked on & yet it feels a Century since
I left Trinity Bay

I do Pine for it
& if I were a Real Poet
I would Rhyme of it!

Though I know T.B., N.F.L.D. is no place special, having now
traversed the Continent, still it do have a Pull on me, comprised
of:

Beach & Farm & Piano, Attic
Island, Cellar
Thicket of Berry & Thorn
Jennie's Dinners
Father's Store, working the counter & sorting the Post
I did not relish it at the time but now these tasks seem A

Vacation
My breaking of Lightning who Father joked was half Moose
& who worked so hard we thought him part Dog too
& let us leave the rest unnamed for now before I start some
waterworks like Bob detests
& therefore start another fight between us

I do try not to vex him but he's easy to annoy   he has got
a Short Fuse & must Keep His Powder Dry   (& now in
the Dark Time we got less to do as there's no boats till breakup,
just some trapping, repairing & chopping to do   & some
waiting for the Sun to return, some prayer for Sanity to stay the
course of Winter, One More Year, long enough to get Home
Again with Cash Enough in Pocket for Father's Plans)

sometimes I am sure the Lights are mocking me!   they
sing out scorn   I am not strong enough! they are Eternal!
I am Not Pure!

down the Gullet with more Liquid Painkiller straight from the
bottle   Bob & me got no Niceties between us anymore

He makes me Nervous
Esp. since the Camp Intruder &
The Justice that was dealt, one week ago

it soured things between us so that most days we do not talk &
there are days he just goes out to the upper camp without no
word of warning & he stays there though we don't got a proper
cabin up at all, it is not finished but Bob don't mind bunking
with the dogs if he got to, he prefers it to a snug warm cabin
with his Brother in it

& when he stays here each has his task & goes about it & each
cradles his drink on his own bunk, the only overlap being care
of the dogs   we neither of us wish to relinquish that

Fitz was his bitch, but I helped raise the rest from pups
        some for us to sell but now we do not want to let any go
as both of us find them company & would miss them should
they leave us   but I know this winter will be tight as
many rigs now are coal goers & do not need us at all & business
is slowing & Father's debt is growing & we may have to sell the
whole litter & forfeit a team ourselves to make it through at all

next time Charlie the Indian comes up I shall ask after who
needs dogs down Village

them Indians do be good for trade & we could use some of the
food they got stocked up for such occasions   esp. coffee
& molasses or sugar which we have had none of since October 12

Bob's face is a little leaner now but he is none the worse for that
& he looks haler, if possible   while I waste away so that
all my trousers must be taken in

        A Patient Skeleton
        Tapping Fingerbones on Table Top
        Doing Time till I get to go Home &
        Trying to Avoid Disturbances Until Then

Note to Self: Tomorrow get rid of Evidence of Intruder straight
& move something to cover the Spot   It would not do for
Charlie or Anderson or Quailey or the dago to see it
        & though not my fault I could be what one would say
Accompliced To It

if no one knows then we are none the worse off, except that we do not speak to each other   not that Bob really ever was one for the Gab, like Daisy or Kate or Ernest   or that Jennie Chants

but it was nice sometimes to hear his voice & to practice my own too   the simple things we used to say have faded out of the days now   & something in me is powerfully sad for missing the chance to pipe up now & again with ordinary things like —Have a cup? —How many cords did you pull out? —There's ice closed over the hole again   or other normal bits of daily conversation

do Bob care about the silence? I cannot tell   he just seems more soaked than normal   which makes him sleepy, or causes him to simply sit & stare into the fire

except one night when we had Company & there were stories & a few tunes going around   & late into the night when he'd enough Fire in the Furnace, Bob let his voice out   he got a voice like a dark, heavy bell that takes you by surprise   & he knows a song or two from home that I cannot bear to hear, so I had to leave on some excuse into the night lest Anderson or the rest might see me cry

> He do not sing when we are alone
> He do not look my way
> & I think he is ashamed of me & how
>   Weak I am, that I would fall into a dead faint like that on

seeing what had happened   that trap around the ankle of the Intruder   his trouser torn back from it, the metal teeth gripping just as effective as on the Wolf & Lynx haunches for which they were meant

the Intruder unconscious & I thought dead at first, & then when
I saw he had breath rising up out of him, that is when I was dizzy
        the thought that we had trapped this man by Accident
& now his Fate was in our Hands

Bob does not have patience for my ways & when I came to again
he had his back to me, flicking snow on the Intruder's face
        the man was in a considerable amount of pain, I suspect,
from the teeth snapping into the bone   & I had doubts of
his walking again & doubts even of the possibility of recovery,
him having been out here a while from the state of things   &
the dirty trap being favourable to poisoning your blood, I suspect,
& much of that already spilled, regardless

I worried about Death

would Death come to him, here, in our wood yard?
& how do that mark us forevermore?

Bob shouted at the man   —can you hear me?

The Intruder couldn't speak or maybe was in shock   he
said nothing but he trembled something fierce

—Man! Say something!   Who are you & why are you on
my property?

The Intruder started grabbing at Bob, a whimper spilling out of
his mouth   he clutched Bob's leg   Bob kicked out
at him a bit by instinct, then he drew back & kicked him again
quite hard & square in the mouth

—Bob!

his boot hovered above the face with small drops of blood now
falling out
—who are you?

the face crumpled up & the sounds coming out were not our
English ones

—he don't speak the language Bob   sounds like one of the
boiler boys on the Dawson   from over in Holland or Russia
or somewhere   maybe Hedy could talk to him

Bob was hot   he didn't know what he was doing because
if he did why would he hurt this man who already been half
dead on account of us?   stoving in his face with his boot,
three more hard cracks that set the Intruder to whimpering

—Stop now Bob   we must get him out of the trap & we
must bring him in & try & see what we can do about his leg &
find out who he is

but there went his boot again, hard, on the face that was just
lying there now, waiting for it

—Bob!

I grabbed his arm   he hit me hard in the neck
without sparing me a glance   I saw some stars
& staggered back   he got the Intruder by the coat, got
him sat up & was shaking him, nose to nose there on the snow,
Intruder's blood spraying out onto Bob's face & marking him

—Fucken tell me your name
(Intruder trembled & made a sound like wounded goat)
—Fuck! Don't make me!
(slobber & bleating)
—I will hurt you!
(baa baa baa)

Bob Slugged The Intruder in His Bleeding Nose

I held my neck, called out feebly   —Bob, take a breath
now, what are you doing?
—he was in our yard, we don't know him   (kick to ribs)
he's here to fleece us   why else would he be sneaking
around?   Right, Man?   a Camp Robber, is who you
are   A Criminal   (kick)   Did you kill a man? Did
you?   Did you Kill a Man & drop him down the Scree?
          You fucken Murderer! (kick)   Murderer!

he took the Intruder by the throat & looked half ready to shake
him free of this Mortal Coil   The Man wasn't
trying to fight   weak as a newborn pup   his
blood going everywhere

—Bob, you got no evidence
—look at his eyes   Killer's Eyes, Duke

Bob grabbed the fellow by the chin & roughly twisted his head to
face me   The Intruder looked sorry to exist   I didn't
know how to help him   Bob got more brawn than me & is
brutal too, when he's in the mood   Intruder said
something we didn't understand

—Dutch he is I think
—I don't give a fuck what he is   he's here to rob us
          or worse
—you don't know that   he could be lost
—fucken better talk now
(bleat bleat)
—can we bring him in
—once he confesses
(baa)
—can we take off the trap then
—once he confesses
—Bob

he looked at me   Father, you were looking out of his eyes,
that look that is like the spark of flint   A Sharp One

he got a length of chain from the dog shed & trussed the man
up even more, looping it around his neck   as though
Intruder had enough strength in him to pry the trap off & try to
run for it

—please, Bob
—go in the cabin & get some bread & a blanket
—it's not enough
—it will suffice   Trespassers will be Punished
—he don't have nothing
—not yet
—if someone knows you got him chained out here, though
—no one'll know
—Bob
—& if you tell I'll kill you
—Bob!

—if you tell, I will
—stop
—I will, Duke   I will   I'm sorry to do
it but we're too far gone now   look at him   no
judge will like this, don't matter what the truth is
          we have to deal with this mess ourselves
—you're scaring me!
—& so I should   get the fucking bread if you want him to
fucking eat tonight

I did so, & then I went back inside & lay down in my bunk with
the Painkiller beside me, knowing full well that when I woke in
the morning the Intruder would be frozen solid out there,
unless he managed to free himself of the chain about his neck
& then gnaw his own leg off, like a few determined foxes since
I've been here (whenever I find a paw in a trap, it gives me hope,
& I keep my eyes out afterward for that crazy three-legged fox,
skidding around in the forest, & I take the paw home & clean it
well & put it in an old mustard tin I keep expressly for that
purpose   I take the pile of them out to look at when I need
Resolve   there's six in there now & I do not wish to add a
Human Foot to my collection (I would need a larger tin, for
starters)   all the same, I would prefer that to the alternative
I found in the morning, covered in the ice fog that had settled
overnight, blurring his features   under the fur of frost
the blood in his veins was frozen to pure, black ice like snaky
Widow's Lace all over him)

when Bob took off for the upper camp that morning, I was
relieved, though it meant I had to deal with The Corpse myself
          I have no experience in that type of Work
          (It was best to Burn him, there was no burying possible,

& that way I also warmed up too, for a few hours, though the Aroma of Roasting Human is not one I wish to entertain again)

twere gruesome in its way but I surprised myself with my efficiency & calm, no Excess of Nervosity as would have been exhibited had this incident happened in previous years
        though I did have a start when some chicken or hare would make a noise & I thought A Neighbour had come to the yard   but none came, I were Lucky

& when it were done & he was gone to cinders I felt some Pride at my Accomplishment

& I hope Bro Bob knows this is my greatest act of Love for him, bigger than Our Constant Lie to Father

I only regret I did not get the courage up to take the Axe to the Intruder & make of him some Dog Feed
instead of wasting him to ashes

Poor Pups are Thin
We all been Hungry

April 5, 1925

I minds now that first time it happened
When I saw my first Proper Mountain

& my Heart did this spasm dance which began in my Throat
& my Breath stopped there too a while

Both Breath & Heart in Throat

Throat Cavernous

It was roundabout 1906, in the springtime, I'm guessing late
April, when I headed up to Vancouver, to meet up with Clare, in
that stint I did as foreman up & down the Yukon   (some
Energy then)   that was when I first saw Mountains

the far-off blue-white Mounds of Paradise drawn close around
Vancouver's harbour, making all our little N. F. L. D. cliffs look
like bedroom stairs

beautiful, so many Bosoms perked up & pointing to the Sky
          (do not take Offence, I speak to you Man to Man as
honestly as I can, take it in that vein & do not deny that you've

noticed similar Shapes sometimes, yourself, in the things around you)

going upriver that first time, I saw how the mountains kept on changing

so different once you're among them   no longer just Nature mimicking the cool heaving shapes of Jennie's breasts, as though she were lying on her back, just so (~~you know the Shapes I mean!~~)   Jennie's breasts, multiplied & strung out in a line, hugging the water

the closer you got, the meaner those mountains became
        sharper & more extreme   hard stripes of rock & ice
        pure black & white

what once seemed Nipple-Soft now started to slice the Sky
        how could something that big look so flat? like the double image in a stereoscope before you take the eyepiece to it & it jumps to singular Life

        Up Close, the Mountains
        Turned Man To Dust Mote,
        Maggot, Nipper, Tick on Dog,
        Dandelion Seed, Parasite

but right as your thoughts went black as the rock, you would find yourself deep in the Hips of the mountains, & colour would start to come back out of the black until it was all green & brown & grey & younger green & lighter brown & blue-white & those sharp lines turned jagged & complex & a million trees appeared before your eyes

& you'd sigh relief because them trees is familiar to you, they are the same at home: scraggly struggling green with unkempt dead ones in among the living, what hold the dead up & keep them from rolling down the mountainsides

& your neck'd hurt from tilting back to take in where the peaks of it all're stuck into the sky

& when you're right up close, you start seeing shapes in the rocks   I remember seeing hands mostly   out flat, or palm to palm (as though praying)

& what looks like veins of snow one hour turns out to be waterfalls by suppertime   that water falling further than fifty of Sandy Cove Beach stacked skyward on its side

& what looked like N.F.L.D. trees this morning would show themselves to be too big to put your arms around & unbelievably tall

all of it making memory of Home shrink smaller
& again smaller

& what used to be all my Life & Care
became as a Speck of Dust in my Mind:

INSIGNIFICANT

(this feeling lasted for a few minutes, I recall   long enough to jolt me out of My Purpose for just one instance, to make me question You & Your Use of Me toward your Own Ends   & it is this instance that I blame for my later Trouble   though it has taken till now to recognize the Mountains themselves as

Catalysts for my Doubt
& hence my Imminent Separation from You
& thus from EVERYTHING
& EVERYONE I knew—
EVEN MYSELF!)

now that you're gone, I feel I can talk to you more frankly than
I ever did while you were here   (you can't Discipline my
Tongue now, Sir!)   I loved you so much I was blinded
by it & I was so scared of you I was cowed & I were led by you
always even when you shunned me & even when you brought
me up before the Judge, yes, even then I would have given
anything for you to forgive me, though you never would, it were
not in your Nature to change your bent   Em said I should
not seek Forgiveness, for it were you who did Wrong, not I
        do that matter, in the end?

my only hope of holding any ground were to converse by letter
or by lawyer, what else would you have me do?   you took it
all from me & from poor Bob too & then tried to paint us Villains
not just to the others but to the whole of Trinity Bay   you
had your claws dug in deep   most men I called my friends
no longer knew me once you had your way   why should
I not join the Union?   am I not a Fisherman?   that
is what I am drove to now   why should I not order from
Clare's Store?   is he not an honest businessman, & your
nephew, & the only ~~Tilly~~ Tilley now to be in the Trade at all?
        what harm does it do?   why must you hold iron-
strong & stiff on every issue & keep those who love you far from
you so we may never feel your tender heart-heat that we suspect
may still burn beneath all your frozen words (they sting like
Hail)   I didn't think you'd ever die, ~~you old bastard~~

I didn't think Bob would die either, & look what happened there
         he should have come Out, not me
      it is one of the Big Regrets (thus far) in my Life
the thoughts of him in there alone when it happened, miles
from anyone but the Indians, them thoughts make me sadder
than I could ever feel for you   him sitting down to his
little supper of beans & rice & duck meat & his heart just stops &
when they finds him a few days later he's still sitting there, froze
stiff with a surprised look on his face, a pinch of salt in the palm
of his hand

a better way to do it than yours, these last few dreadful months
when you did not know us, you would not eat, you hit at us, at
Bert & Eva too when they ventured too near, which angered Em
so that she could not be around you for several days   other
times you thought Emily were your own wife, you screamed
down curses on her   accusing her of Harlotry so purple it
were humorous to think of Miss Priss going at it   then you
would turn right quick to weeping   —do not leave me do
not leave me, think of the children, they are not all grown or dead

who could stand it for much longer? Emily threatened to abandon
me several times & return to her Mother but in the end did her
duty by me through all your burning epithets, your weak fists &
your soiled nightshirts

(that is how you know it's Love!)

me, you usually took for your brother Robert, what you thought
betrayed you when he ran the Templeman store out of your
building, after it were repossessed   in your demented state
you sometimes spoke so lucid that I learned some things I am

pretty sure are true   you thought I was Robert & Robert
you never forgave, for certain, although he have tried his best in
recent years to help you, from what I can see   it is true
tis sneaky business to work for the rival merchant out of your
brother's store, but it were Bank Crash days, Father, you all
needed money & you must show mercy on Robert as I tried,
every day, every minute, to show to You, even when you called
me names so blue that the S.S.Dawson boys would have taken
offence

in my letters I told the others what to expect but they were still
taken aback   Ernest, Daisy, Kate & Genie all trickled in
this week   we could tell it was soon upon us, you were so
weak then, you could only lie in bed, though your voice was
undiminished by the ravages that were taking place both in
your body & your mind   Daisy couldn't hardly sit there a
hot minute   she couldn't look at you, her breath trembled
with the effort it took to hold her smile   you told poor
Daisy she was dirty   when she came in the room, you
asked who brought the stink   —who let in the pigs? you
said   you accused her of Soiling herself, hissing to Em to
get her out of there right now, & that was the end of your Reunion
       later I heard Daisy & Kate in the kitchen, Kate trying to
tell poor Dais she didn't look dirty, she was looking quite good,
it was a lovely dress, she was in fine shape, it was just Father's
mind gone off   Daisy said no wonder she hasn't been
back here to see him, why did he have to be so Cruel   did
he not love his own children?   I went in & sorted
her out

—Father does not have his Faculties now & is at our Mercy
       this is the time to show we Learned our Lessons from

Him & to be Christian in our Conduct   we should be
Compassionate as one must be to any Dying Soul, no matter
what they may or may not have done to us in their Life Time

Kate stared strangely at me   —Dry your eyes, Dais, I said
          —go on in again & give him a kiss   he won't bite,
he haven't got the strength

but she wouldn't go back in until You was dead & done, two
days later, not until Alice & James showed up, too late, too late
on the same train, though she from Leo & he from St. John's,
huffing their apologies & looking relieved to have missed the
Ordeal of Your Passing   (though it were no ordeal, really,
those who were there can attest   You slipped
most peaceful into Death from the depth of some dream, your
toes twitching a little & a puzzled look on your face, brows
drawn, as when about to correct something

I was surprised by your Death
Somehow the moment in its Smallness was disappointing
No match for Your Life & Its Scale)

it is the first time we children are together since we have all
grown, & it is queer indeed to be seated here at table in the old
home, no Bob no Baby Arthur no Mother & no Father to Preside,
the others of us with our heads bent quietly over our dinners
          this is my table now, we all agree, & the paper from the
lawyer seals it   this is my House   the others do
not wish to live here & think me daft for wanting to stay on, but
I can think of nowhere else I fit in this world   (& I paid
for it, along with Bob, two thousand one hundred & nineteen
dollars, so it is proper I do claim it for us both & make of it a

Better Place than when You were Head of Household)   my
Brothers & Sisters cannot wait to leave again & go back to their
respective Happy Families that bear no resemblance to the
Example of Our Childhood

no, in their own Houses, my Siblings & their Families laugh
together, play shuttlecock & listen to the radio or read stories
out at night   they have wiped their souls clean of guilt by
making the journey to see you off, & I wish them safe travels
home again, every one   once you are in the ground
tomorrow we'll shut the door to your room & leave it as it is,
with all the things you loved so much you'd polish them:

    Globe   Bible   Razor

    Ledger   Barometer

    Belt

I shall not hove you out altogether, as you did Me & Mine those
years ago

    This is my Manor now, I am its Lord
    I Shall Act As Befits My Station

When Mabel used to read my cards I always would draw the
same one   same old Three of Spades   Mabel said
this was a mark of Constancy & Determination

—Tilly Stubbornness, you mean
—yes, she said   —I suppose   you will stick at a
thing oft-times too long & against the grain of good sense
but this steadfastness is also your best strength in Life

most days I love the sameness & aloneness that is more strong
here than anywhere I've been, Outside   I love it when I'm
working   but when alone in cabin by fire at night I am
like a great sad stone, bone-tired, heavier than the heaviest of
living things & weighed down with dark thoughts, squid-ink
clouds of them

I never been one to crave much Sociability, though when folks
come through it is a Holiday for my senses all the same, what
are grown used to nothing but the trees & ice & wind & stares of
animals as I catch them in my traps & take their skin away &
break down the carcass quickly into usable parts for my meals
& dog feed, both

when Charlie ~~the Indian~~ or Joe Roberts or Anderson come by it is most welcome & I don't mind spending Sugar, Coffee & Bacon on any visitor & anything else I may have put by

sometimes we gets a good yarn in before they must be off again, & I must walk back out to my sawhorse & keep on working the trees I felled this week

I shall work through tonight by Northern Lights & reflection of the snow for what else have I to do Christmas Eve all alone in woods by river with only Fitz & Mike & Fang & Murph & Pad Bar to keep me company (if I chooses to leave the comfort of the cabin & go & visit them, that is, holed up in their lean-to & curled around each other for warmth)

though it was always forbidden by Bro   (they are not Pets, Dukey)   I do think tonight I may invite them indoors with me   there's no one here to care if I have dogs for bedmates
a sure sign I am letting go of the last stitch of my Civility

the work is much slower now that I am By My Lonesome but I works extra long all day to make up for it, & keeps myself occupied well   Idle Hands are of the Devil, to that I can attest

Bob has not sent word now since Winter set in as to how he's faring   we do not talk of what happened at all
          I think of it from time to time but what use is that?
Best to Keep the Past Buried & Forgotten (Buried as I could not bury the Body, it were too cold) I got no one else but Bob & he don't want to see me, I reminds him too much of What He Did

~~Have There Been Others, Besides?~~   ~~I cannot help but think on it~~

I suppose he could be townside tonight with his Eva, but knowing him he'll blow in there for a Christmas Kiss & head back out to his traps again, cradling his Real Sweetheart, Whisky, in his Arms   Back out to his Peace & Quiet, Thankful there is no one else around, including his own Woman

(I do not quite got the Loner Bug that bad & craves Company more than he do

I will admit it! I do love to see another Human at least once a
          week!
Otherwise I starts talking to trees & asking them questions
          about their families & their dreams!

     A Life with only Dogs & Prey
     & Occasional Indians for Company
     Is too Tough a Life For Me:
     The Lily-Livered Good Son
     Of the Tilly Family!)

Every Morning
There's A New Hope Born
& Every Evening
Finds Me Mourning

my ghosts are stacked thick now
they are my main possessions

it is queer how when you got time by yourself & are getting on
in life your brain can play tricks   you might be having a
normal morning   putting sheep shit on the vegetables
          & then for no reason at all you get this wave of memory
come over you so strong you have to sit down there in the dirt
for fear you might keel over

probably some stupid little memory   something you
haven't thought of for years   but it comes back so strong
you feel undone   you have no defence against it   &
then you're crying into the shit & the strawberry plants & no
one can tell you to stop it or hand you their dirty pocket rag to
dry your eyes with, because there's no one left   you finally

got the Peace & Quiet you thought you was after all these years
        & now that it's here, you wish there were something to fill
it back up again

I say You but I mean Me   these days I live more in my
mind on the ground   the Past seems more real
than what I spend my time doing

for instance just this morning I had a flash of memory about
Jennie again after all these years   about Jennie or sort of
about her   about after she started going with Boys and
what I did to replace her, to get back that warm flesh feeling,
proof that you're alive:

I made friends with a Barn Cat & snuck it inside!

when Father finally caught it he killed it or made it disappear
somehow   maybe banished it to live with that band of
wild cats in the woods, abandoned ones & runaways that would
wait outside the circle of our beach fires, with their eyes
glowing, making sounds like The Dead come to The Party

that Barn Cat slept across my chest at least two months before
Father found it   warm soft fur belly with feel of Woman's
Hair   the motion of breath & Rattle in the Throat that
Vibrates Your Arm   & with your hand on its side you could
feel even the Passage through Intestines of Items Consumed
On Their Inevitable Journey to Excretion   the feeling like
that of a warm earthworm moving just under the soil's surface,
the memory of which gives me pause for grief regarding the
demise of that Barn Cat what used to lie in my bed & prove,
through its Proximity, the Veracity of my Existence

(you cannot doubt you are alive when you can feel another
warm body's Bodily Functions)

Ernest would tell me some rot about animals being created by
God to provide A Service to Our Living, them being our Foodstuff
& Workmate   he do not think they have a Conscious
Mind or no Soul, neither   I am Dead Sure he is Dead
Wrong on this   (& many other Things!)

Animals got Souls   I knew this from Barn Cat & from
Lightning back then   & I suppose I knew it from the
more savage Alaskan Beasts, the Wolves & Bears   as well
as ones we catch in Traps & Nets, or with Hooks   (&
Murph & Fitz, Callie & all did prove it)

from looking in their eyes
& seeing something there
that looks like you

ANTHROPOMORHIC IDIOT

(Yes   even if I says a thing or two all wrong
for school, I done my reading   & the bad
grammar is Affected, not Ingrained   if you
MUST KNOW)

I still Kill them, Animals, & Eat them too
& I do still find their Flesh to be Delicious

HYPOCRITICAL MORON

I got a few more names than that stored up to call myself, too
     & I lets them all out in a cloud sometimes as I pounds at
my own head with my fists like a Champion Boxer of the U. S. of
America

there's no one here to keep me from it
they're all gone & left me

I am happy for them
for everyone I knew or was related to

they got clean of the Stain that I leaves everywhere I goes

I CANNOT HELP IT

~~I am Slug~~
~~Where'er I Make My Path in Life~~
~~I Ooze My Poison~~

Christmas Eve, 1908

A letter from home is fine & precious when one goes fifty or 60 miles to get them   I have got none at all since October & I don't know why, as I do write them   at least a few nights a week I am sat to table   though they do not get a chance to be posted but 2 or 3 times a month when someone on the River is going to Town

Bob is at Tanana for Christmas Dinner now, I expect   he still wants Basic Tradition to be held although he do not like to go there much & would rather keep to Himself than sit snug up at Homestead with his Family

I am staying home, if Home is what you calls the wood yard cabin where I have been installed since Summertime this year

I saved up a few squashberries for today, as a special treat for Christmas time, my fancy being to do a Klondike representation of a traditional N. F. L. D. Duff, such as M— or Jennie or Kate might make for Sunday Dinner

my Duff will still be made tonight, by gum, although I had featured Bob sitting down to a portion beside me   having, as in some other years, grown tired of the Missus early & lit out

the 2 of us putting away all our arguments & sharing a meal that would Soften his Heart toward Home: Boiled Taties with Drawn Butter, Rabbit & Gravy, Salt Cod & Brewis, Scruncheons & my Newly Invented Squashberry Duff
          (whose tartness will hopefully be compensated for by a Generous Dousing of Rum Sauce)

What a Silly Reverie, a Christmas Dinner for Two Brothers!
          it is just me & the dogs tonight, as always   as twas last year too, & I recall I floated myself on Painkiller and sang carols till the tears fell out   I do not wish to repeat that event again, it were dire   I will not cook so much & so rich just for myself, but I will make my Duff & soak some Fish & Tack as well   & yes, maybe boil a Potato or two BUT NO RABBIT (never my favourite) & NO SCRUNCHEONS (I got a delicate stomach for some things these days, & too much Fatback will incapacitate me straight)

I got the squashberries by the fire & the fish is in a pan of water since yesterday afternoon

I am so sick of eating rabbit & duck & my tongue is prickling now thinking about that fish & the salt of it

          A knock upon the door!
          My heart knocks loud against my chest!

the sound is startling   the Indians & Anderson & all never knock, just come on in   none who live up here got much niceties, & I includes myself in that camp

          KNOCK   KNOCK   KNOCK

A Stranger?   INTRUDER?   the raps like gunshots
making my heart leap after days of only fire & wind & dogs

I draw the latch, but with axe in hidden hand, to be sure
I been here long enough to have Precautions

it is a tall & unknown man with long moustaches & grey eyes,
standing in the yard by himself in the snow, wearing a cap of
bright red blanket cloth stitched up with old boot-laces

—Bonjour   Hello   Do you speak French or English?
—English
—C'est Bien   My name is Jean-Claude Ripart   I am
lost & see your smoking cabin so I come here to see where I am
finding myself
—John?
—Jean-Claude Ripart, that is correct
—all right, you're on the River, at Duke Tilly's wood yard, & we
are about 70 miles from Tanana Proper, which is the nearest
town
John is crestfallen with the news   —Ah
—you were trying to get there today, for Christmas?
—yes, oui, I have une petite amie you know who lives in Tanana
& I was bringing her some gift for Noël Christmas & some good
food for souper aussi
—that is hard luck, boy   you've got a day's walk to go yet &
the wind is picking up   if you already lost your way tonight
I fear you'd perish if I let you leave in these conditions
—so you say I will not make it
—there's no way it's possible
—Pauvre Annie! She will be very sad to miss me
—I can imagine

he sighs & looks around   —your name is Duke? That is
not some other word?
—It's short for Marmaduke   it's my middle name
        William Marmaduke   supposed to be an old name
in the Family somewhere   but you are correct   in
English a Duke is also a type of ruler, lower down than a King
or a Prince, but in the old days they would be the ones in a castle
overseeing the town & tithing all the peasants
—I see   Duke   (he says it nice like dee-oo-kuh)
—let's get you settled away   you'll bunk here tonight
        my brother is at his wife's you see & lucky for you I already
got a start on a nice supper, seeing as it's A Special Occasion

John is misty in the eyes & he's trying not to show it
        I am embarrassed for him so I look away & let him have a
minute as I busy myself with the taties

—I come from N. F. L. D., John, & there we like our salt fish
        I hope you brought your appetite!

though it is his hardship, I am thanking my lucky stars that
Fate brought me John's company for Christmas Dinner
        Distraction in the form of a Mysterious French Gentleman
Estranged from his Sweetheart on Xmas Eve   Hopefully
he will tell me all about himself in that smoothed-out sounding
voice that takes the words I know & turns them into music of
the sort that M— might have sung, once, to put us to sleep

though the salt fish is soaked & the Duff has been executed &
smells right good, we do not eat it   John has brought
with him all manner of food & insists we consume it, for it is his
way of thanking me for allowing him to stay here & though

I protest, he asks me to sit while he goes about his preparations
& I have a rare sense of how Bob used to feel those nights
last year when he'd stop up a few days, with me busy making
grub & him stretched out cold junk on the daybed having a
snore or whittling spoons & spitting his tobacco in the stove to
make the fire steam & hiss   (& though at first it is
uncomfortable for me to sit there with someone else working,
I grow to like it soon enough!)

John is a grand cook, he has for us a roast of Bear, which I have
not had before: it is not Tough as I expected, more like Beef
coming off the Bone   & also a Ham, sweet & crisp on the
outside with not too much Fat for my taste   & a real Brandy
Pudding, which he sets on fire   & he did up Potatoes, cut
up thin into slices & bubbling in a sauce he made of Flour,
Butter, Salt & Milk   & he did also make a Mince Pie, which
nearly makes me Swoon with Pleasure (~~LIKE LOOKING UP
SKIRTS WHILE CLIMBING UP LADDERS!~~)   all those
Raisins & bits of Apple soaked in Rum & the Crisp Pastry holding
in the Buttery, Spiced Ooze & the Fruit   we eat till we
are hurting & have to undo our trouser buttons & lounge by the
stove, trading songs back & forth despite my weak voice
he is happy nonetheless to learn a few new ones
& sings for me in a passable tenor some French ditties
with words like pretty drizzles of Molasses   & every so
often we leave off singing so that we might eat more

Thank you, Baby Jesus, Born Tomorrow, for sending this
Frenchman here to Distract me from Myself on what can be the
WORST DAY OF THE CALENDAR if you are Alone & Inclined
to Dark Feelings at the Best of Times, let alone on a day put aside
for all to come together, BE IDLE & feel Happy for Themselves

Thank you, Baby Saviour,
& Thank you John
I Love You Both

& if I Eats More French Food
I Fear I'll Say So Aloud
& Embarrass Myself!

May 2, 1923

I knock on the door & no one answers   another mate
arrives & he just goes on in so I follow his example

tis fairly tight with men in here, in shirtsleeves for the heat of
the crowded room, with pipe & cigar alike a-blazing

they don't know me & I got nothing to mark me out as Peculiar
            just a new man in old clothes, like the rest, or most of the
rest   (there's a few better dressed than others, but to a man
they are down to shirtsleeves & suspenders & the Atmosphere
is Collegial)

so why do I feel as I did when I was a lad, gone down to the
school where none would fraternize for I were Till(e)y's Son &
every boy was not to play with me   we had to make our
own world with cousins & with siblings

Spittle, Rotten Egg, Cow Plops, Rock
these were my first communications from the other children
& then, once courage was raised, cruel things were shouted
            threats of beatings in various barns up & down the

shore, several of which were accomplished quite effectively, dunkings in rivers   once I was tied to a tree & left till Bob & Ernest found me, hours later, with DADDY'S BOY put across my forehead in ink that wouldn't come off until Jennie rubbed my head half-raw with lye soap

soon enough I learned to run, &
had a knack with spots for hiding
which ensured my survival to adulthood
for I were never a fighter like my brothers

NOW I AM GROWN
I should not have this feeling: mouse on kitchen floor, craving its hole

—BE A MAN!   Father's voice booming in my head, though he would tan me proper were he to know I was here tonight, in the Lair of the Enemy (or one of the Enemies, for they are Plentiful) (he lost privilege to direct my Course when he did Banish Me the Second Time   here in Port Union I may do as I Think Best & he shall be None the Wiser)

there's a few men here my age & many older   a gent gone white pulls a chair out beside him
—Wilf Rideout
—Bill Tilley
—Welcome, Bill   you a first timer?
—yessir
—where you fish?
—Melrose
—aha   fine spot   that's good   for a second there I thought you were one of them Elliston Tilleys   but

sure what'd one of that crowd want with the FPU?
—right   I've heard of them of course, probably related somewhere back in England, I suppose
—let me tell you, Stuck Up is not the word
—we're just fisherman out our way   not much to be stuck up about
—no, none of us have, eh?
—that's right   (& Wilf passes me his flask)
—that's why we're doing this, he says   —for those of us, that is the most of us, with Nothing   we have to stand together to be heard
—I believe so, Wilf, I really do
—we're not all the Chosen Ones, see   we don't all got Life handed to us, Lording it over other men how well off you are & how fine & fancy you can dress your wife while us poor slobs is out working hard for our keep, which thanks to the Ryans & Templemans & the Elliston Tilleys & the rest is far less than what we deserve & barely enough to keep yourself going on, let alone a family
—you're right there   tell me, do you Speak? you're a Natural
—Me?   Wilf laughs   Me? I'm just an old shit with a grudge in my heart against them that kept me poor
          I don't have the gift of Gab, myself, I don't think, boy, no   there's a few here real good at it though (he points at a big fellow with walrus whiskers & a natty man cleaning his specs on his vest, speaking intently to two older gents)

—Wait till you hears the man himself, Wilf says   he's Genius

we toast the Union with his drink
& he introduces me to some more of the Boys
I am that warm I am also down to my shirtsleeves now, rolled to

elbow, unbuttoned to my breastbone as Em will not let me do at
home on even the doggiest days

We are all Here for the One Purpose

I am Among The Working Men, A Working Man Myself

Together, We Brace to Fight the Oppressors of this Country
& See the Ones in Charge Get their Justice
For the Boots Kept So Long Upon Our Necks

Murph is Dead   I do not wish to be the one to tell
Bob about it

Murph dead   & Fitz with a wounded paw
no use of sled till we gets a new dog

Bob always did like Murph, who we depended on to keep the others going when they flagged   it was damn Quailey's dogs what did it   he got a few that aren't fit & I like to keep them separate when he's up here but this camp is smaller now than the last & he just hove them in with our dogs when he got in yesterday afternoon

the snow was starting &
he did not ask about it

I had laid out Tea, Smoked Salmon, Bread & Jam   we were getting on well enough, considering his Taciturn Nature
      (he is like Bob, twenty years in the future, I was thinking to myself, & trying to contain my smile)

then I heard the most piteous shrieking out of the dogs & much murderous growling   I looked to Quailey & his face told the tale: he had his 8 shoved into the lean-to what should only fit my 6   by the time we got out there three of his dogs were on top of poor Murph, the others keeping my dogs at bay as Quailey's savages tore at his throat & back legs

it was a horrible sight & Quailey did not hesitate but drug his team out & shot the three dogs there & then   & with a nod from me he shot Murph too because to do otherwise would've been a cruelty, his throat tore out & more of his blood on the snow than was still pumping through his body   my other dogs cowered together in the corner & whined at the sound of the rifle going off, then they all lay down quiet as far away from us as they could get

—I'll cart the mess away with me   & sorry about yours, I'll owe you when my bitch has her next batch

he headed back inside & helped himself to another slice of bread like this kind of thing was Ordinary   so I followed him back in & made more tea, we carried on like that for half an hour, & then he got his remaining dogs hitched & threw the dead ones on the sled, & called to the team to take off, & they did, leaving me here with a bloodstain to remember old Murph by, & a gap in the harness, that's all   I will have to tell Bob about it, & he will be mad as Hell & maybe go after Quailey a bit   they never been Bosom Companions

Fitz's paw is not good   I have doused a rag in St. Jacob's & lain it on her to cure any infection but that did not work to its full purpose & she has some dangerous-looking fluids seeping out

& I know the Oil do sting her bad   I hate to put it on her

I am in there with the oil & she's snapping at my hand a bit when
I hears a few people in the yard, voices high
                    Children!   or Women

      I hold my breath to hear better

WOMEN, at least 2, talking to each other

I don't know too many Ladies up here save Mrs. Bob   my
heart starts jumping from how foreign the sound is

one calls out for me   —Mr. Tilly!

I back out from the lean-to in what I hope is a handsome fashion
& turn around to face my visitors   two young women
          Indians done up as Outsiders, down to their Buttoned
Boots

—how do you do?   I manage, though they are a sweet
enough sight to make me lose my speech
—fine, thank you   we are down for your Lynx, your brother
wants some mitts from them   I am Mrs. Dick the Pilot's
Wife & this is Mrs. Herbert   we got camps further up

Mrs. Dick is as pretty as they come for Indians   she is
smooth of skin   black of hair   friendly eyes & a smile
like Sunday   the other one don't say nothing   just
darts her eyes around, sizing up the place

—mitts eh? well, we got 2 lynx at the moment   is that
proper payment for those mitts?

—yes   your brother said one for the making, one for pay
—that seems fair enough

I invite them for tea but can see they don't want to stay here
alone with me   Mrs. Dick asks when Bob will be back
—I don't rightly know   he comes & goes days at a time
—I will have them done within the week, you can say to him
        my husband or I can bring them by
—ah good, I haven't met him yet

Fitz is whining in the kennel, a sick sound   Mrs. Dick
stops to listen

—why is your dog so sad? Do you beat it?
—she was in a fight with one of Quailey's yesterday, hurt her paw
real bad
—oh

the other girl smiles small, I don't know why (don't she like
Animals?)

—Quailey's dogs killed one of mine, Murph was his name
        & Fitz's paw is not good
—that's a shame, says Mrs. Dick   —Quailey always got
them mean ones
—he must beat them I suppose, I jokes to her
—yes

Mrs. Dick looks at Mrs. Herbert, who wishes she were not here
right now, & says something in their other language   Mrs.
Herbert looks none too merry but heads off toward the trees &
Mrs. Dick says she sent her for some bark that they will use to

make a compress for the wound   I take her to the dogs
          she stands a while at the entrance to let them smell her
before she tries to get to Fitz   the dog lets her take the
paw & gently probe it, crouched on her toes & humming softly to
herself   Mrs. Herbert returns with some bark & twigs some
minutes later & I boil the kettle   they steep the bark in
hot water like making tea & use the juice on a piece of cloth
with a pad of moss which Mrs. Dick binds to the wound, taking
care with the knot so it do not pull too tight & smart the paw

          —use this at least 4 times a day on a fresh bandage &
the disease will all come out   make sure it's always hot
when you put the dressing on

they take the 2 lynx pelts & head back upriver   I watch their
shapes slowly getting smaller until they disappear, reluctant to
lose sight of that rarest of creatures:
          Human Female
          in Alaskan Bush!

I shall make extra effort this week with my traps in hopes of
enough pelts to request a pair of new mittens for myself, as well,
the next time Mrs. Dick comes around

February 2, 1909

~~(will she need to take my hands' measurements?)~~

February 4, 1909

LYNX   LYNX LYNX LYNX

Here lynxy-lynxy-lynxy

Come to Dukey

1 ~~G.D.~~ Marten in the Traps

February 5, 1909

Checked traps early A. M. still no bite
Chopping Wood this day as much as I can manage
Fitz's paw looks good, there is no Pus
Bob is still not back

Mrs. Dick come by again with husband Dick the Pilot

I heard tell of him before   he works for the N. C. & C. Co. &
Clare used to be on his boat   & I think he thought the Pilot
rather too fond of himself (funny from Clare!) because he
never would talk highly of him though he could not fault him
for any certain wrongs   when I sees him though I knows
why Cousin Clare was turnt   Mr. Dick is a handsome
bugger & TALL, which Clare is not

(My Dear Cousin always got to wrestle the Green-Eyed Monster,
he got some bent toward Vanity, he's been that way since Birth)

Mr. Dick is home till breakup & is our closest neighbour here in
the upper camp   we shake hands & he got a firm grip but
not like he's trying to prove anything   he looks right in
my eyes & keeps my hand for a second too long till I looks away

& studies the woodpile   Mrs. Dick looks on with her hair
rolled up the White Way & pinned to the top of her head
            (I wants to see her in them Indian Braids,
or with loose hair lying down her back all straight)

—the mitts are not finished, Mr Tilly, did your brother come back
yet?
—no Ma'am, he's still missing   it's been eight days
            should I put out a call to the Judge do you think?
(she does not think this funny)
(Mr. Dick intervenes)   —I think Bob is capable enough
in the Bush to last a week or two (she nods)
—yes, I dare say   it's the lack of warning that gets me,
when he leaves   please, come in, sit down

I get the kettle on   Mrs. Dick's dress is the brightest thing
yet to grace this house, not accounting Emily's postcards, which
I have tacked up over the doorway, Kind Love from Newman's
Cove blessing the house where Father would have placed The
Cross He Hung On   Mrs. Dick's dress is a deep pink colour
like wild roses, with lighter pink at the neck & the wrists
            my cheeks flush to match it   I lay out the tea things
& the Painkiller for Mister but he brushes it away   —I don't
indulge, myself   thank you (Clare's dislike for him coming
clear all the more)   I put it back on the shelf without a
slug for myself either lest I seem rude, or unseemly to the Lady
(Bob always drinks in front of his Missus but I don't know what's
the Rules for drinking in front of Women You Ain't Married To)

I am that jumpy with us three hove into the tiny cabin that I slops
half the boiled kettle on the floor when taking it off the stove
—we'll go skating on that in a minute, I joke & Mister has a good

laugh & Missus gives a smile that shows her front teeth just a
glimmer   (she has them all!)

I search around for other things to serve them   I made a
Pudding yesterday but it got Rum in it, which could offend Dick's
senses   I settle on some Bread with Butter & Smoked
Salmon

—say, this is good, Mister says   —you ever think of selling
it?
—not rightly, though we've traded for a few things   not
everyone does the smoking up here but it sure is a change from
the salt
—I'd buy some, don't have much to trade, myself
—I'll have to ask Bob about it, if that suits   we're partners
on everything
—that's fine
—I'll give you a piece now though, to take home
—that's very kind of you, Mr. Tilly   (that is the Wife talking)
        how is your dog?

I am pleased to bring them back to the lean-to & to see her once
more in the entrance, standing quite still for a few seconds to
let the dogs smell her before she kneels down & gives Fitz her
hand to sniff   Fitz sitting with her tongue lollygagging
out of her mouth while Mrs. Dick takes her paw, unwraps it,
lightly tests its movement, brings it to her face & smells it, then
turns to me

—you can leave the bandage off now unless you see more
coming out, then back to the bark water as before
—thank you, Missus (she bows her head & smiles)

(me to Dick) —your wife got some good sense with animals, I tell
you that
—she's good with all kinds of things   her father's a healer
so I say it's a fair bit in her blood, but she's a quick study too
        can't keep her in Books
—I used to be the same, at home   we had a good library,
Grandfather had the works, he had a room full   my father
used to sell Saturday Evening Post & I would read them front to
back   heck, I would read the Ladies' magazines too!
                Interesting Research into the mind of the Fairer Sex!
(I wink stupidly at the Mr.)   what I wouldn't give for a copy
of the Post now, that would pass away an hour or two!
—I have not read it, Missus says
—what a shame! perhaps my sister would send one up   she
lives Stateside now
—no, sir, that's not necessary
—it would be a payment for your help with Fitz, you see
(Mr. Dick interrupts)   —really, no   though a piece
of that smoke salmon, now, we wouldn't turn down

I pack up a big fillet for them in a bit of clean sack

it pleases me to think of them eating it, later that evening, cozied
up to their little table, Missus tucking Handkerchief to Mister's
chin, her dress glowing like a Ruby in the lamplight

the taste of my smoke salmon the cause of a Shared Smile of
Pleasure & Warm Feeling Between Them

Augmenting their Conjugal Happiness

February 6, 1909

It is my birthday   25   though no one here knows it
but Bob   I assume he has forgotten, birthdays not being
the sort of thing he fusses with   neither did Father, but
M— or Jennie always would make our favourite dinner that day
        mine was Roast & Potatoes with Fig Pudding for dessert
& if there was no Roast it was Fish, good fresh Fish, not this
blasted Salmon   I'm nearly half Salmon myself now, from
eating so many of them

if I can make some money off em they might taste sweet to me
again   Bob thought it was an idea   I told him the
one day he came by here in the past 2 weeks   he said it
was a good idea & if I can get enough people who wants some
then smoke away   I handed him some to taste anew, he
said that it was good, all right   & when he packed up
again to head up Redlaw way I stuck a piece in his kit when he
wasn't looking   it keeps well in the bush

—when you coming back?

he shrugged & shoved his hands into his new mitts & on the
way out of the yard took the last of my lynx bait & I cursed him

(in my head, not aloud)   he were here no more than an
hour & in that time he could barely spare a word that wasn't
begged for   what have I done to make myself so Hateful
to him who is the same Blood & Kin as Myself?   I know
I am Cowardly by Nature but still I did stick by him & did Burn
the Evidence & speak not a word to no one
        have I not Proved Myself?

when Mrs. Dick came back with his Mitts a few days before that,
I was in a state, halfway through skinning my first Lynx what
I had caught that morning

Skinning has never been my favourite part of Life   but it
got to be done, to everything you wants to Eat, so you must be a
Man & Face It   & sure by now there is no shock to it, it is
Ordinary

it is My Lot   I am a Trapper whose life is bound up in
Killing Creatures & Skinning them, for Food, Trade & Money
        More Trapper than Logger now   a Sourdough but
in Dreams, Foolish Dreams Dreamt before I got here, & in Lies
still Writ to Father

Mrs. Dick came up behind me when I was stretching the skin,
my hands gloved in blood to the elbows, & I may have been
humming The First Noël, for some reason, though it is well past
Christmas   —Mr. Tilly?   & I jumped a mite I think,
& let out a small sound like a mouse's squeak when startled

she was tittering then, a small light laugh that could also be a
mouse's sound, her hand over her mouth, in her other hand the
promised mitts for Bob, a fine dust of snow in her hair & on her

shoulders like powdered sugar   I reached out to take the
mitts from her but my hands were slick with blood & I had
nowhere to wipe them

—you'd best lay them inside for me, I'm rotten, I said
(she laughed again) —I see you're trapping Lynx yourself now
—I am
—what a coincidence

I could feel her eyes take my measure   I turned back to my
work lest she see me colouring up   in a moment I heard
her turn toward the cabin, her White Woman boots squeaking
in the snow   I finished tacking the hide out quick so I could
catch her in there & make her stay to have a cup   I used
my shoulder to open the door to save cleaning the blood from
it, shoving it open in a far too abrupt way, not how I wanted to
do it   she had her coat off, pretty pink dress exposed,
pan of water on the stove & the kettle set to boiling   she
touched the water in the pan with her fingertips, added a handful
of snow & brought it forward to me, so I might wash myself
she had a smell of starch & pine needles   the steam off
the pan rising about my face as I set to washing myself up proper
& she got the tea things out   when I was good & done
I rose & tossed the pink water out into the snow   .   she had
my tea with the sugar in it already, as she had seen me take when
she was here before   I sat with my hands on my lap,
feeling My Courage Growing Bold

—I'll get another this week, I said
(she looked at me)
—Another Lynx
(she smiled)

—I should like a pair of your Mitts   for my own use
—I can come again in a few days' time   will your Brother
then be home?
—I cannot say for sure, but tis not likely   & if he is, it's at
best for an hour, in the morning, & then he's off again before
lunch
—oh
—I like the company, when you visit   & Mister, of course
—we like it too   gives us some occasion to the days
—you do not make your own occasions, then?
(she smiled into her cup)   —not so often   no

(a pause long enough to hear my wet socks on the line spitting
their drops down onto the stove)

she got up to go   she got her coat & mitts, I started to
rise from the table, then thought better of it & sat back down
       she turned back to me in the doorway with all that pink
covered up   A Secret Nosegay in a Brown Wrapper ~~as
I used to make for J. C. from wildflowers, wrapped up in butcher
paper & stashed where only she would see, at the very back of
the pantry~~   ~~or up in the Attic~~   ~~pink
hillside roses, bluebells & buttercups & such, hidden in a parcel
of plain paper so no one would notice them were they not
seeking them out~~   ~~she would put them in a milk bottle
under her bed & keep them there till the petals crumbled into
pink & yellow dust~~

—I will be back in a few days with yours, then
—thank you, Mrs. Dick   I shall look forward to it

she shut the door after her & I slumped forward, my head quite
heavy on the friendly wooden tabletop

February 14, 1909

This log book is a funny kind of record to one who knows the
whole story & may read between the lines   all my notes
for this week got to do with Lynx but Father would not know
what that word Lynx really meant, were he to see it writ

Feb 7   Splitting down below the cabin   Warm
         Indian kids down for Lynx Body
         (meat)

Feb 8   started to cut wood INSIDE the cabin
         it is so cold all bottles have froze
         no hope of checking L. traps

Feb 9   Bob here 2.5 hours before heading up to Redlaw with
         my last Lynx trap
         ~~BASTARD~~

Feb 10   Cutting wood

Feb 11   Ditto   traded flour baccy & salt for new trap

Feb 12   Ditto on the wood   trap set   no catch

Feb 13   D. O.

Feb 14   Several Miracles: Warm Again!
                                     Lynx in trap!
          FINALLY
          I been sleepwalking for days
          WAITING & it weren't till this morning that I had one
          caught

if Father were to read this, or Emily, they would just think it a
dreary record of these February days   but for every word
I puts on paper there's a garden of hundreds more, blooming in
my head

that lovely, lucky lynx   such a beautiful Cat   I have
just freshly skinned her & am breaking up meat into pieces for
the Indian Kids

I have not resorted to Lynx Roast yet myself for they look too
much like the Barn Cats we'd have at Home, just overgrown in
size, but the Indian Kids do like it & I gives it to them when I have
it without trade, it is good to give out to your neighbour now &
again   (like I done with the Dicks & the Salmon)
(Smoke Salmon for the Salmon-Pink Mrs. Dick)   my
hands are going through the steps needed to break down a
carcass into smaller parts   my mind is filled with the way
the cloth of her rose pink dress looked against her skin in the
lamplight

Mrs. Dick! Please visit me again! I beg of you! You are the sweetest
sight I have lain eyes on since October, 1906!

& sure enough when I thinks of her, she appears!   coming
up the path, a laugh like the tinkle of icicles sliding off the roof

in Spring   it is such a strange thing to think on her and
have her materialize   I have to wonder if she has some
kind of magic to be forming from my thoughts like this

—Mr Tilly   do not tell me I am catching you in the act, again?
—I am beginning to think you're going to show up every time
I start skinning something, Missus
—maybe   who knows   should I come more often,
to improve your trade?
—I dare say you should   it's been slow this week
—I have your mitts   (she holds up a knotted cloth)
          will I put them on the table for you?
—I'll be right in

I get done as fast as I can with the meat & carry it over to the
storehouse for when the Kids come by next

she's got my bowl of washing water heated & she's got the tea
fixed   she is in a new dress   it is a pale yellow
that looks even prettier than the rose

—you're like the sun, or a spring flower, in that dress
          something welcome

I should not have said that   it is not proper talk for a
Married Lady   she stands looking at the table
          looking very sadly at it, standing very still & not breathing,
her face going pale so I take haste to go to her & offer her a seat
          I do not wish for her to Faint Away   it has happened
to me before & is not a welcome sensation

—please, Mrs. Dick, sit down

I take her elbow   she clutches at me, suddenly, with force
        I am afraid   she pulls at me like a body drowning,
pulling on my shoulders with her hands dug deep into the
muscles   heavier than I imagined   I take her face
in my hands   her eyes are brown & her face is worried
        it is the sweetest vision I could witness   —you are
all right, you're fine, don't worry   I try & lower her into the
seat & she presses herself to me   she's shivering
I bend over her then & kiss her   she is quaking
I feel my Bravery Quicken

she says —We shouldn't

I back away

she has a hold on my sleeve & she pulls on it
—I would like to, though
—so should I   what is your name? your given name?
—Nell
—Nell   you are so beautiful   my name is Duke, or
William, whichever one you want to use

she kisses me

it is a deep one

she is hungry for kissing like I am   she is starved of it

the smooth yellow cloth   I dare to run my fingers along
her neckline, she lets me do it   I go now with fingers lower
onto Bosom & she makes the pleasure sounds   I press

her Breasts with my hands & Kissing is now the world in its entirety, Kissing & the Press of Flesh   I bring her to the daybed   I say   —are you sure you do not wish me to stop? for I will understand   she says   —I have been waiting two days to come to you, I had to wait until my husband went to Fairbanks, to be safe
—I have been waiting too, not waiting but dreaming
I didn't dare to hope   I take her hand, kiss it, it is warm & firm   I put it on my Self, she does caress it, she kisses me, she is smiling   I bid her turn around & begin a slow unbuttoning of the fifty or so buttons down her back
          Sweet Lord I will make the most of this   it is my first day for this Activity & may be the only day I have like it in this Life, so I shall make it Last

when the buttons are all unfastened I guide the dress down her arms, slide my hands over her skin to remove it, inhale the scent of the nape of her neck & take her hairpins out
—shake out your hair   (she is blushing)   please, Nell, shake it out

there is nothing so beautiful as Nell in camisole & drawers shaking her hair out so that it falls in a perfect sheet all down her back   I gather some up & rub it in my fingers
          —that's better   & I remove her other garments then in the light of the open stove door   I kiss many parts of her   I taste of her like I seen Clare do with Bessie   & the taste is somehow familiar, although I never Adventured in This Territory before

she is moaning   my Soldier standing straight at Attention inside my breeches   I cannot wait   I push her

onto the daybed   she smiles up at me & grabs for my thighs
          I drop my trousers on the floor   press right
into her   right inside   I had wondered
how it would feel, not having had a Full Education until today
              hot hot as inside the stove but wetter than that &
rocking like the rhythm of the ocean, back home

I can see now why some seeks it out like Painkiller & pays dearly
for it, too

—Nell!   You are beautiful!
—yes
—Oh thank you, God!
—you hold on, keep going
—I can't contain myself!
 she digs her fingernails into my buttocks —you hold on, Duke
—OH!   not if you say my name!
—roll over
—OH!
—roll over now
—how do you mean?
—let me lie on top of you

she kisses me & I roll over & she sits astride me with her hair
coming down over her body & hiding her so I brush it back with
my fingers to reveal her Left Breast   she makes a throat
sound   I pinch her Nipple gently & then harder when I see
she likes it   she slows down her rhythm on me & I can
feel every tiny movement of her skin on mine

—you're not done yet, she says   I shall have my way
with you first

I am speechless   There is no world at all save Nell
locking round me, slowly pulling me toward a Glimpse of the
Divine

—put my breasts in your mouth

I do as the Lady says   one after the other   I am
greedy enough to try both at once but my little mouth is not up
to the task   one then the other   slow sucking to
match her   she is moving so slowly I feel like screaming
          I can feel every cell as it shifts & slides against the next
          I am trying to hold onto my Self-Control but fear I am
not long for it   she is moaning now   she got
one hand over mine on her left breast   we are squeezing
it together as I suck on the right   she is moving faster
on me now, faster & harder   less teasing & more
demand   I bite a little   she kisses me hard then
sits up straight

& Works with Quiet Determination
Until We Both are Moved

we lie on the daybed   I run my fingers over the skin of her
arm & put a line of kisses down the top of her head   she
allows this for some minutes & then she gets up & begins to
dress   & without mirror she knots her hair back into its
tight perfect coil on top of her head

before she goes she unwraps the parcel she brought with her,
which has a piece of pudding of her making folded in wax
paper, as well as my new mitts   they fit perfectly, the
same design as Bob's, but smaller

—I noted you had finer hands than your brother
—I hope they pleased you
(her eyes drop to the floor) —yes   I need to go
—must you?
—yes
—will you come again?

Nell says nothing for a moment, then she makes her way to the door

—there's no need to worry about any outcomes, she says
        I'm barren   so it's no matter about what happened
        & that you let it out

HER ADOLESCENCE

They give Eva one part mustard to four parts flour, and she knows she has finally passed that unseen and unspoken threshold between child and adult. It's taken long enough. Here only the true babes get eight parts flour in their poultice, and those she takes care to steer clear from, lest she end up as their unofficial caretaker. She has just escaped from such a life, from what had seemed already a lifetime of it.

'Escaped,' yes. The body knew that the way out was to waste itself, and it had started without her. But her soul and spirit and mind and whatever else had caught up to the body again, now that she had time to rest. She had nothing but time to rest, in her new clean bed with hospital corners. Because this is a hospital, isn't it, this place where she is now. A kind of hospital in a meadow in a forest with a river down the hill somewhere. A hospital for just one type of patient, and everyone looks alike. Sallow, shrunk, grey and tired—but nonetheless some others are also enjoying their luck, having worked themselves sick doing for everyone at home before they caught the real thing and got shipped off, just like her. Duke writes *Who Will Look After The Children?* as if she was not carted here because of them. He wouldn't care if he caught it himself and sickened and died right this minute, he's been trying to kill himself ever since she was born as far as Eva can understand— though his weapon of choice is wet, blunt and ineffective, and his suicide attempt has thus gone on for many years.

So, has TB really acted as Saviour to a hard-working Bonavista Bay Girl, sweeping her off her feet, carrying her on pale grey wings to the gracious oasis of the Sanitorium? Yes, please you, Jesus, and praise You! Amen! Bonavista Bay Girl is Reborn Again!

It is not all roses. She was shocked the first day when they brought the tea with cold cups and used the same leaves four times over till she'd rather drink her washwater. Mrs. Tilley would be scandalized, her daughter forced to drink *refreshed* tea, *her* daughter only drinks Fresh Tea, don't you understand, you Nursies? You did not mind your lessons well. And now it's time for sleep.

Sleep is better outdoors and these smart Nursies know it. They know many things about her and how things will suit her best. She sleeps in a proper bed but on a balcony, not indoors. The fresh air is all about her and the stars above to see, the crickets going and at dawn the birds to wake her, no need for anything more. Life is simple and it is sweet. The other girls in her ward think so too, or most of them do. Some who are stronger now are itchy to hop it to St. John's proper, they want to be back in life, and miss its buzz. Eva does not, and neither do the other tired girls around her on this end of the hall. They listen to the echo of the talk and laughter further up the corridor and feel no need to participate.

She waits for Nurse to come and bathe her. She watches the sun come up in the sky and feels its growing strength upon her skin. She eats wholesome foods, even if the tea is weak; they have some malt powders that she did not have for Mrs. Tilley at home, which may have nourished her, you mix them with water and drink down many of the vitamins you need. She will write a letter to Duke about them when she has the strength.

She has been here just two months now and some things are more effortful, if that can be considered a proper word. Writing is more effortful than reading. Standing up and sitting down are more effortful than walking a short distance. Talking is effortful and laughing more so. Eating is more effortful than anything else, but she tries to eat anyway, as she knows from experience how it hurts the Nurse's feelings if the Patient doesn't try. A slap, really, isn't it. So she swallows down all of the stewed prune or milk custard she's given, and she chokes the malt down too. A Patient must have patience and try her best to please her Nurse by eating every bite.

Did it make a difference? Perhaps. Each day, when instructed, she walks a little farther on the lawn, with nice Nurse Barnes for help if she feels weak. The Nurse is neat as a pin and Eva doesn't like to lean on her for fear of making wrinkles.

On the San grounds is a bench by a small fountain where the birds land and drink. Eva can see it, across the lawns, and each day she takes a few steps closer, and it grows larger in her vision, and she knows she will walk all the way some day, and sit there, and maybe make a picnic of it if Nurse Barnes will allow. They can bring their toast and Marmite and a jar of jellied peaches and sit there for an hour. It is a simple goal to have, perhaps, but a large enough one if you are a Patient of late-stage tuberculosis just starting on a regimen of fresh air, rest, exercise and foods of health. No further treatments yet, and she prays to stave them off, as she saw poor Melody Maloney and Edith Bennett and the state they were in after they started 'the more rigorous course.' Melody says it's done with wax, they seal up the rotted parts. Dripped down into your lung, how can it be? She doesn't want such things, no Lucite pellets rattling around inside, no ribs removed, no nerve crushed, as Mrs. Tilley's had been, ineffectually.

Eva's fate had seemed romantic when told to her by Mabel, she had seen it as a fairy story, and yet it all had come true, more or less, in lopsided and disappointing ways she hadn't imagined then. Words could mean many things, she supposes, for she'd thought the leaves had foretold of Love, a Stranger meant to be her Husband. A rescue from her life, yes, from her mother and the children, but not in this manner. The long package: a needle. She now knows it well. The tall man: Dr. Leonard. She is the sad lady, she and her mother both. She is the one who wastes in grey. The long journey. Removal past wonderful. Sad lady fades to dust. It hurts her to laugh but she thinks laughter to herself. How fate works. It is a good thing to mull over in her mind, during these hours when she lies here too tired to read, to speak, even to watch the leaves move in the trees beyond her balcony. How did Mabel know the truth, and why couldn't she have said it plainer, so that Eva could prepare? She might have guessed her life would be one of illness. She's always taken after her mother, everyone says so, why not in this as well? It makes Eva sorry for those times she'd been impatient with Mrs. Tilley, with her groans and her sighs. The world does not have to hurt you quite so much, you know, she used to think. From the way you carry on you must enjoy the misery. Now she knows this not to be the case, although it is true that as time goes by pain becomes more familiar, and she imagines that if one day it were to disappear she might miss it, her only constant thing to count on, her only sure fact. A thing to occupy her, to ground her and to keep her thoughts steady toward a Higher Aim and not mired in some stupid muck of who has necked with whom and who cares about it. When you are sick, Sins are absolved. Eva would never forget this, she swore, no matter how hale and hearty she grew, nor how long she lived. She would rise out of this place stronger in body and moral courage both, she would be pious. She would deny all men her heart, and, more importantly, her body. First though, God, she would like to stay here, just a year or two. She would like nothing more than a slow, graceful recovery in her bed at the San, till Mary and Bob were old enough to feed themselves. It's not a tall order. All she would like is more time.

When she dreams at night it is of this place, and it makes her infinitely happy. Plain food. White walls, white beds and white-clad Nurses. No visitors allowed. Slow walks around the lawn, and starlings in great clouds each night at dusk, circling across the red and orange streaks of the setting sun like infinite variations of the Mobius Strip folding in upon themselves.

BOOK FOUR

• PATIENCE •

For me there is Heaven & Hell, little else in between
   by which I mean to say that the passing of each day is
but a means to An End
(Bad or Good, hard to say)

I am Waiting   stocking up money for Father

this Life I am living now is nothing more than waiting for the
other Life to begin again, so I try to see myself as though in the
Post, in an illustrated feature: Here is Dukey working hard!
  Here is Dukey, Felling, Dragging, Sawing, Splitting, Piling—
the Cycle of the Alaskan Lumber Man!   Here is Dukey,
Cheeks Gone Gaunt in Winter, Sadly Clutching Empty Traps!
  Here is Happy Duke In Springtime, Catching Salmon!
So Much Salmon!   & Here He Is Writing Uselessly in his
Useless Log Book, waiting out his six or so years till he gets to
go back home out of it   that is the length of time it will
take to get Father in the clear by my current calculations

I keep the thought of Hell close by me, to warn me not to stray
too far   carved into my walking stick:

Hell & Sin

the letters still as deep & clear as when I put them there, before
I left home, 1906

I need the stick now more & more   my Bum Ankle is worse
in the cold times

Sin is what I lean upon   yet in acknowledgement of that
fact do I hope to stand straighter & reach Baby Arthur up there
in God's Country someday

Ernest used to tell me to knock off with all that religious
nonsense, it was Father's way of controlling us   he thinks
God don't even exist

—but Ernest, don't you feel Him?   don't you sometimes
feel His Presence?

today for example   today it was so cold that once I poured
my tea into my mug, two breaths later I turned around & there
was a skin of ice on the top of the cup   This is a Hard &
Pure Kind of Place to be Living & that frozen tea just about
made me crack up   you have to melt ice to make water &
then no sooner is it boiled but it turns to ice again   I've
thought on ice a lot, these past few weeks   like the frozen
river, now 12 feet thick in spots   we got to use full saplings
to keep our fish holes open   jam the trees down in the
holes every six or eight hours that we can manage, the river
freezing so damnable thick here & having the most
confoundable habit of filling in your holes overnight   & it
is A Job to make a new Hole so we tends the dozen we got as

best we can   wouldn't be so bad except Bob traded our Auger for some Tobacco & Painkiller with Cross Jacket John & now digging the river is twice as hard & if all holes are closed it's a day-long chore or longer, now that the days are short   & a man don't want to be out in the dark too long because all but the Oil is Frozen & you're as like to get frostbite as stub your toe

Ernest, I go out there in the dark to the river by myself with the axe & the sapling & the dirty big bucket because our darling brother Bob is passed out cold from drinking & going out of his mind with boredom & being caged up with me in the cabin because it's too cold these past 2 days for him to tramp down to the other camp to be on his lonesome again & it is the all-dark season & you can't do anything much outdoors so we're confined to sitting & mending our traps & keeping fish holes open & baited & pulling in the ones we catch & he's got some meat curing & I'm writing letters home & doing some baking & puttering about   IDLE   it sure got Bob into a celebrating mood, which didn't break till very late this afternoon, cooped up in the cabin with the bottle having himself a grand party on the daybed & singing snatches of them Irish songs he got off one of the saloon boys in Fairbanks, very lewd

neither of us is very used to Sharing Quarters anymore   & though I longs for him when he's up river, I can't stand him when he's here

I am half glad my tea went to ice & Bob is now passed out   it is good to have a bit of peace for a change & maybe a reason to go out here onto the river by myself in the middle of the night when it's so cold you think you're breathing knives

So Cold it would Shave a Brass Monkey, as Clare likes to say

I put Bob's coat over mine & thank him silently for his generous
build   our two pairs of moccasins one over the other &
my Indian cap on inside my double hood with face-flap
buttoned tight across my nose, tickling when I breathe
          working down each hole with the sapling, pounding it
through the slush ice that is starting to honeycomb itself into a
solid thing once more, stopping every now & then to hear what
the forest is saying & to listen to the chandelier tinkle of the
Lights that some think are Angel's Voices, Whispering

when I get them all pounded clear again it's nearly morning but
I don't care because the sun isn't going to come up, regardless
          I lie down for a minute on the ice just to look at the sky,
although doing so is life endangering   but something in
me wants the sky more than anything, & I would die just to look
at it   so I lie there for a minute & let myself sink into the
vast black majesty of it with the bands of colour rippling
through & the million pinhole pricks twinkling away in their
random patterns like ladies' jewels, spilled upon the shivering
green & orange

& I know I am a Nothingness
& I smile because this Comforts Me
& I cry because I can feel the Presence of God in the very
coldness of the air freezing my tears to my cheeks & I know that
I can Mend my Ways & Become A Good Man if I continue to
Atone & Be Patient

One day I will understand what it is to be A Part of Everything
          Alive & Full of Feeling

I get up shivering & go to the cabin, bang open the door with
my shoulder as my arms are now gone numb   ice spills
out of the bucket onto the floor with a clatter, broken shards of
ice from the fish holes   I curse soft under my breath
—Son of a Whore

& then I drop the bucket altogether when I sees them

it is too much for me, for My Little Heart, which threatens to
Stop Beating

     When I sees them, I nearly Dies
     My Sight Goes Black & Blotchy
     & there is A Loud Something in my Ears
     A Roaring
     (Like Waterfall
     After Rainfall
     Rushing Hard)

it's the yellow dress tonight, folded & laid quite carefully on the
back of my chair, which is turned away from the table

they cover up quick with the blanket but I saw enough
the sight shall never leave me

     I am God's Fool
     Ol' Daftie Duke, The World's Rube

     I will Fall for ANYTHING

—don't mind me, I'm just grabbing a few things   think I'll
go see the dogs

Bob curses & sits up, shoving Nell toward the wall   he
hocks the contents of his lungs into the spittoon & lies back on
the daybed with his feet sticking out, a large hole in the left
sock exposing his filthy toes   Nell covers her head with
the blanket   I put some ice in the kettle & stoke the fire
          strip out of my wets & throw on some new clothes
I grab some Smoke Salmon & a bit of Bread & Lard & my
blanket from the top bunk & head out again with nothing else
said between us

like Nell, I let the dogs grow accustomed to me before I crouch
among them & let them crowd around me, a warm, breathing
world of dogs   the press of em   nothing but dogs
in the world, dogs & me

I am shivering, raw
full of the night sky   I feel like I swallowed it

Fitz has her nose right up to mine, we stare into each other's
eyes

—You're True, aren't you, girl   You're my Good One
          My Fitzy, My Friendy   My Wee Sweetie
     My Wee Pup

May 25, 1906

Clare looks about the same as last year, before he disappeared
from us   though I got to say his face looks thinner even
with the whiskers growing out & waxed at the tips to little
points

he is Dandy enough for this town, where I do feel my Plainness
more than ever, Vancouver being the sort of place where every
lady got a posy on her hat brim & a tuft of lace at her throat
          the fashion is wasp-waisted, the corset-mongers make a
killing here   (& I will admit the sight is none too heavy
on the peepers for a simple Bird Island Boy like myself)

were it not for Clare I would be lost before I left the station,
where train did bring me straight across from Massachusetts
          it were a long journey but as I had splurged on a cabin
with bunk it weren't too bad   & I saved some cash by
forgoing meals except one day that I et breakfast in the middle
of the trip, full breakfast with Blood Sausage & Runny Yolk Eggs
& Buttered Toast, it was Delicious   the rest of the time
I contented myself to look out of the window at the scenery
passing by, with two cups of Tea & two Scottish Biscuits daily
          this is enough, if you are Idle & have no need to Exert

Yourself & may for most part lie abunk & Conserve Energy
        Train Travel is civil in the utmost & I do prefer it far more
than Boat though I spose I must buck up now & get happy for
the water like they say all N.F.L.D.ers are constituted, from
Birth, if I am really to go Stoker with Clare in less than a month

the streets of Vancouver are the busiest I seen, busier even than
St. John's   streetcars on their electrified tracks shrieking
up to the stops where you waits with your coin   the cable
up above keeping them on course, so once you been on them a
few times you can be sure you know where you are headed,
there will be no Wrong Turns (though the sparks that shoot out
occasionally give me a start)   & they got plenty of auto-
mobiles here too, some are even taxis you can pay for a ride,
though who got cash for that   & the horse & buggies all
seem very posh as well, like this town got in on the money good
& is feeling its Pride   though maybe that's just the places
Clare & Bill Clouter take me, & elsewhere in this city there's poor
ones down on their luck with no hats or socks to speak of
them that don't speak English

Clare showed me some of those   the Foreign Types who
come here to work on the railroad or else to work the canneries,
what I imagine is somewhat comparable to Viscoloid but with a
different smell   I worked the splitting table for Father a
time or two & would not relish a whole factory of it, without no
breeze to cut the stench   they were Chinese folks who do
be very small & though not brown or black they are not white &
have faces that are young no matter what their age & do not
smile at us but give us wide berth   & in their part of
town all the signs are in writing that looks like the scratching
the hens make in the dirt   little lines put crosswise through

each other in patterns that look mighty difficult to memorize
          Clare did laugh to see what a start I had when we
walked into the sea of people stepping round us wide like we
was catchy   staring at us or else averting their eyes,
calling out to each other like they were angry, but Clare said
that was just The Chinese Tone of Voice

he bought me some kind of their food, which was like a soft bun
that was white & steamed in a kind of reed basket & there was a
type of spiced meat inside
—Dog Dumpling sure is good eh, Duke?
I knew he wanted to get my goat but all in all I could not be
sure if it was a joke or serious   though I ate it anyway
          any food to me is welcome, especially on another's dime

I did not start with as much cash as I hoped for & what little I made
since then got sent to Father straight   he wrote me last
month in Leo & was unhappy with the amounts I have been able
to post to him thus far & I tried to explain the circumstance &
how it do cost me to Live   I got room & board   & it
was $20 for my kit to go up river, which did seem costly but Bill
Clouter paid $40 last year in White Horse so I suppose the $20
spent now at the Hudson's Bay on Granville is a bargain, though
I am not accustomed to putting out that much money on myself
          & Grandma needs $5 & Kate a loan of $6 (which I did not
tell him) & Bob Hobbs is owed for the lamb last year   but
no matter   if I send $10 or one hundred it will not suffice
when Templeman be at him & he don't even have enough for
the winter's worth of coal & can't go up to our land for wood
this year as that got seized till we pays so the house is cold as
a tomb, I expect, unless he's borrowed something, which I know
would eat his Pride   I need bigger money than what I can

get in Plastics & have hopes now for Bob & the Yellow
        though the job on the S. S. Dawson is all right for pay too,
$75 a month (or $85 if we fires with coal though we don't know
which it will be till we starts)   & that includes your Bunk
& your Slop so there's one less dollar a day I got to spend on
myself   but Vancouver is a town where you wishes you had
some money to throw around as there's much to spend it on & it
all flashes right new & pretty   & if I could get Jennie one
of them Chinese dresses with the flowered silk brocade in red
& white I would be most happy   I suppose for now a
postcard of Chinese ladies wearing same will have to do
I am in no state to send her gifts & sure that would raise Father's
ire like nothing else, with him in such a fix now   (—what
do she need Fripperies for?   —who is Jennie Chants
going to impress in the Cove, dressed like an Oriental?
—good for a mummer, maybe, nothing else)

no, if I want to rain down money, I got few choices but to try my
luck with Bob once the Dawson gets me upriver, or go the
dishonest route like the Grey Fox   though he is a Criminal,
most do not hold it against him, he is so courteous to his victims
        he do not commit undue Violence against them (unless
he is provoked)   & has been known to have a dance with
the fairer passengers as his boys hijack the train, the entire
incident taking on the air of a Party   his mug was in
the paper while I was travelling up & I could see a resemblance
to Clare around his eyes, which do not quite surprise me as the
Grey Fox has a reputation for being charming with the fairer
sex & leaving them sighing while his boys relieve their male
companions of watch fobs, money clips & any other prize
        could I join his gang? once he busts out of prison? he
has a group of younger lads to help him & there must be cash in

it or why would they try? rumour was the CPR lost $300 000 the first time & that's a sum so heady I could live on just that figure swimming in front of me for at least a few days, to gain so much the first time out & then, when finally caught, to have robbed nothing but $15 & some Liver Pills, tis a shame really
        when you see his face in the paper from the trial last week, you can't help but sympathize

Duke, the Gentleman Robber, protégé to the great Grey Fox but stealthier, less easy to catch as he is better at staying unnoticed, he got no Love Darts in his Eyes   (Ha! even in my daydreams I cannot feature it, I don't have the Gumption to live Outlaw like some might)   I suppose there is no easy money in the world & even genteel crime got its price, as Grey Fox can attest to, now that he's on the other side of the iron bars again   & I knows I got no heart for jail but it is nice to dream a Life where I got more guts & daring & the money flows to me & removes my problems quick rather than at length & with the price of working hard for many years before you sees any Shine to the Bargain
        Clare would be better suited to that kind of life, if I thinks on it   he has the Derring-do & the Charm   though for now he keeps it confined to his card games & his dalliances in the Houses I dare not visit, where Company awaits those who will pay for it   —save up your coins, my boy, & we'll get you some Tail up river   you can't afford what's on offer in Vancouver   & what you can afford is none too fresh

Clare always got a way to make me feel his seniority & greater experience in life so that I knows myself a proper Bumpkin
        I am not much for Courting Females & besides I got to scrimp my pennies so I waits for him in our bunk at the rooming

house or goes down to the zoo at Stanley Park & gawks at the monkeys & the bears & parakeets, & the seals what look the same as those at home but no one eats them—a cheaper pleasure than many others & one that keeps me occupied—& he comes home late, whistling, smelling of eau de toilette & smoke & dockyard brine

I keeps my mouth shut tight & asks him no questions, no matter how late he gets in   for though I love him dearly, I can't stand Cousin Clare when he looks so smug, just like Ernest's little lap dog, Pearl, that time she got into the butter dish

September 21, 1911

God
God!
~~GOD IS A JOKE HE DOES NOT EXIST OR IF HE DO HE~~
~~HATH FORESAKEN ME~~

God the Father hath done what Father did & bade me leave him
till I can prove myself repentant for those things I have done,
which he will not name, will not utter, will not allow to soil his
SANCTIFIED TONGUE, pure white as a cod's tongue it's that
Holy   (or so he would like us to think)

how do God exist if things like this can happen, this silence of
years after a start full of incident?   can it really be a
full four years ago now that the Intruder were dead in the yard,
froze stiff, & Bob threatening to kill me?   & then pushed
off to make more & more cabins for us, empty cabins, so he
could have somewhere to run, no matter how I tries to follow
him?   I want him back   I want
someone here to take the edge of Wild off me, & Bob is all I got
to hope for

I know tis not long till I eat my boots or some such, gone mad
from this solitary life, each hour marked out by the axe biting

into another tree, the moan & shriek of it falling & the sweat
freezing in beads as I haul the wood down to the river

the dogs my only helpmate & company

The Dicks have pushed off months ago now   that time
with Bob were the last time I saw her, & I do regret it as I would
have liked to talk to her about it, & ask if she told him   ~~do~~
~~he know I dipped my Nib in his Inkpot~~   he gives no sign
either way, though I have had little occasion to study him in the
time that's passed since then

I has but dogs to speak to, save an Indian or two on the way to
camp or maybe Anderson who never had a word for me anyhow
            he, like Bob, been at this so long he almost lost his English

I do not wish to become like that & so persist in writing daily in
the log book   but now, this many years in, I got little
News to report & when I looks at the pages they seem powerful
sad with their evidence of the Nothing that is my Life
(the slow decline of my Penmanship mirrors my Inner Collapse,
& the letters get more ragged toward the recent pages, and
more sparse)

who do I write for?   is it for Father, to show I was here &
worked hard for his money, little & late as it may come?   to
prove we are trying, squarely trying, every day that we're alive?
            some part is just to know what day it is & to remember
their order

lately I do not wish to write at all & would rather sleep
& each day's entry blends into the last

June 5   Warm, 50 Salmon, 1 rabbit
June 6   Warm, no Work, fish
June 7   Hot, Mosquitoes Bad, 2 Chickens
June 8   Traps all empty
June 9   Ditto
June 10   Ditto
June 11   Ditto
     12   D. O.
     13   Do
     14   do
     15   —
     16   —

after keeping up the habit for some years I wonder what do it
count for in my Reckoning   & I would long since have
abandoned it, save I think it is the thread keeping me loosely
tied to Humanity   I dare not let it drop   I do not
write the real substance of my days   I cannot put on the
page the other things that have happened & are true & which do
haunt me   so this list of rabbits caught & cords chopped
must serve as a record of my Life, pathetic as that is, a life added
up in fur & lumber, unwritten loneliness & the feeling I am losing
what little was left of myself, of that real Self within me

soon I will see my face in a mirror & think I am Total Animal,
suitable for eating & then sit here humming contentment while
waiting for my leg to boil up (good with some Taties & a decent
dose of Thigh Gravy)

soon I shall not distinguish between me & dogs & shall look to
Fitz for my advice & consolation & laugh right hard when for

both she bites me   (I have got in the habit now of sleeping out with them on occasion, it brings Comfort to us all)

soon enough I won't know what to do when Folks appear at random, which is the only way they appear around here
          soon I won't recognize them as Human, or rather, all things shall seem Human:

          Dogs, Lynx, Birds   Trees, River   Fire

Poor Duke Tilly got a Fairer Constitution than what do suit this Country & did bite off more than he could chew (of his own leg actually!   now ain't that a Grisly Frontier Story!)

OH GOD! Father of All Fathers! You are stuck in Long Ago & Far Away   When I was young, I thought that You were Everywhere   But You are Not   I see that now as clear as I see the snow falling

Oh Foolish Child, Foolish Duke o' days past
OH GOD OH GOD
I am your Stupid Son what didn't get the joke till late
          Oh foolish foolish Me

OH GOD OH GOD OH GOD
Have Mercy on My Soul
~~If You Exist~~

Grub moved up:

200 flour
~~one slab Bacon~~
1 case milk
4 lbs cocoa
6 lbs Raisins
1 Ham
50 lbs sugar
50 lb Rice
10 Rolled oats
6 lbs tea 5 coffee
24 onions dried
spices one lb
~~4 cans Butter~~
6 cans cream
spuds
18 lbs White Beans
10 lbs Split peas
~~6 cans cream~~ 1 slab Bacon
20 lbs lard
1 can coal oil
4 cans Butter

1 lb soda
2 yes two CAKES

Although I get no visitors to speak of I shall eat good this
winter   I do not mind the extra paid for Cocoa Raisins
Sugar I got to have some Sweet to my Days   Bob spent
some extra this year on Doctor's bills so he cannot say nothing
to me about how much I have put aside for Father & how much
I have kept to myself
          of us both, I am still Paying the Lions Share
          he keeps more to give for his kids, which I am happy to
          support
          it is a small amount I am spending anyway on food
          compared to some
          I do not have a huge appetite but wants to eat well when
          I sits down to table & that is not a Crime

it is true times are bad here   Bob been telling me that
since I arrived   he been spelling doom since I landed but
I have not listened or have done so with One Ear Only, thinking
he was a Pessimist & that we would Make a Go   it is bad
here for living, it makes you Old before your time   we
works & works & then half the riverbank is washed away in two
of our camps & we loses 100 or more cords what took us a whole
winter & spring to pile up   that's $600 we lost to the river
this year   the rate is dropped clean down to $6 a cord now
& that number $600 is a hard one to swallow when you wants to
make enough to have a start, at Home

Bob might have gone Out this fall but for his Missus breaking
her arm & now he has to go down to her more often to help, chop
her wood & that kind of chore   Isaac is still too small for

it, though he is a good hand at many other things, they all does what they can to help   Bob don't like going in to the homestead too much   the arm was infected where the bone came through the skin   we gave that Doctor a good $100 or more of our money this year & Missus still is not mended & took too much of a shine to the Ginger what she was first taking for the pain   Bob said she asked for another 3 bottles when last he went to Town & she never been one to Imbibe any Medicines, before   that Ginger do make a Man feel well for his Rhumatax & I have been known to use it some myself   it is also good when his Heart is Sore & he wants to Forget the things he holds Private to his Person but you got to drink a good quantity for that & most Men got no Stomach for it on account of its Taste, which is Quite Strong

I don't know if Missus would ever go back to N.F.L.D. with Bob   I can't feature it somehow, not because she is Indian (though that would surely cause a stir in Bird Island Cove!)   but because she is not like Nell, who looks natural in White clothes   on Missus they are somewhat ill-fitting & no matter how good her sewing she don't look right & is more at home in Bob's old trousers anyhow   Poor Bob, now that his Woman is weakened he got to go to her a couple times a week & is not quite suited to the task   she is getting on his every Nerve   she gets on the Ginger & then she starts in crying   he don't know what to do with tears but run from em, as I can attest   & he can't bolt with the chillians there too & the youngest but a babe in arms   all he wants is to be out on his own & having a nip himself, which is a different situation than with Missus as Bob can oft-times control himself & some may say he even works Harder when he's Soaked & is a Better Shot, that's sure

I started a letter to Father about all this but have not finished it
        I keep it in the back of the log book   it is too much
to write out & my hand do not like the task, it is stiff & not much
good for small work   "we did not do as well as we had
hoped this past summer but we are sure of a start next year & if
we gets that we shall surely come out this fall"   last year
we said this very same thing & we believed it too & then we sold
less than 70 & had to work at others' camps a few days here &
there to have enough for our grub list come October   &
though Anderson is my pal I do not fancy working for him, he
got a different face then & keeps his eye on you hard so you're
more likely to make mistakes than if he weren't watching

Quailey is worse   last week a sheepdog loose from the
Village wandered to his yard & his dogs took one sniff & tore
him up dead, I would guess they were half starved
        so when you work to Quailey's you got your ears cocked
        on the lookout for any Surprises

        Kate got married

I did not even know till now because our mail is so late
        married four months before I heard it   Genie
wrote all about it & about Kate's dress & her flowers & what they
all ate & how perfect it was   it were just the Leo family
there, Father of course did not make the journey   I do not
know her man but his name is Butterick   he is from Leo
        they will live there now & I suppose she is happy
I did not think Kate would marry at all, but I am often Wrong
about Women   Emily is not going to like to wait another
year   I know she is already planning things with her
girlfriends for our wedding   she likes to think on it

she got handkerchiefs, tablecloths & bed linens ready, she told
me, in a chest with the other truck we'll need for our Home
        she finally sent me a photograph of herself (& her sister)
last year   it were a good one   they got matching
dresses on & matching curled hair but Emily is the prettier &
looks the younger though she's not, she is older by a year

I sat them over the window   I got her sparkly postal
cards strung up on a bit of twine along my walls   there
are a dozen in all now, most with flowers, & they spruce the place
up right enough   she will be spitting mad at the news
but I suppose it won't matter too much   I am too far away
for her to get steamed except by letter, & when she sends me
angry ones I just use them to start the fire

she gets vexed for show, more than anything, I think
it been too long a bargain for either of us to back out now

November 21, 1912

Sawed five trees set 12 snares
Mr. Green chopping while I am sawing
While I gets my traps full Mr. Green does the skinning
While I does the splitting Green does the piling
(is this what it feels like to be Husband & Wife?)

Green came out of nowhere about two weeks ago   he is
British   he is older than me, more like Father's age, but
very sprightly on his feet & don't mind any work a man can be
tasked with   Mr. Green was not looking for me in particular
but happened on the camp & called out   I made sure he
was a Good Man, then asked him in to tea   he was in
decent gear but it was worn & his boots had seen a lot of
walking   I asked him of himself & he told me he came
out here for Forgetting & then he didn't want to say any more

Forgetting seems unlikely to me here, where there is nothing to
do but mull over the details of your past life, Outside, but I did
not say this, not wishing to Discourage him

He is a sad fellow but is often boisterous & merry & though
I understand it to be playacting it is cheering all the same   it
does me good to have another body around the place   he

needed some work so he's been here with me since   & I am
paying him cash for the balance after room & board & I think
though it is paying out a bit it helps me get my cords in fast, so
maybe I can get out first thing in Spring rather than stay here all
Summer   that is my thought on paying for labour when
the wood is not yet sold   that & the Solace of Human
Companionship   but I will not tell Father about Mr. Green,
& I hope Bob do not either

who knows what they write to each other, if they ever writes at
all   Bob says little to me these past months when he
passes through, he been sick this winter   & he never asks
me to join him on trips, not to go to hunt or to Tanana so I got
no news of His Missus Eva & Kids, either, & cannot be sure he
do not collect my mail & withhold it from me, for it is certain
my letters have dwindled into a thin amount what used to be
plentiful as salmon & I think about ceasing writing at all for I get
nothing for it & have to do so much work to write them
           it is hard when you have to travel so far to send them &
are never certain of reply   my hand is not working soundly
on the fine tasks like writing anymore   but perhaps I DO
get them & Bob just keeps them & reads them himself & maybe
even writes back replies, writes from me to Emily, some of his
crass jokes that have made her think me sick & that is why it
has been so long to hear from her   NO   No
even Bob would not be so low

he was cross with me for taking on Green without consulting him,
& got more hot when I said I knew he would have done the same
in my situation (& he had to agree) & then he went to crashing
round the yard all night, drunk as a Bum & doing violence to
the smokehouse as though it was the manifest of all his

Problems in Life   it took two days to fix it & I lost a few fish too but did not reproach him (for that is the worst way you can be with Bob   it makes his rage keep its heat where otherwise it would die down)

Mr. Green took a couple dogs hunting yesterday   Runner & Mike   Chicken are thick around the yard these days & he was to bag a couple for our dinner as I made the Bread   (is this what it's like to be someone's Missus & Helpmeet?)   every now & then I could hear the shots, so I hoped he had good luck   them Chickens is the easiest bird to get, they just sits there & lets you take aim & then if one is shot the others fly up in panic but fly back down & settle in the same spots again once they have forgotten what scared them, which takes about two seconds, they got such tiny brains   Mr. Green came back about 6 pm   he had three birds but looked none too happy   when I went out to the skinning table to see his catch he had a sad sad look in his already sad eyes & none of the usual Pride in his bearing   & he told me old Mike died on the hunt   —he took a start when the gun went off & then he died, it took a couple of minutes but seemed painless enough   from the bang of the gun, I suppose, Sir

Mike!   he had not been too strong for a while, our Mike, but he was still the best for nosing out the hunt   I did not think poor Mike's old ticker would give out, he seen a mite worse than a damn Chicken Hunt & lived through it

~~FUCK YOU GOD YOU GOT NO SENSE OF DECENCY~~
How many dogs I got to lose to Alaska?

It is Not Right

June 10, 1930

—Do you have a spine at all?
—yes
—do you?   for if you do, I see no evidence!
—stop
—'stop'   you sound like a little girl
—stop
—you sound like Eva!   'stop'
—Stop Now, Woman
—He's dead, Duke, he's been dead for years already so it's time
   we made changes   we don't have to keep all his old ways,
   some can bear to be improved upon   why can't you figure
   that out?
—it's not that   I made a promise
—it is not right, never changing anything so that we must live in,
   what, a Museum? or a shrine to your parents forever
          I can't do it   it's too sad in here
—you're going to change that, are you
—yes
—it's not possible   the whole house is sad, you can't fix it
   it's in the wood
—I'll try
—Em

—we need a fresh start   he's been gone 5 years & your
Mother was hardly here, was she, before she left?
—don't talk about her
—& why shan't I?
—she isn't for you to talk about   you never met
—we have to make room now, we got another coming, & where is
the nursery to be when you've got three rooms still full of your
Father's things laid out like he's coming back tomorrow
        it isn't right, & I dare say it's queer in the head, you are not
right upstairs, you know & I don't know how to help you   if
I had known how your mind goes
—yes, say it
—& that I shan't   I don't need to say it   I am going
to clean out those rooms starting tomorrow, I got Jennie & Mabel
coming over   we are going to get it all done quick in one go
—the three of youse is ganging on me now
—they don't think it's right for you to have it all like that, like he's
coming home any minute
—it's not my place to change things
—Duke, it's your house
—it shouldn't be
—not this again
—it's Bob's, he should have come back first, it is my fault
—there's plenty of things that are your fault   don't take on
the things that aren't
—empty comfort
—Bob would have died if you were there or not, you know it, & he
would have come home if he wanted to   he was just as
stubborn as the rest of you, I'm sure, you weren't going to be
changing his mind

she touches my hand with the back of her own

—please   let's make it ours here, let's clean it out & make
it new
—all right, girl
—we could even get new wallpaper
—sure
—bring in my pedal organ from the barn!
—we can put it in this room here, where the piano used to be
when I was a boy
—lovely   soon no one will remember twas the store at all,
twill just be Our Home

& then Eva's footsteps are coming down the hall   I wipe my
eyes   it will not do for her to see me in a state   she is
rangy as Queen Anne's Lace & growing about as fast, too

The Lord In Heaven Love Her & Keep Her Safe (her cousin
Jessey were only a few years older when she got in trouble, up
in Alaska, at the Mayo camp   the story sits in my mind
more & more, now that I see my Eva with her Womanly shape
just about to Bud & Swell   Bob had to go to the
Judge   he went to the Judge though I know he
didn't think it were true   he thought Jessey was bringing
Trouble on herself being up to the Camp at all   (& I do
think it was foolish for her to go there, yes, but foolish do not
mean an invitation to that sort of doings in my books   she
is a pretty enough young thing but has the walleye just a touch
          The Hardest-Working Girl in Alaska, I used to call her, &
it was pretty close to true, she mothering all them other
chillians, with Missus sick on Ginger)   the men were on
charges of Rape & although the Judge found them Not Guilty
Bob had been doing business with them & that went sour pretty
quick   he wrote to me about it but did not give too much

detail & I suppose for that I can be glad enough   though
perhaps not, for now I got my own thoughts filling in the holes
of how it's written   & I am sure what I imagines is a
thousandfold worse than the Truth

(for starters, if she weren't already roughed up bad by them
gents, I worry some that Bob give it to her good for ruining his
business   depends how Slick he were at the time I suppose)

(The thought of Eva ever having to go through that type of
Trial makes my eyes go blotchy black)

Bob always cursed that he had Children
he was not like me that delights to see em
& finds them the brightest part of Living

even now that Bert have grown old enough to see through me &
knows me to be a Drunkard & a Fool, there are still odd days on
the water when he looks at me like he might want to know a
thing or two from out of my Brain, & that's a True & Chuffish
Feeling)

Emily is right   it is still Father's House, not ours, despite
His Passing   it is chock-full from the Attic to the old
Shop with His Energy like the crackle of sparks from the stove,
& it makes it hard to keep from thinking of Him, Always

    Biding by His Ways, His Rules
    Trying to Make Him Proud
    With Every Daily Action

(but I would like to keep it so, & she will never let me)

Bob comes by he says to me take a break from that wood & let's
go moosing

I been chopping cords for a week straight   I have no time
for traps these days or smoking fish   barely knew it was my
own birthday yesterday, except for making my marks in the log
book   a day like all days   just checking traps, making
water & chopping   I just wants to be at the cords what
have money, promised money attached to em   I can see our
profit building up on the banks, there's still five steamers I know
who take wood & I don't know all of them, surely   I got
nearly enough logs now to pay one passage back home & I know
Bob got at least as many at his camp too   now I am cutting
for extras like a new suit to go home in, a bunk on the train,
some Vancouver silk for Emily to make her wedding dress
          cutting & sawing & with each log I am figuring what I will
do when it turns into money in the spring   I could keep
going like this all winter   a little hunt off the yard, though,
might be a welcome sport   no harm in a Change, it is
Healthy

—moosing?   you seen tracks?

—yes indeedy, about a mile back to my place   Hurry Up
—A Moose Hunt with you for Company, sounds like a Party
—hardy har
—well I guess you're better than talking to the stumps

truth told I am glad to see him   I would be gladder to see
another, but Bro Bob is good enough   I get the feeling
he is always disappointed in me no matter what I do & I cannot
figure out the trick to fix this, so never know what to say to him
as a result

& he is not the gabbing kind, least not with me, though Hedy
did say what a riot Bob was when he works down in his yard,
telling all manner of stories & giving out a few songs too while
he's sawing   so it's me that turns him quiet, I suppose

Moose Hunt for three or four days he said so I pack up enough
provisions to last us   Bob hitches the dogs   I gets
the Blankets Painkiller Tobacco Axes Flint Grub

we heads down Bob's trail a ways   back downriver toward
Tanana Town   Bob is driving the dogs & I am walking
alongside   he always drives them when we are together
although we are partners on the dogs & every other thing, he
thinks himself leader by virtue of being born a few years earlier
or being here longer (or both, I suppose)   we both are
men now & full partners in this life but even so it is the small
affairs like how he is always the one to work the dogs, it is those
things that have got me turnt   not that I express it to
him, for I also fear his Temper, what I have seen emerge a time
or two   I do not wish his Wrath upon me as I have seen it
poured on others in past times, which I do not care to dwell upon

he been good to me   he let me stay here with him
back in '06, when he could've sent me home again with nothing
but a smack on the arse for my troubles   he split his
work with me   he showed me the things I need to know to
Survive here   simple things: Salmon Wheel   Moss
Roof   Don't Thaw Your Spuds Before You Boil Them Or
They'll Ruin   & also things like Killing Is a Part of Life &
We Must Not Shirk It   & Alaska Has No Law, It Is Get
Your Man Before He Gets You, just like the judge told me when
I went to see him that time, before crossing the border, back
when I was green & scared

I got my Sins too

Bob's far better to me than the others, really   I would
shudder to think of me & Ernest up here for this long together
          (& Bob is the only one still good for Father, the others
are all turned) SO I will vow now on this Moose Hunt that I will
make some kind of Improvement of our Lot Together by Virtue
of Conversing on Topics other than Wood, Pelts & Salmon while
we are in the Bush

Does he have news of Clare? (No) From Leo? (No) Europe?
(No) What did he hear at the Post Office about the Banana
Wars? (he fancies joining up for any fight that America got its
mitts in, now that Alaska is A Territory   & the Banana
Wars got the allure of a warm climate, beside   but he has
told Father he would come home next fall for the business, so
he cannot join anyway, as he do not like to go back on Promises
          Bob figures the fighting will get much bigger before it
dies out and there would be a lot of work ahead for one cut out
to Soldier

I cannot join   I got bad ankle, bad nerves & I got Emily
to think of

Bob does not think of his Missus   he would be glad to be
clear of her & to have more to shoot at than Bear & Moose
        he would be a good hand to have on your side in battle,
he would show no mercy as he cut them down   or perhaps
I misjudge his Character   & as Bob lay dying in Nicaragua
somewhere, he'd suddenly feel bad for those he'd killed
praying earnestly for the first time in his Life, for forgiveness
        for Mercy
& as the shots went through him, he'd fall to the ground with
Real Tears in his eyes, crying out his Missus' name:
O, Eva!
& Missus would hear the Echo of his Cry,
        Far away across the Foam
& know that Bear Bob Loved Her, He Really Loved Her
        Despite All Indications to the Contrary
        Throughout Their Many Years of Married Life)

dogs panting, straining forward   Bob's commands ringing
out   the squeak & crunch of my footsteps & my laboured
breathing   sled runners swishing smooth over snow

I CAN FEEL THE BEATING OF MY HEART
& A NEW HOPE STARTING

July 14, 1930

Em have had her way   we have begun to throw Your
Things out   some we have sold & a few repurposed to
other uses (shirts cut into rags, etc)   she wants you Gone

I was right glad she weren't in the room with me when I tried
the cupboard door   that cupboard in the wall you told us
years ago was stuck shut   it yielded easily to my hands &
offered up its Secret Bounty: every one of my Alaska letters &
Bob's too, every letter we wrote Home between the two of us
          all done up neatly in a rubber band & placed within a
chocolate box

there were two handkerchiefs in the box too, old ones, of
Mother's   I took it all & went up in the woods, the same way
I used to go when I were a young lad, far too young to imagine
leaving this place long enough to merit Writing Letters

I headed up to the nook under boughs by cliff where I did like
to keep some eats & books when I was young   to my
surprise there was a jar there still after all these years with
many moulds growing one on the other inside of it   A

Libation for the Dead which may once have been Spruce Beer
   I squatted down on the moss beside it

it was a hard chore to start reading, but once I began I had to
finish them & did not care whether Em were looking for me or no

the letters telling it all & yet leaving it all out, too   my plan
to come Out pushed back year after year, almost comically,
when you read them all in sequence & see the years slipping
away while the words stay the same:

> June, 1910 —I don't know if I shall get away this fall or not
> I don't think the two of us can so it's likely the two will stay
> if we can't both come out

> December, 1911 —I shall try & get away as early as possible
> from here & come direct home

> May, 1912 —I wanted to come out this year but cut my foot
> & had my fish to take to town to sell & it kept raining all
> the time & I couldn't move until after the last Boat for the
> Outside so it was a case of stay or walk out & I tell you it
> was a hard time to walk to Fairbanks as I were already
> crippled & now my foot is cut open so I had to stay so by
> one thing & the other I didn't get away but if I live until
> next fall I shall walk out if I get frozen in so you can see
> that I am bound to come & Bob is likely to come too

(Lord on High, how much Painkiller did I tip down while
writing that one?)

> February, 1913 —I think that I shall get out of the Yukon
> pretty cheap this fall

(& that time at least I were as Good as my Word)

I wrote plainer sometimes than I remembered, & now it made
me shake to read it:

> —I notice what you said in your letter that the place was for
> Bob & me when we came home & that we could fix things
> between us & I guess that your ideas are good but I must
> tell you that Bob & me don't get along very good together
> he is one of the most ureasonable men that I have
> met yet (God Rest Him)   —I left him last fall &
> started to work about 2 miles above him   I seen that
> was the only way to get along for I can tell you true that
> I am not stuck on any of these dirty abusing rows like
> Martha Baker used to have (Pardon me, Bob, for saying so)
> —Now I am going to tell you something that I have
> been thinking about once in a while & that is THIS I think
> they all think—that is Ernest Jim Bob—that I am trying to
> get all your place because I stood by you & done my best to
> help you & make you happy & what I've done was only to
> keep my promise   —I told you when I left that if I got
> the money you would get some too & my word was good
> but you was doubting you said you'll be like the rest of
> them out of Sight out of Mind but I could never have you
> to be beholding or see you want if I could help you, Father
> no one else cares much about one but their Parents
> & you was all there was, sick & not able to work & with Sons
> out in the world & able to help & would not
> I think men of such stamp are too low for anything

the final letter is not a letter, but a telegraph, the first one I ever
sent, as I recall:

September 23, 1913

Mr. Arthur Tilly,
    Elliston,
        Newfoundland.

Dear Padre: —

I am sending you by mail M. O. #18116—to 18124—inclusive
Tanana to Elliston, N. F. date 9/22—for $100 apiece, this to
be held pending my return. I am leaving today or tomorrow
for your place & will stop over at Leominster, Mass. for a
few days to visit my sister, write me there if you choose.
    Everything here I am leaving in good condition & in
charge of Brother Bob—who I tried to have come back to
you instead of myself but he would not do so.

Hoping to be with you soon, I remain your son,

Bill W. M. Tilly

(my name looks odd spelled out that way, & I don't immediately
recognize it   when I sent that message, I thought my
troubled years were over

Ever God's Fool, resting sweet & easy at the start of my long
Journey Home)

why did you keep these letters?   did you read them over
before you sent your lawyer after me? I hope not   I hope
my naked words of devotion & LOVE, Father, would have turned

your heart back towards me, had you read them over
& you would have been able to see the wrongs you did

but I suppose it wouldn't matter   you were always Too
Proud to admit your Errors   & we were supposed to pay
the price for it without dropping our smiles

I do not wish to Emulate Your Pride
I do not want to be like You with my Children
Emily is Right
We must Clear it all out
Wipe This House Clean

Everything Gone, All Traces of You
All Except this Box of Letters Addressed to You, From Your Two
Sons Up North, Which I Shall Hide in My Trunk Up in the Attic,
with All The Other Things From That Period of Time That Em
Don't Like Me to Mention
For Fear of Giving the Children Ideas

(I Were Not Civilized Back Then)

February 9, 1913

Three days in & we got not much left to talk about   we
have covered many topics from World Events to Tanana Gossip
to Memories of Puddings Past   Bob did tell me things,
though at first it were like he was chewing on a molasses taffy,
his jaw working away but no words coming out   I think he
started talking just to make me stop, I was nattering on to him
about a story I read in the Home Journal that I had Kate send
up to me for Mrs. Dick (ah well, good company in Bunk!)
      tis about a Sailor's Sweetheart who sneaks onto his ship
as a stowaway & later gets discovered & gets put to work as the
cook but then it's her who's killed when they are attacked by
Pirates & the Sailor has a period of brief but deep bereavement
& then uses the loss of his Beloved Sweetheart as a catalyst to
his own heroic deeds & eventually becomes a Great Captain &
leads his men to Victory, keeping Sweet Whatever-Her-
Name-Is firm in his mind like a Patron Saint, to Steel his Nerves
during all manner of Daring Sea-Battles   Bob wanted to
jump in quick enough then   he hates reading them
stories & hates it worse when I recount them   I knew at
some point I could wear him down   but now after three
days of naught but talking & walking the moose trail we are
down to just a few untouched subjects & those shall remain
untouched, by either of us, as they are Volatile

we shall turn back tomorrow afternoon if we do not find our
game & then it's two more days to walk back out   & in
Black Moods too from not finding our Moose

bedding down tonight I ask Bob to sing   he has a
handsome voice
—fuck no
—& why not?   you sing down to Anderson's camp, they
tell me
—go fuck yourself
—no need to be so crass, Brother   if you don't want to, you
could just say Duke, I do not wish to sing right now, thank you
—'Duke I do not wish to sing right now, thank you'   how's
that?   or how about 'Duke I am so sorry, I am not your
trained monkey put here on this earth to entertain you'
—I accept your apology, thank you, Brother
—well, take it & apply it to your arsehole
—goodnight   I'm turning in

I get settled in my rabbit coat & blanket on my boughs at the
side of the fire   Callie, Spot, Runner, Fang, Randall & Fitz
are a warm wall of breathing fur at my back   Bob stumbles
off to have his Evening Leak, which he follows with a final slug
of Painkiller before hitting the sack   I can hear his steps
crunching away toward the trees & then the steaming sound of
hot piss hitting the snow

—Duke is a child's name   I think you should give it up
          it makes you sound   well, something
(even my name do itch him   what can I do about it?)
—it is my NAME, Bob
—your NAME is William Marmaduke   Duke sounds so

high & mighty   why not take up some other part?
—Marma Tilly might be nice, you're right
—you should be an entertainer
—you should
—William is a better name than Duke, Dukey
—It doesn't sound like me   though Kate calls me William,
from time to time, for a joke
—I'll call you Bill
—no! Bill was our ram, remember?
—& for that the name does suit!
—& Bill Clouter! I'm not sharing a name with him!
—what odds about it
—let's call me Marma if you hate Duke so much
—Marma!   Fuck no   Marma'll be what you cry out
when I strike you in the face for being such a ragdoll's cunt
—Bob! Good Lord, you're horrid
—& you're a Sop
—so?   it's my prerogative

he settles down on his boughs with his blanket & dogs, the mirror
of me across the fire

—a fancy-talking ragdoll's fucken cunt   Prerogative?
well oh well   you think I've never read a fucking book my
own self? (he chortles & hawks one)   we're a perfect pair,
eh Bill?
—don't call me that
—baa baa Brother Bill, have you any wool?
—I detest you
—yes sir yes sir, three bags full
—good night
—good night my wee ram

—I may attack you in your sleep
—no you wouldn't, I'd hear you coming, you & that bum foot of
yours   & then it's MARMA! for you   (he sets to
laughing)   MARMA!
—MARMA!
—MARMA!
—MARMA!   it's quite a fun word to shout, isn't it?
—yes, it is, Bill   I'll enjoy yelling it good & loud the night
I finally decide to kill you
—Ha!   that's rich   I say
—well something should be, & it ain't either one of us
—now that's the Lord's truth

Runner shifts around so that her nose is now resting on my
neck, & little clouds of steamy breath rise up around my face,
smelling of Dog Fish

This is A Good Night in The Bush

March 1, 1923

My neck aches from clenching it in the cold

Eyesight Going   part from writing letters by Kerosene
Light for all those years & part Genetics

squint to see the paper   squint to hammer nails in   to
thread a Needle   most letter-writing over now   Hand
very Shaky
too much LIQUID PAINKILLER in my adult years

~~IS THIS~~
~~ALL THERE IS?~~

~~IS IT ALL THERE IS?~~
~~IS THIS IT?~~

~~ALL THAT THERE IS?   HOW CAN THIS BE IT?~~
~~HOW?   HOW CAN THIS POSSIBLY BE ALL THAT~~
~~THERE IS?~~
~~NO NO NO NO~~
~~NO NO NO NO   What have I to show for~~
~~The breaking down of my body?~~

all those who once meant something to me are evaporated
I have no Family save Wife & Youngsters   I speak not to
Father, or to the others   we talk through Proxy   I have
a Lawyer who writes to Father's Lawyer & in this way we are trying
to Mend our Fences   or at least Divide them Equitably

this is an anticlimactic way to finish

I try so hard to pretend that I am Happy, Better Off & Strong, but
surely any Barn Cat looking in my eyes would see I am awash &
drowning in a veritable Lake of Sorrows full ten times wider
than the likes of Lake Laberge

Melrose is fine, it is as fine a place to be as any
          & I do think myself blessed to know the men that I knows
now but still & all it is a struggle to work with Pride when I know
how he despises me & wishes all I ever toiled for to be taken
back again

I am tired of this fighting   a fight by Lawyer & Letter is
as hard on a Body as the Fists

I want to return to our Home in Elliston
I long to Rest Again in the Bosom of our Family

~~I AM SORRY FOR WHAT HAPPENED~~
~~& I AM STUCK, EXILED AGAIN~~

~~WHY WHY WHY WHY WHY WHY WHY~~

if you need other proofs of why tis reasonable for me to join the
Union, look no further than your mirror, Father   even did

I not believe The Message, I should mouth it, just to Spite You

(but I DO believe it   & am happy to say The Words)

February 16, 1913

GOD IF YOU ARE THERE IT IS ME, BILL

ME & BOB NEED YOUR PROTECTION MOST
DESPERATELY WE ARE BOTH SINNERS BUT WE WILL
REPENT I GUARANTEE IF ONLY YOU WILL SPARE US
WE WILL DO GOOD BY OUR PROMISES WE WILL GIVE
UNTO OTHERS WE WILL NOT STRIKE DOWN OUR
BROTHERS OR SISTERS

HELP US TO LIVE

HELP US OUT OF THIS PLACE

Dear Father, if you could only know what has happened to us
        there will be no one to tell you of it & no way for us to tell
you ourselves   I did not bring paper or pen, I thought we'd
be gone five days at most   I should have known better
I am no green baby anymore   but I did not care to worry
& now Alaska shall win out

Dear Father, we are sorry to leave you & to let you down
        this Country is a hard one & it do not give up its riches

too easy, despite the stories you hear   the luck is only for a few men & we are not those men, we are Nobodies who are soon to perish on a Moose Hunt like a pair of green babies who just made their way here from Outside   Dead on a Moose Hunt, their arms round each other, the frozen bodies of the two doomed brothers will be the sure-fire making of a great Frontier Legend like Soapy or the singer with a gold nugget wedged up between her front teeth (to kiss it is deemed lucky)   we will be like that, talked about years after: —Did you hear about the two sorry arses who went hunting in February up the river when a storm came up? Brothers?   they had to eat their dogs when they ran out of food?   then they lost the flint in the blizzard & could not relight their fire & just sat together arms round each other cracking jokes in weaker & weaker voices till both their hearts slowed down so much in cold & hunger that they died one right after the other (not saying which went first) frozen together in a fraternal embrace with a mound of dead & half-skinned, half-eaten dogs on one side, & a few miserable skinny ones shivering beside them, still alive & terrified?

that is how our Legend will run & some Folks I know may shed a tear for us, others shall not

you see, our Luck has run thin   the odds are against us
we got no one to be looking for us so we are not likely to make it past tonight   I do not want to upset you, Father, but you will never know how we talked of you in our last hours together, how we talked frank about you & what you done, Good & Bad, & it were a relief to utter aloud some of your deeds that I have not mentioned to anyone before, kin or no   & some things Bob said did shock me but it were good to know them

& I go to my Death somewhat unsure of what I have accomplished in my time but I did try to make things right with you, I tried, I gave my All to it

(is that enough, in the end? I feel it is not adequate   Bob feels the same   we talked of this together but we know not what to do to Remedy the Situation)

when they find us they will alert his Missus   she will be distraught, I'm sure   he could barely speak of it, his words coming slowly, but he worried for his Eva & how she would manage the six children on her own   though he hardly goes there, just knowing he is near is a help to her   her arm never worked good since that accident   them kids is young   he did wrong by her leaving her there alone   he should have took them up to the camp   she is a good hand when sober, a better trapper than him

she needs the little money we got put by, Father, & that is why we got nothing to send back with our ghosts when we floats by Elliston on our way up into the sky (or when we sinks down to Hell, two sinning stones   it is not for us to choose which way we goes this time)

I told Bob about ~~Mrs. Dick~~ Nell & me   he chuckled, said she was a trim little morsel of a woman & that I was lucky to get a piece   he did not seem surprised by the news & not angry neither that we had shared her   truth told, I felt my shame the more that he was so easy about it

—but I committed offence against poor Emily who waits at home betrothed & knitting socks for me & against Nell too, &

you yourself when you get down to it, though I didn't know it at
the time

Bob would not have this talk   he said this is my One Life,
I should not feel Guilt for what happened, & besides that is hardly
the worst thing a person could do to another   Em & me
are not even Married yet & been apart for years   hell, if
I didn't nail anyone out here there'd be more of a problem & he
named several members of our family who've been afflicted with
similar vices   some a great surprise to me
—these things happen all the time

I know he meant to comfort me, but my Sins still weigh heavy
on my Conscience   it don't matter whether half the world
done the same or not, my actions are Regrettable   Father,
take care of Emily if you can, she is to be heartbroken by this
         I know there can be no wedding if the groom is a Corpse
         (what a sorry joke, the kind you tell & no one laughs)
Father, I am glad Jennie came home to you before you have to
grieve us   I know she will be good to you & care for you
while you sorts out what to do next without your two partners
sending money out   I know you can make good yourself,
you were always Clever & if your Health do stay this year there
is no reason you cannot make a start yourself   You do not
need us, though You think otherwise   & You shall
manage all right on Your Own

DEAR GOD PLEASE HURRY HERE

WE NEED YOUR FUCKING

HELP

I tell Bob I am thankful for all the things he's taught me & I am
glad to be his brother, proud to be here with him now
—dying like an asshole?   don't be fucken proud of that
—at least I'm not alone
—oh boo hoo
—I lost my way hunting rabbit a couple years ago & was out a
few days, no food at all, no dogs, got turned around in a storm
          it was my 1st winter here alone, what a numbskull I was
          I thought I was going to die that time, didn't happen of
course, but I didn't want to tell you about it afterward
—don't blame you, Bill   I would have roasted you
—you would have for sure   who will roast us for this one?
—I wouldn't mind roast anything right now   I wouldn't
mind fire
—I wouldn't either   ooh, a cup of tea   hot tea, now,
with Painkiller
—let's not talk about it

WE ATE ONE OF OUR BEST DOGS, WE WERE THAT DESPERATE, GOD!   DO YOU KNOW WHAT HORROR IS IN MY HEART FROM SKINNING CALLIE & TAKING HER MEAT FROM HER BONES?   FROM THE SMELL OF HER MEAT ROASTING?   IT WERE

AWFUL AS BURNT INTRUDER BUT MADE ME SALIVATE AS WELL

IT WAS TWO NIGHTS AGO BEFORE WE LOST OUR FIRE BEFORE THE BIGGEST SQUALL & THE WIND THAT SENT OUR KITS FLYING (FLINT & ALL MANNER OF THINGS LOST IN THE DRIFTS & UNFINDABLE, THOUGH WE SEARCHED FOR HOURS) WE ATE CALLIE BEFORE THE END OF TOBACCO, THE END OF PAINKILLER BEFORE PAD BAR FROZE STIFF & SO DID NOSEWORTHY, ANGEL & THE RUNT WE GOT AS MANY DEAD AS ALIVE & HOW WILL THE OTHERS COPE WHEN WE TWO PASSES OVER? SHOULD WE SHOOT THEM NOW TO SAVE THEIR PAIN, LEFT ON THEIR OWN & STARVING? HOW ABOUT OURSELVES? BOB SHOOTS BILL FIRST, & THEN HIMSELF, & WE DIES AT OUR OWN HAND & NOT ALASKA'S?

GOD COME & HELP US

OH GOD I HATE YOU & YOUR NEVERENDING TESTS OF ENDURANCE

—I hate you, God

—Amen to that, Bill   God Can Stick It In & Break It for all
I care

(& then the wind dies down!   the snow settles!   the
two brothers hold their breath to make sure the storm is really
over, & they then start to laughing!)

—curse out God & he'll stop the weather, eh?
—guess so, Bob   we should have tried that a lot earlier

(night comes to a happy ending, & brothers drift asleep in the
new calm, grateful for the end of Wind & Snow, hopeful that
come daylight their trail will once more reveal itself)

I wake to the sound of Bob swearing under his breath & shifting
away from me to reach for his rifle

—what?
—shush!

my eyes start to adjust to the dusk, it is not yet morning
          Bob slowly points the rifle to our left   what is it
there, that something, there in front of that tree?   that
something that moves just a tiny bit   a crunch of snow
under paw?   under hoof?   crack of rifle right next
to my ear, SO LOUD   CRACK! Again & then ONE MORE
each CRACK tossing Bob back a bit, he is weak from starving
these past days

sound of something falling, stumbling

we get up as fast as our cramped muscles will allow

Bob got rifle, I got mine ready too

huge   what is it   got a strange shape & seems to
have too many legs   No   Oh No   it is Cow
& Calf   the mother Moose fallen on the baby &
both of them dead now
Bob laughs   —any other day this would be a curse
        today I say we're blessed

he's right, it is Good Meat for the Starving   but you do
not shoot Calves (nor Cows if you can help it), never, it is not
right & gives me a queer feeling to see it

Bob wastes no time   he got to let the blood out fast or else
the meat will spoil   we got to work now quick, we who have
been sitting days on end with naught but thoughts to chew on
        the switch is hard   my brain do not want to agree
with my hands on what to be doing   Bob is the most
efficient butcher I seen but this time it takes him a minute to
remember how   I do not want to skin the calf
I cannot do it   I set to helping him with Mother
instead   when we have her quartered Bob slices a big piece
for himself & starts to eat it straight   —we're not going to
make it otherwise   we still have to walk out

he offers me a piece & I take it   warm, slippery with blood,
& heavy in my palm   the carcass reeks of entrail   this
is what it feels like to Chew Something, to feel it go into your
Body & give you Nourishment   what a Joy, what a Delight!
        I will never again complain about Too Much Smoke
Salmon   as long as I have Grub Enough to keep Belly
Full & Death a Mile or Two Away, I care not what it tastes like!

I Am No Fancy Lad
& Flavour is Pure Luxury!

The Meat gives us strength to continue our work & once Mother
is disassembled & her scraps are given to our starving dogs & a
good piece of her right flank too, I am that happy with Life that
I am smiling & going to work on the Calf without another
thought to it   Bob is right, this is Lucky, & not all Luck
looks good at the start   it would be worse to have killed it
& not to eat it, that would be more Wasteful & Disrespectful of
Baby Moose who tastes different than Mother & is easier on the
jaw

there is so much Meat now it is a funny thing to two who are
near-starved   there was nothing but snow for days white
white white   nothing else, even the trees disappeared &
now we got sun coming up to expose this Colourful Scene
        Bob & I both coated in blood, the fur of our coats sticky
with it & matted down like we ourselves been half-skinned &
are just waiting for the Trapper to come finish His Work

I hug him   he is grinning   he eats another piece of
meat & I do too   our dogs savage their way through the
bones, barking now & then with pleasure

DEAR GOD
THANK YOU
IT WAS A RICH JOKE TO PLAY BUT I AM RIGHT GLAD
FOR THE PUNCHLINE

we loads up what must be six hundred pound or more onto the
sled   with only 5 half-dead dogs left, this is a hard go

Bob & I get in the harness too & hitch ourselves up
            we all will pull our meat out   Bob got to stop every
few minutes to regurgitate himself so I finally makes him get
out of the harness & stand on the back of the sled, though this
makes things harder for the other 6 of us

but we feel Fine   we are strong with Meat   we can
keep on pulling for another few good hours with the thought of
Home in our sights   Bob is steering us, between further
Emptying of his Accounts   we follow his voice & swerve
as one between the trees, hoping to pull our way to camp by
tomorrow morning

Dear Father, if we Lives, I am coming Out at the nearest
opportunity

Alaska been too long on my dance card now
& I am growing weary of her Company

HER ADOLESCENCE

Christmas at the San could not be cozier, the room decked out in paper chains that Eva and the gals slowly pasted together, sitting up around the table in the common room, as the Nurses wanted them to do for at least a few hours a day, to build their strength. For Christmas morning she wants nothing but to sleep the day away in her lovely bed beside the lovely window. She knows there will be carols, and a special dinner tonight, something rich that she will not want to eat, like ham perhaps, and mash, and pudding. She will go into the toilet later and make it all come out again, for it is bad food for her body, which wants nothing but water, tea and dry bread. Eva is sure these foods are enough to nourish and sustain her without all the other noxious, odorous and overly flavoursome things which Nursies One through Ten all try to tell her are good for her and necessary to her continued presence on this earthly plane.

It's sad to lose her stomach. She can remember when she was a girl and would scheme how to steal jam out of the jar without her mother noticing. Mrs. Tilley kept count of the biscuits, but jam was harder to keep tabs on, as were fistfuls of sugar, straight from the sack, swallowed quick in the pantry while fetching some for Mother for the Church trifle. Duke sometimes had a twist or two of licorice hid in his coat for when they would go up the path together for blackberries, chawing like conspirators. Mother could not say a thing about their blackened teeth, for berries were full of Vital Energy and she approved of their consumption. "Only don't make such a mess of your face, girl. Husband, why do you let her get away with this?' Mother. Eva wasn't allowed to call her that while she taught school. Mrs. Tilley it was, and Eva didn't like to say it. Mother had the right idea. Put a door between you and your family. Stop talking. Lie down and wait for it to end. But Eva knows she can't give in, she can't. This place of rest is not her destiny, the tea leaves said as much. There is more to come for her, and she knows she must grow strong again if not for herself, then for Mary, Bob and Bert, whom she has finally begun to miss, and for Duke, who needs a woman there to help him and to keep him from his slide downward into his own abyss. Mrs. Tilley left these burdens to her oldest daughter and Eva is determined to carry them.

There is a package from Duke and one from Aunt Kate and Aunt Daisy and the Stateside family, and a little one with no return address. The Nursies had hid them until this morning, and when she sees them at the foot of her bed, Eva allows a few tears to form and nearly break across the surface of her eyes before she conserves them. A patient does not expend their precious fluids, unless in urgent circumstances.

Duke's parcel is packed in a wooden box, which she knows he's made specially for the trip. It has his trademark lack of adornment, and yet how well he has taken care to sand the edges and to keep his script neat on the address. Nurse Ford pries the top off with a letter opener. Mary and Bob have made some drawings of the house and garden, and of Duke with the dogs and the sheep. These she has Nurse Ford hang beside the window. Bert has put in a note about gossip from town but there's nothing too juicy in it. Her father has put in some cod liver oil and brandy. She sees Nurse Ford's expression and understands she will be allowed to keep neither, though Nurse Ford will no doubt have herself a little snort to ring in Christmas as soon as this ordeal of the parcel opening is done.

There are some sweets, and several apples he must have been saving up special, as they are usually all et up by this time of year. And in the bottom of the box is a bundle of several plain-covered notebooks, tied together with a bit of twine. Inside the front cover of the first book is a note written on a piece of ledger paper from the old store:

Daughter   I hope you are growing well   My hand is not Good so I will not write long but wish to say we hope to welcome you home as soon as possible in the New Year once your strength has returned   the children ask after you   the fish was slower this year than in many & I have not had great luck with the garden neither so excuse the lack of substance in this package

I hope this will help pass some time   You always asked to read my Klondike books

Do not Judge me harshly for know there is much I did not write down & know that my life was different then & anything I may have done I have atoned for & tried to make right in the years which have passed

Take the Oil & Brandy twice a day & if you should need more send a wire about it

Your Father

What is that, dear? Nurse Ford tries to peek inside and Eva snaps it shut.

Some lessons my Father sent up.

Even on Christmas?

He believes in hard work.

Eva will read them later when Nosey Nurse Ford goes off duty and Nurse Distracted-by-the-Doctor comes on shift. Nurse Ford cannot understand why the sight of a book of lessons should make a girl weep, but Eva doesn't care what Nurse Ford thinks and lets the tears fall freely now. Just holding those forbidden volumes in her hands makes her homesick. She used to get the belt sometimes for searching for them. Her father hid everything of interest in the attic and when she thought it was safe she would climb up there and rummage through the old canvas sacks and metal trunks. There was a special belt he had for her, the oldest one he owned, no longer fit to wear. It kept its place in the wardrobe solely for these moments. It did not have hard edges. Mother had a birch cane at home, just like the one in school, and she was deft.

Nurse gives Eva a handkerchief for her nose and removes it when she's finished. She dabs Eva's face with cool water. "None of that, now." Cecily in the next bed wakes up with a start and wants to know what's happening.

Eva's Aunts sent her magazines from America which rouse several squeals from her roomies. She can trade for whatever she likes after this, even Meredith's copy of *Little Women*, she is sure. Cecily already wants to know if she can have a look at The Delineator, when Eva is finished of course. She wants to know everything about everyone, always, and Eva will have to be careful to keep the log books hidden from her and only read them when Cec is at her treatments.

Eva's Aunts also sent up some pretty pink combs for her hair, and a pot of rouge. *Dear Eva, Do not tell your Father or he'll get his britches hot! All girls need a little Vanity.*

It is quite ridiculous to think of rouging her cheeks here. Who to impress? She has foresworn impressing anyone ever again. She imagines that rouge would look like warpaint on her grey face. She opens the pot and daubs some on each cheek. "Cecily dear, would you like to freshen up?" Eva passes the pot over and Cecily liberally smears the rouge. Eva laughs, it was as ghastly as she had imagined. Nurse Ford tuts. "I'll leave you to the rest." The rest? Ah yes! The third package, a small one really, no bigger than a can of sardines. *Ms Eva Tilley, Care of the St. John's Sanitorium*, and no hint as to who it is from. She rips the paper off the box and pulls out a little something wrapped in a bit of flour sacking. A kind of wooden locket on a chain, an oval carved in two parts, with a little wire hasp. Her heart beats fast, quite quite fast, and she thinks Walter! and pries the locket apart. Instead of the love note/photograph/apology she thought she might find, there is a tendril of hair, someone's hair, quite red, and the tooth of a fox, or a wolf, or a dog, and a dried berry, a partridgeberry, and a thin sliver of red velvet, which she recognizes, knotted several times and circling everything.

Who is that from, Eva? Cecily wants to know.

Oh, someone back home.

You have a sweetheart, then? You never said.

Well, Miss Nose, some of us don't tell everything.

She carefully closes the locket and fastens it around her neck, not to be removed again until she leaves here, except at bathings. The Doctors can think that it's their care that cures her, finally, that it's their supplements and infusions, their rehabilitation regimen and dietary monitoring, their wax (yes, it did happen, nine months in, and she fought and bit and was finally put under with the horrid gas that gives you a day-long headache afterward, just like Cecily told her would happen). Nursies can think they've cured her, but Eva knows the difference, she knows it is the power in the locket, in those talismans that Mabel bound together, just for Eva, in the words that she said as she did it, in her thoughts of Eva's good health. When she gets home from the San, Eva will set to work harder than ever. She will praise Mary and Bob for even their most mediocre accomplishments, and hold them on her knee and kiss their foreheads, even though her heart is cold now, colder than before. She will visit Mabel regularly, and talk to her, and try to learn from her the things she knows—the things she is able to pass on, at least. For the rest, Mabel was born like it, she always had her voices and her strange ways and Eva knows she can never be like her, wholly, and also never wholly like regular folk. She will learn what she can, and for the rest she will work.

A grey lady. A shadow. Removal past wonderful.

Time going still again, like playing at going to sleep.

BOOK FIVE

THE HOMECOMING

December 15, 1913

It does not feel the way I supposed it would

it's as though I am in one of those Pictures I went to with Clare
& Daisy & her man in Vancouver (they like the Movies, all of
them)   A Fool There Was   it is as though I am
Edward Jose in the Picture but I am actually watching it too,
Edward watching Edward running from Theda Bara (do not
Corrupt me, Vampish One!)   watching myself sitting in
this train car, Going Home

HOME

I have reached the Island & now it is just a matter of Time

it felt strange to travel back the way I came eight years before,
most things being the same, but some things different   &
I could feel how Alaska has aged me, how my body carries its
Afflictions & how they've Changed Me   Clare still looks
the Devil, he will not grow old in this Lifetime, & still got the
taste for Doves though he said Bess have retired from the

Business to marry a Town Signatory & she is a Respectable
Woman now, very fine   her new Station makes him Desire
her all the more, of course

He always liked A Challenge

we traded all the news we could muster   Daisy is looking
as well as can be hoped for, Jules too   they are tight but
making do with what comes   I sent them 400, it put me
back a year but I was happy to do it   when I saw them they
did not ask me for anything more   they knew I would need
it all for the Wedding & getting our things together before we
can fix our own place   we are getting some furniture, bits
& pieces when she finds it   Emily has been storing it in
Father's barn what only have the cow & old Lightning anymore
            there is lots of room in the other side & Father does
not mind doing for us like this, it is really part my barn too for
I have sent the money to build it & buy the hay & oats, me & Bob
have, so it is all right to use it, I write to her   it cheers me
to think of them talking together, her having a reason to visit
him once in a while   we will live with him till we are sorted
            there are five bedrooms, only two is occupied so it shall
not be tight   we will not stay long, just until we have start
enough for our own digs   1 year if Business is good
            Father, Me & Bob is Full Partners in the Store & Farm
now, though Bob is not coming Out this year   he decided
to trap another Winter but is sending the money from it & will
come Out soon

my collar feels tight around my neck, I am not used to Collared
Shirts   I have Lived Rough & have forgot a mite what it
is like to be Dressed to the Full

in Vancouver I asked Clare to take me back to Chinatown
          I had dreamed of it a night or two since we went there,
1906   the red & gold & black (trapping colours), bold
slashes & strokes   the butcher shops   the smell of
those Dog Dumplings   the women in brocade dresses &
dainty needlework slippers   these things have come into
my dreams sometimes, mingling weirdly with scenes from the
River in a manner not unpleasant

Clare & me wandered through the throngs of people   we
were so happy to see each other, it was the first time since I headed
for Bob in the fall of '06   & though much time had passed
we picked up talking like I seen him last week, that is a thing
about Clare   he's Comfortable

he bought me a meal   the people around us small & very
neat & here I was a torn-up mess with uneven haircut, ragged
jacket & boots with soles flapping 2 sides   I never wore
these boots for 7 years (the moccasins do suit better up there) so
the stitching has rotted from lack of use

I can't have anything Good it seems, I do Waste it, or I Save it till
it falls to Ruin   & I have spent my lot on gifts, I have no
money to fix myself

Clare bought me a meal, same as that first trip up   we
didn't know how to order so he just pointed at a few things &
made 'two' with his fingers to the girl   we ended up with
something with Meat, Carrot & Cabbage, very good & another
dish with Fish & Green Vegetables that I did not like as much
          it was too Spicy

my stomach sometimes acts against me   I ate more Rice
to calm the feeling
Rice is familiar   but in Alaska it is Plain, Salted, Buttered
or with Smoke Salmon
there was no Spice   it were not Chinesey

we talked of Clare's adventures these past years   he is
still working Boiler   he likes it, he gets tired of staying in
one place   to Clare that is Murder   he is still mad for
Bessie though she is Unavailable but he got another one up in
Fairbanks one in White Horse & a couple in Vancouver who are
Quite Acceptable Substitutes   there is a funny one I met
named Ella who came to the pictures with us, dressed as Charlie
Chaplin   they looked cute necking on the streetcar, all
right   I said Ella was a good 'en & he coloured some, so
I think she got a bit on him, & that's a trick for Clare
          sometimes in the Winter he takes off down South to San
Francisco, Los Angeles, big hot cities where there is fun to be
had if you are Man Enough   sounds like a lot of energy
necessary for that type of life, & much spending of your money,
but that is Clare, he will burn bright until he snuffs out quick as
a wink some day   & most times I admire him for it

I went to see Kate in Leominster before I headed home
          Kate Butterick now   Mrs. Katie B. I calls her to make
her laugh   she is looking well enough   she got a
youngster & may have another soon   5 or 6 months I would
guess, though I did not ask the details   George is a fine
man   he is a quiet one, which did surprise me, Kate being
the sort who likes a bit of a laugh & a swagger to her fellows as
a rule   but they are well enough, they have a nice home &
their little one is good & fine & healthy   George have a

good job at Viscoloid as a Supervisor   the money is
Good & Steady

Kate told me she had met a woman who knew M—, a woman
from Ireland who came here young & settled   M— knew
her, back when she left us, after Babby died

she'd come down Stateside, it was when we couldn't find her

she was tutoring wealthy children in the good part of town, &
this woman, Mrs. Daly, she was the cook at one of the houses, she
would feed M— in the kitchen once the lesson was done
Mrs. Daly said she was a Good Soul, very Sad, you could tell, &
somewhat Desperate   she played around town with any
music man who needed a piano player, it didn't matter what kind
of establishment, & Mrs. Daly wouldn't say more on the subject

M— had some story made up about her whole family being dead,
she were A Widow to all she met   she said it happened
in a shipwreck, & I imagine drew some realistic details from
that time with Father & the S. S. Eric
          Kate & me had a good laugh at how Father had acted as
          though she were dead, those years
          & she was doing the same of all of us, Stateside
          & then we both were crying
          & then she got the Gin &
          Poured us both a Stiff One

—she might as well have been dead, for all we knew   she
never even wrote
—I know, Duke
—huh   It's Bill now
—what?

—Bob's been calling me Bill, I spose he didn't like Duke
        thought it was too childish
—Bill
—yuh   my man Mr. Green knew me as Bill only, in fact
—it don't suit you
 I laughed   —that's what I told him, but you knows Bob
        stubborn as a whipping post
—wouldn't know him from Adam   I was a kid when he lit
out
—that's right   well, no matter   he's a lot like Father
in terms of putting his mind to things, & a lot bigger in stature,
just picture that

~~Poor Kate I love you I miss you I want to tell you that I love you~~
~~the most, of all of Them   (I do not care if that is Sin, it~~
~~cannot Stain a Soul already this full of Trespasses)~~

I am frozen to the core, that stiff my teeth are chattering though
it is toasty in the train car   all hands have coats off, save
me   I am buttoned right to Chin

~~Will Emily still Love Me?~~
~~Will She still Love Me~~
~~Even though I'm Not the Same~~
~~As When Last We Saw Each Other?~~

~~I Am Old~~
~~I Have Shakes~~
~~I am Bones In a Bag, Katey said~~

I take the train all the way to Bonavista   you couldn't do
that when I left   the country is changing & I can see it will

be good for business   we shall get our stock much quicker
from St. John's   we must strike a deal with a Dry Goods
there for special cloth, sundry goods etc & offer more choice
than Templeman or Ryan so we are in the race with them for
the main trade but have our own specialties you can't get
elsewhere, maybe more notions, buttons & the like, candies of
all kinds, magazines & books

Emily would like that

As the Train hits the Peninsula it's all memories of drives in
buggy, my heart is hurting it is pounding so hard, memories of
this land, of the land itself, barrens, ponds, trees & shore
      wind whipping at the tuckamore to toughen them to the
      trials of Living
      it is a Hard Land too, this Land
      Hard & Beautiful

at Bonavista Station I sees Philly Clouter, Bill's uncle, who
looks about the same as when I left but with a touch of grey to
his hair   he got the same pipe hanging out of his mouth,
it seems   —Philly!

he turns but do not recognize me   —Philly! It's me, Duke
Tilly!   he frowns a second   I done my best to clean up
      Kate & Daisy would not let me leave for home without
new suit & haircut   but the fact remains I looks different
than I did 1905, since Alaska had her Way with Me

I Have Grown a Bit Crooked, Am Leaned Over to One Side A
Mite & with a Limp to my Walk, Hands Not Too Good for Small
Work & Face do show Signs of a Few Odd Hardships with the

Rosy Cheeks of One Who's Often Used a Bottle to Fend Off the
Cold

—Duke Tilly, well Holy Ghost I didn't know you!
—I knew you straight away!
—what's it been, five years?
—eight
—Sacred Heart   Eight Years   that can't be true
—it's been a long time, Philly
—your father know you're back?
—I wrote him September I was coming but didn't give particulars,
  hard to estimate, you know, but I said before Christmas
—it's a long road, I figure
—it is, though faster with the train in   what's all the news?
—oh, sure Jennie will tell you that when you gets in, between her
  & Emily you'll have an ear full soon enough
—I imagine   are they all well?
—even better when they sees you   that's a good surprise
          will you ride out with me or do you have someone coming
  or what?
—I don't   I was going to ask around so you saved me that
  job
—we'll have a good gab on the way in

he hops to & throws my kit on his buggy   we get on & he
clicks to his horses   I will see Lightning in just a few
hours, no colt now but an old thing like me
          like Jennie   Father   Emily

I don't know what to say to any of them, though I have brought
them all Gifts

Father: Rum & a Nugget (which I bought in Dawson off a Drunk
         got a Good Price   had to bring back a touch of
Colour, as I'd Promised to Bob I would keep Our Lie standing)

Emily: Beaded Moccasins of Eva's make, seeds for her flower
garden of a few kinds we don't got at home, white silk for nuptial
dress, white Viscoloid comb with roses on it for her hair & white
Viscoloid pearls to match (Kate chose them)

Lightning: bag of oats that I picked up in St. John's

Jennie: Chinese Lantern from Vancouver
         Red with Black Designs & Gold
         You can put a Lamp or Candle Inside It
         & It Glows Very Pretty, Round as an Orange

July 22, 1905

Kate is on my back about this Dance they have all the way over in Catalina & how she wants to go right powerfully & Father says she must have an Escort & Kate says Jim do not want to go & Clare has a date already   Mary Blake from Bonavista   & will I go with her to a Dance in Catalina where we knows almost nobody & me not liking Dances at the best of times   but she got that look on her mug she knows will hook me   the look of a Barn Cat sitting pretty in the hayloft, a mouse's dead little head laid at your feet

she says she knows a girl or two that shall be there so by the end of the night I will be sure to get some dances in   I smiles at her but it feels like a Death's Head

how can I deny her? I know she don't half want to dance with Clare far from Father's Kingdom, with less chance of word travelling back   & I wonder can I arrange this somehow   I will make it a goal for the evening, give me something to think about besides my Nerves   I always been Shy at such Occasions   some other folk (Clare) are Pure Social & it is no Effort for them at all

I do envy them but do not have the guts to move so big or talk so
loud when other people are about & can see me   & when
alone I have no need for such exaggerations & so have become
a man more silent & still than otherwise

    An Invisible Man, Unseen, Unheard
    A Mere Gaze on the World

    That's all there is to me
    The world passes through me
    It fills me up
    (I am but The Cup!)

—Kate you know I must love you
—well, yes now   I know you wouldn't get this spruced up
  to take Daisy out
—no, my duck
—you're my good brother
—you're my runt

  she swipes at me & gets me good on the shoulder with her nails

—you're mauling me!
—let us not exaggerate, William
—fine, Katherine   do I look all right though   my hair
  is unforgivable
—it isn't stellar   but it'll do the trick
—are you sure?
—get Jennie to give it a trim, then, if you're so worried
—can't you do it
—I have to do myself!   I shall be gussied up proper tonight
       we have to leave in an hour!   scoot now, Duke
       I have to see to my stockings & iron my dress

Kate bolts up the stairs hard & heavy like Father detests
        he feels we should respect his Ears, what are tender, by
leaving no audible trace of ourselves inside His House

~~I have Learned to Tread Lightly up Ladders~~
~~& have Memorized the Whereabouts~~
~~Of all the Culprit Creaky Floorboards~~

I run a comb through my hair & make a parting & take the
scissors to the back part myself   I have no designs on
Wooing Women & hope rather to pass the night uneventfully &
above all costs avoid embarrassment   (& to have a good
chuckle getting Clare & Kate dancing
                        it should be better than a Serial!)

I go out to hitch Lightning to his cart   the stars are starting
to appear over the water, so I have two times the constellations
        M— had a book with them drawn out in it, but she took it
with her & did not bring it back again   I remember
Cassiopeia of course & the Ursas, but the others are all soaked up
into the general twinkling mass of sky & I can't pick them out

this shirt is James's & a mite tight around the neck   if
Succumbed with Emotion of any kind I may pop the top button
off   I must be Calm in these clothes & Appear Confident
        this shall be somewhat of a trick as I feel my Nerves in
my Throat already & we haven't even left the Farm

I give Lightning a drop of water & try not to waste it on my
trousers what Jennie pressed for me this morning after she put
the Porridge on   Father says she is to stay here tonight &
cannot go Dancing   & you know she don't got a Beau or

two somewhere on the Shore   & would give anything for a
scuff, that one, her & Kate are mad for it   their faces getting
red & shiny & very happy looking, on the fast ones   &
serious, open, & smaller somehow, on the slow

hair damp at the neck & unfurling from coif into little curls as
babies have, what smells so good when you put your face there
& breathe it in

INNOCENCE!

Girls got that too, after dancing a few reels, I have had only a
few occasions to observe   after dancing, they lets you see
things about them what you wouldn't in usual life   they
got their guard down & out comes their real faces, which are more
relaxed than usual   & we can now smell their authentic,
intoxicating Odour which is like Baby Scalps & makes you sure
there is a Hopeful Future for us all, Somewhere

(if Girls let you smell them like that all the time, the world
would end   no one would be able to work or think, the
beautiful Scent not permitting us to concentrate on any task for
longer than 2 seconds before collapsing into a glorious Sigh
over our Desks or Nets or Woodpiles

it is a Scent best left to the end of a Dance in a Town You Don't
Know with your Sister's Acquaintance holding your Elbow after
you have Drunk some Blueberry Wine & are A Little Tipsy Turvy,
& are thus Permitted to Collapse into The Damp & Curled
Hair of a Female Stranger in All Its Olfactory Glory, & She Will
Graciously Pretend Not to Notice, Nor To Remember it,
Afterwards)

that will be the best possible outcome for tonight   & I have a wealth of stars before me to wish it on   but I must be careful to make sure I pick a STAR & not a reflection in the water, for wishing on a star's reflection can grant you distorted wishes, twisted past recognition of what you thought you wanted when you made The Spell (WHICH IS WHAT WISHING ON A STAR IS   OR SPILLING SALT   EGG CRACKED IN GLASS OF WATER ON THE WINDOWSILL AT DAYBREAK   BREAD IN YOUR POCKETS FOR THE WOODS

Mabel taught me that)

Christmas Day, 1913

Praise be to the Saviour, born this day in Bethlehem, for returning me to the Bosom of my Family

safe at home in Trinity Bay!   & it is better than when I left for we are back in the Store again, back in our rightful place as Tillys!

tis better than when I left, for Emily is here with us this evening & this evening I shall finally ask Father for his blessing, for we hope to be married quick come 1914, she has waited too long she has waited away eight years on me & I feel myself growing old, sure everyone else in the family got youngsters going   I got to seize my life now & make something more of it I will be **30** come February without wife or children & it is too much to bear

Jennie is letting Emily help her with the Ham & they are boiling Fruitcakes, both wearing aprons over their dresses in the steamy kitchen   aprons from the same pattern, made with the same cloth (Jennie is Economical)   both of them out there working aside each other &, as I take it, best of friends since I been gone   they got the girlish whisper going like a couple of Sisters

I wonder do they speak of me but I will not ask it   why
should I rekindle those Dead Fires that did no one no good &
are long forgotten by all but myself   still I wonder have
Emily & Jennie talked frank of me?   do Em think worse
of me for it?   is that why I have only had three kisses since
I been back, & those were chaste & quick ones? Mere Pecks?
            or can she smell Alaska on me   can she smell the
traces of my life up there, of Intruder, Moose Hunt, Nell?
            I have washed my face plenty since coming Outside but
I catches a whiff of Alaska myself, sometimes, Gamy & Sour

she wants to wait till we are Married to do more than those
chicken peck kisses   I may not hold her on my lap & we
have not danced again   although sometimes she will let
me take her hand when walking or sitting in the parlor in
evening time

she says I must know her feelings & why cannot I wait a little
more we have been at it this long already won't it be perfect to
be wed & then to BED to go TO BED FOR THE VERY FIRST
TIME IN OUR LIVES, THE BOTH OF US, AS PROPER MAN
& WIFE

I promised to ask Father today
I been putting it off since I arrived

he only wants to talk of the Store, the Stock, the Loans, how I can
make us more with other Enterprises   he wonders could
I sell Smoked Cod, could I breed Dogs   & I am that tired
once I works on Father's plans all day I do not feature much
beside my supper & my pillow   so it do not hurt me too
much when my Emily got no time for me & Jennie too

I am like her cousin now, or a brother who moved away when she was young, she do not know him but pays him basic familial courtesy   she is polite & this is more than I could have hoped for, I suppose, but it hurts me anyway

(O for a taste of the Frenchman's Mince Pie this night, & some of his French singing!)

where is Bob now   is he at Tanana with Eva & is she feeding him good grub?   will he toss in the Indian's blanket?
          yes, I will admit I misses parts of it already, though when I was there I was dying to get Out   I did not know how strained the silence could be here   I had forgot what force Father has   his Mood is everywhere & if it is a Black One you had best just wait it out, there is no changing it
I suppose that is much like Bob, but Bob I have got used to after our years together so he do not bother me as much   &
with Bob, there was always another camp upriver somewhere, & miles of stumps to put between yourselves   when I came home I didn't know what to expect, but hoped for a smile, a hug, a handshake, a list of questions, some fleeting sparkle in his eye   instead Father came out to the cart & spoke to Philly about his lambs (they had been sick the week before) like it were nothing to him that his Son who been gone Eight Years now is Come Home   I did my best to like it   I smiled & clapped old Philly on the shoulder & shook his hand before he left   when he was gone round the bend & there was no one else, Father had to look at me   he stood there with hands at sides   —come on in, then, if you're back

it were Jennie who asked the questions though I noticed right enough that Father listened to my replies

one thing I learned off Alaska is that you got to temper Pride
        you cannot let it be All or you will Suffer   the
Indians know how to be Proud & Humble both   Big Jim,
Crossjacket John, Charlie & the others that I knew were Proud
Men but not above asking something of you if it were needed &
you could do the same with them   I wish Father had a
little of this in him   it would do him Good

Jennie looks much the same as I remembered   more
thick about the middle maybe or maybe it just been too long
since I seen her & I had whittled her down a size or two in my
thoughts   she did not hug me or smile too much but at the
time I chalked it up to Father being present   (now I knows
she just is Different, as am I)   she pelted me with questions
about my Frontier Life the whole night till we run out of oil in
the lamp & had to turn in & the whole time I did not get a chance
to ask about the Family or anything else   Emily did not
come over to The House that night

it was too late in the evening &
Father was Tired

he seems to like her   he lets her cut his hair if that is
indication   but he don't have much good to say of any one
& I wonder if his health has worsened & he will not let on
        he is slower then I remembers to get up & sit down & to
go up the stairs   he got a stoop between his shoulders
almost like Templeman left his boot there a mite too long & his
hair is now pure white, though it has thinned none   &
there has been a time or two I think he forgot who he was talking
to   I AM SORRY it took me eight years, Father, but I came
back to you all the same, as I promised I would

he is on the daybed now   he is pretending to be asleep so
as not to talk to me   he will talk Business till the End of
Days but don't want to have no other words between us
          the Girls don't want Business on Christmas   they
wants a Merry Day or at least a Calm One   I got to talk
to him though, I got to get this sorted   Emily made me
swear I would do it before the New Year

—Father   will I get you a Whisky?   the dinner will be
ready soon   (he pretends sleep   I lean over him)
—Father!   (his eyes pop open   although half-
expecting it, I still have a start)
—Boy
—Do you want a Whisky? before dinner?
—I heard you   don't repeat yourself   folks would think
you're soft
—sorry
—Whisky
—yes sir

(he likes a good big glass full & no water, one before dinner,
one at dinner, & one before turning in   I can match him,
now that Alaska has trained me in Drinking)

—I have a question for you   I am sure it is no secret to
you that Emily & I have had a promise together for some time,
& I wanted to ask you, you see, for your consent to finalize the
match
—well   how considerate
—will you give us your blessing?   we'd like to marry as
soon as we can
—how considerate of you to ask

—of course we'd ask   but still, you have known I wished to
marry Emily for a good long time now, & we will plan, if you
agree to it, for as soon as we can manage in the Spring
—if I agree
—your blessing is important
—you care what I think, when you've had a secret arrangement
with that one already how many years?
—it's not secret   I wrote you I had plans before, I wrote
several times to you
—did you   must have been one of the many letters you
say you sent me that somehow never arrived
—that's not a fault of mine   you know the post is tricky
        there were months when I had nothing from you & then
you wrote mad with me for not replying to the letter I never got!
—don't raise your voice to me, Boy
(the women are quiet in the kitchen)
—I'm sorry if you didn't receive Official Notice but you had to
know   Emily's been visiting you for four years now, nearly
every week   at any rate   we intend to marry as
soon as you'll allow
—you just got here & now you want to change everything
        you've been here a few weeks & you think you can do
whatever you want   we are just getting started
—I'll still be your partner on the Store as we planned
—you'll be too wrapped up to care about it
—don't be foolish
—don't you EVER call me that
—Father please   I just want to marry her   I will be with
you all other ways   we're not leaving you   we want to
live here till we gets our own place, to see to you   Emily is
a good hand, she has lots of energy, she can help Jennie, or even
mind the shop sometimes, she is better than me at sums

—you think you will live here?   you've already decided
that? what else have you figured on?
—I'm one-third partner of the place   there's five rooms &
just you & Jennie here   it only makes sense
—you think you can come here & just do as you please?
—no sir, of course not
—you want my business & now you want to live in my house &
you have it all decided between you?   how will I feed
another mouth?
—I'm not out to take nothing from you   we will work
together like we planned   we can do more & get more
money, I'm certain   Emily shall be no burden   (I force
a laugh) besides she doesn't eat too much, she is so small
—I know you're trying to hoodwink me, Boy, & I don't like it
—yes sir, no sir, I'm not
—I am HUNGRY   JENNIE
(she comes scuttling out quick)
—when will we eat?
—just a few minutes now   sit to table, Arthur, & we'll bring
it out
—you've made Turnip?
—yes sir, I wouldn't forget

(Father sits to table, I follow, & we say nothing more till the
women in matching green flowered aprons bring out the Ham
Turnips Pease Pudding & Potatoes, at which point He starts the
Prayer)

The Women sit with heads bowed over plates & fingers clasped
tight   Ears reddened from the things they've overheard
          & I feel Sorry for Afflicting Them
                    This is a Man's Affair

The dance hall is the church hall over in Catalina   they
have brought in wild roses & other flowers from the gardens of,
I suppose, the Junior Ladies' League that organizes such things

& there is Cherry Cake & Jam Tarts & a bowl of Punch that I make
for straight away, only to find it untainted with Drink of any sort

—Catalina's dry as a bone, my love   I say to Kate & hand
her a glass
—not while I'm here, my dear   she reveals the jar of
Grandmother's Homemade that she smuggled inside her bag
 —Kate!   you scamp!   you're the worst of us!

she takes a swig straight from the jar & winks at me then sloshes
more into her glass to mix with the Ladies' Punch

—hold out your glass, William   it'll give you Courage
—I was thinking of waiting outside for you
—not tonight, dear   you have to risk it sometimes
—my heart is not good
—not good?
—real bad   real bad, Kate

—racing, like?
—yes, racing, jumping   it's skipping beats, then there's
these lurches   oh God   I'm like to Die tonight
—it's all right, it's your Nerves is all   have a good swallow
then cast your eye around   there's plenty of girls here &
most are real nice too   & some are even pretty on top of
that!   Lord knows we're all hungry for a new Man at these
things, you'll be dandy (she finishes her Punch in one go, she is
a Natural, like Father)   I'll take a stroll & see who I can find
          get your mood in a better situation & stop your sooking
          I'll be back in a minute
—I'll be here by the goodies, unless I see Clare

(Kate turns red on the ears & walks quickly away
          Success!)

now that I am alone I got no excuse for not widening my gaze to
include not only the decorations, food & libations of the evening,
but the PEOPLE as well   though truth be told, to be
immersed in a group of folks most of whom are unknown to me
feels like DROWNING   this could be my last night before
God's Territory   I got Heartbeat coming out my Ears

there are no chairs over on this side, & across the room it seems
that most of them are full   besides, I do not dare the trip
across the dance floor   I lean on the wall instead, like the
other few fellas who have adopted a similar posture
          though they look collected about it, & that makes me
wonder what the exterior appearance of Duke is, to these
strangers here tonight   do it match up to how I am feeling?
          my guess is it do not, as no one has approached me yet
to see if I need Medical Attention

Kate's doctored Punch is strong   I am not one for Drink,
most days   the taste is abusive to my Throat, & to my Head
afterwards   like M— I got no real Stomach for it   BUT
once in a while I sees the Fun the others have, like Clare (& Bob
when he lived home, boy he was bad for it)   & there are
nights I think it would be fine for me to go on it hard as they
can do   (mostly when out in a group like this & feeling
like I got no skin & no voice either   & then I slug it back,
to see if it makes me into Someone Else till sunrise:

A Bravery + Foolishness Elixir)

concertina & fiddle are playing fast together & the dances are
starting   I see Kate come running back with some strange
smile on her   like a mask on top of something else
          she grabs my hand
—let's dance for this, Dukey   it'll get us going   after,
we can find some others   I didn't see many of my girls
yet & don't think you should settle for Ellen or Mavis really, so
that's that   come on   please   I needs the whirl
about & you're my good partner
—at home with just us
—same thing   just look at me   we'll have a laugh

I give in, because what else am I to do here besides try & shrink
away to nothing (which, deep down, I recognize is impossible
          no matter how powerfully I desire it, I cannot actually
vanish!)

Kate gives me a swallow straight from the jar & I chase it with the
half & half Punch, which feels harder to take than the straight
Gin, then I gets a fresh glass of the clean Punch without Booze

from a small, slight girl in a plain navy dress well fitted to her figure, with mouse-brown hair pulled back from a pale kind of too-young face (which you find pretty & yet feel you should not, she looks so much like a girl of twelve)   she smiles at me as she serves it & touches my fingers briefly around the glass
        she has pretty eyes, which are brown like the colour of Lightning's flanks

I got no tongue to tell her thank you, but turn away & gulp the sweet stuff down, in hopes I may desist in smelling like a Public House   then Kate & I get in with the other couples lined up on the floor, men on one side & ladies across, clapping, waiting for all to gather so we may start   the Promenade has always terrified me, but by now I got some ripe new Gin coursing through, what Grandmother made only this month
        & which, by rights, could be mistaken for what they use to sterilize bandages

my feet seem to be stamping in time to the music, & my hands are clapping along & I got a smile on my face (is it like Kate's, a shield on top of something else?   I can no longer tell)

the first couple starts the Promenade through the centre of the floor   we are near the end so I got some time to get my Nerve together, for it's like a wedding aisle in the middle with everyone watching & clapping you on & noting what you're wearing, who your partner is, if they have seen you before
        & I guess they does this early in the night for all to cast eyes on each other & spy out who might spark your interest, for later on   it is practical, if a tad transparent, but I feels inadequate to the scrutiny & it's only Kate's misery what's keeping me here at all

some of the girls is smart looking enough & they are also good
dancers   but none of them holds a candle to those I already
know   I have not paid much attention to the gentlemen's
side of the floor, but I am now drawn to the next fella waiting in
line for his turn, for I know the silhouette like I know my own
hand   across the way from him is the one Kate said it
would be, that Mary, who is more Busty than Kate, with very fair
blonde hair & a dress the colour of nearly-ripe blueberries with
factory lace on the trim   & I look across to Kate & she is
smiling all the harder & don't she look half tipped in already
          I wants to shout across that the night is just beginning
& not to give up Hope   Clare may hold her close yet

I want to tell her   —don't worry, it's in the Cards, Mabel
said so!

I don't say nothing, though
& just keep clapping with the fiddle
it's more kind

February 22, 1914

Dear Bob,

I got your letter dated Xmas Eve 2 days ago   I know it
must have cost you dear to write it as you was never one for
letters but still you covered 4 sheets so you must like me a mite
after all   Har Har   I forget what I wrote last time in
those 3 ones I sent up along my trip home one in Vancouver
one in Leo one St. John's   whatever I wrote then is different
now   it is not how I thought it would be   I don't
know how to manage with Him   He is most unreasonable
& I fear it were the wrong choice for me to come Out not You for
You are stronger than me & maybe he would not be this way if
you were home   he do not want to hear my side & if you
will believe it said he do not want me to marry Emily   he
do not want her to live here with us   he thinks I am trying
to cheat off him   ME what have spent so long killing
myself to get him straight

I tell you it is not a good place
          Bob what can we do   I been waiting since '06 to
marry, you knows that   & that poor girl been waiting too
          sure the Whole Cove is waiting on it   they been
asking since I got home when will be the wedding, for Emily
have been talking about it this 8 years now & she is not young

no more I am not either we must not lose our path now because
Father is upsot but he is firm in his view & do not seem likely to
change it   he do not want to talk anything but Shop &
Farm with me he do not care to say me the time of day & poor
Emily thinks he don't like her

I say to her she could be the Queen herself & he would be the
same

he is just Hateful

Bob you know the truth   I wish you weren't so far away or
that the others would talk to him   but they don't wish to
see the ire of Father either, who do?   you wrote you took on
Noble & the old man for the winter I hope they are not so drunk
that they Kills each other   you know Noble don't like the
old man much   it must be fun to listen to them talk
I am glad you got your two Moose so you don't got to go out no
more the winter for Meat   you know I still laughs
sometimes at the thought of that Hunt & how we were fixed but
don't worry I am telling NO ONE   they must have been
Fat Ones to break both Sleighs   I suppose them dogs
were mighty tired after that   you said Noble let Cap run
away & the old man's dogs might have killed him   I hope
that is not so   maybe by this time you have found Cap
or someone caught him   I would not believe Noble that
the old man clubbed Cap   I know he is hard to his own
dogs but he would not hit yours   Noble is just trying to
turn you against him (they got Old Hate)

I am sad to hear you give up Fitz but I suppose she had her
years already & is good for a rest   it sounds like that kid
Carl Paterson will do good by her   can you believe wasting

King Salmon strips on an old bitch like Fitz when she been
eating Dog Fish her whole life?   sounds like a funny kid,
she will have a nice old time with him   is Susannie Rice
as good with Riley   now you have given all away but Fang
& Spot, do this mean once they are gone you will come Out?

Bob I do not mean to pressure you but I ask because if you is
selling dogs to come Out I say to do it fast, it don't matter to stay
on the summer for the money like you said

The Boats are nearly all Coal now & there's no money in Cords
& you cannot stay just to trap when there is so much we could
do here the three of us working together   Come Home
right away because we need you here & I know you could make
a difference to the situation   you wrote that part about
Missus   I know you did not see her for months   why
did you go for Xmas to the Siwash not to your own wife
         I got to wonder Bob if you are saying that you plan on
leaving without spelling it quite out   ~~I know Eva have~~
~~not been good to you   it is best to go your distance~~
~~   the chillians are old enough to serve themselves & they~~
~~are long used to your absence   it will be better to be~~
~~away from her when you cause each other Harm~~

I hope you will not be cross with me
all I says is Brother to Brother

you say Alaska is the deadest place on earth   I say it seems
lively compared to the Store, with just me & Father here
         Jennie is gone   she was married three weeks ago
to a fella lives Champney's East so now she'll be a fair ways
down the shore

Father gave her the stuff for her dress but did not go to the ceremony for she does not have his Permission to leave again & never will & I know he is turnt she is quitting him but he still will not say me to marry Emily who could be a good helpmeet now when we have no Jennie & are fixing our own meals & doing all else in the house after working Store the whole day   this is not a good way to be Living   we need a Woman but his Pride do not let him agree to my Marriage   he says if we does it I will no longer have a place here like it were some kind of Treason against him & not a way to Continue The Family   I tried once to say it were my place too, mine yours & his in equal parts   he did not like this, he says I am the Child he is the Father Till Death Do End It & it do not matter if I am grown   he sees my marriage as trying to steal from him   how do I say it is not like that, that we want to look to you, you are Old & Alone (I must say the Truth but not so he takes offence   I need some other Words)
          I could write James or Ernest about it I suppose they are better with words than either of us   did you know James is in St. John's now   he is trying to run a Public House like about a thousand other fellows   he do not write too often, to me at least, so was not sure you heard

Bob you were twenty when you married, how did it feel?
          I am 10 years more than that   it is what I chose those years ago & now I must fight for the chance to have it
          she got her chest packed to the top with sheets & pillowcases & handkerchiefs with my initials embroidered in lavender thread   she been stacking the stuff up so long it would be a Mortal Sin to say call it off because he is too Proud to let me have one thing, one thing of my own that has naught to do with him

there is no more News here   or none that I knows of
          Emily is back in Newman's Cove till we have some other
understanding with Himself   she could not stay here now
          I know she is vexed that I do not quit him but I say he
has all my money, this place is as much mine as his & if I leave,
it will be as though I went North for Nothing & you know what
a black thought that would be after Slaving that long & working
myself so I am half-dead & broken up   & you after doing
the same

you will be happy to know he got enough Painkiller stored up to
drown a Man   it is a good enough Comfort though I takes
care not to Dent into it too much at once

write me again sometime if you can stomach it   I like to
hear from you   tell me all the news with the old man &
Noble   tell the chillians their Uncle Duke misses em
          I suppose they do not remember me at all now
          come Out soon   we will have a room ready &
I know with us both we could make a change & get a real start

Remember me to all you sees   Bill

June 14, 1914

The priest says to kiss the Bride
I can feel my cheeks pinking from all of the stares

Kate & George   Jim & wife & kids   Daisy & kids too
         Jennie   Mabel & a slew of Pearces & friends of
Emily   & even Father   who protested till the last but
between Jim & Daisy they got him here   they convinced
him I think of the Damage to the Tilly Reputation if he were
not to Show   in fact it were Jim who has turned Father's
mind these past few months what was so set on Forbidding me
this day   Jim wrote & appealed to him to read his Bible
close & see there how he was wronging me & blighting what
should be the best part of my life   (Emily is good at
nicking letters & opening them careful so that the owner never
knows they been read! Whatta Wife!)   Jim is wily enough
to talk to Father in his own language   I got no gift for
that & just want him to do right   Jim wrote to him —Now
is your chance to make a good time or a bad one for your old age
        Father, just think what we lose if we lose Duke
what we will all lose   our old proud position at Elliston

It took Father a few weeks to get over that letter, he was burning, but in the end he knew the sense of it & could not argue

& sure enough a few weeks later when it seemed it were his own idea he told me I could marry her & bring her to live with us, though he would not stand to the ceremony

& now they even got him in the Church this day, against his Word   (I got to learn Jim's trick!)

Emily is as beautiful as she ever been, with the Chinatown silk from Vancouver & the white roses in her hair
        she do not look her age   she looks a girl

we line up outside the church for handshakes & kisses but I don't know half the folks here   they are Newman's Cove folks, all here for Emily   she is in her glee

Emily Kate Daisy & Jennie spent yesterday cooking   they got a lot put to table for the folks all coming up to the house for a drink & a scuff   Philly got his fiddle & Emily got her organ moved up but I hope someone else will play for I want to dance this night with my Bride in my Arms

I do not look forward to our Nuptial Bed next door to Father's, every sound travelling through the wall   I want to take her to the barn or somewhere else where we can be alone, but she is too fine for that, or for root cellar   it would be rough of me to ask & I know I shall not dare it

I did not think on her Body too much in the years we been betrothed, but in the past weeks it has occupied my thoughts, ever since he gave his blessing   I know it is a certainty

now that I will see her in full, & touch her & claim her as my
own & she will do the same of me   I do not know if she
will like me   I been through my Knocks   & if she
don't like me there is naught we can do now   it is Too Late

Too Late for us Both
Time Now to Eat Your Cake & Be Merry
For Life Does Have Some Good In It

Kate got tears in her eyes   she kisses me
—I'm glad for you, William, glad for you both
—thank you   we're glad you're here, all of youse
—it was worth the trip
she presses my arm & then moves down the line to give a kiss
to Emily   my face is tight after all the smiling, I have
smiled at everyone in Town & then some

folks starts walking back to the Store but Emily & me get in the
buggy to drive up   she got me a new shirt & collar &
made me throw my old gear out
—you look like a bumpkin trying to be proper, not like a shopkeeper

(I feel it, Emily, I feel that way too
I have been touched by the Klondike
& there's no way to shake it now)

in the buggy I kisses her & she do not break away but kisses me
back   her soft little mouth warm & wet against mine
          there is no better feeling   I takes her hands in
mine & kisses each one   —I will do what I can to make up
for those years you waited   I want to be a Good Husband

she smiles & says she loves me & I say it back & George who is
driving us says to stop with the mushy talk, it makes him Queasy
—is that right, George?   says Emily   —Kate gets no
lovey pet names, then?
—no   says George   —& that she don't, & she don't
ask for none, either, thank God

we round up in sight of the Store
& then I am laughing on account of Father's trick
It is a Good One

he told me last month we still did not have the money for a
proper sign   I knew it were funny when he been insisting
on going for the parcels himself every time these past few days
          mail were never his errand of choice as it points up to
him that he is no longer Postmaster for this cove, as he was for
many years, back in The Good Times

he must have ordered the sign on the sly & hired someone to
hang it while we were at the Church, for a wedding surprise
          his intention to show me, with inclusion of offspring in
the lettering, that all was, if not Square, then Passable between Us:

TILLEY
& SONS
GENERAL STORE

it must have cost him a pretty penny to get it made & sent
          by the time he comes back from the church, half the Bay
will already have seen it

TILL**E**Y!
E! E!
HEE HEE!

—Emily, this is going to be good   I say   —just you
watch Father, see what he does
—he won't do anything   he'll pretend it's intentional
        he may even change the spelling of his name to suit the
sign & start adding in letters where there never was before

(& though she said this jokingly, she was right about him
        she always is   & the last time I wrote my name as
William Marmaduke Tilly was the wedding registry

I been W. M. BILL 'DUKE' TILL**E**Y ever since)

July 22, 1905

I got 2 things in me at all times, sitting kitty corner to each other & picking fights

One part is shy of the Other Sex, & SCARED of what large feelings they do inspire

& the other part wishes to take control & press into the girl who, so warm I can feel the heat radiate, is now swinging through my arms

these dances can be devious   disguised as sanctioned social interaction & yet, with the many twining steps, weaving through arms, holding hands & changing partners, it's DOWNRIGHT DANGEROUS WHEN YOU GOT SOME GIN-PUNCH IN   I sees Kate now in a knot with Clare & swinging into him & she is turned red & shy & he is teasing her, I think, from what I can glimpse of them as I pass my own partner to the left (Emily Pearce of the Punch Table & Simple Navy Blue Dress & Young Face though she did say she was seventeen when I enquired as our fingers touched, once again, upon my Punch Glass, when I headed back for the third time)

her fingers are bony

all of her is spare
& she is like feathers compared to Kate, in terms of ease with
which I can swing her
& Kate is no hard weight to carry, her own self

she makes a mockery of my hair, asking did my sister cut it that
afternoon?
—why?
—it looks fresh
—it do?
—you don't look too much like a lad who takes care to trim his
hair, on most occasions
—don't I then?
—no   (she laughs)   (I say nothing)   oh,
come on   it's no insult, William
(I glower at her)   —can another girl cover the punch
bowl? (she is taken aback, emits a nearly inaudible & nearly
invisible gasp)   —I didn't mean to offend
—can another girl cover
(she sighs)   —yes I think so
—good   (I crack a smile)   let's have a dance then,
Miss Pearce   (I bolt back my Punch & grab her hand
while I am brave enough to do it)
—wait   (she pulls away)   —Beulah!   can you
do this for a few? I have a dance
—yes, maid   (& Beulah gives Emily a little push toward me)
—thank you, Beulah, maid, much obliged   I say
—if it's that much to you, you can pay me back later with my own
dance!
—if I still have breath I will, it's only fair   though I must
warn you, after this round I may not have the go left
(Beulah laughs)   —I'm having you on, boy   don't

want to dance with you anyhow   you're too homely for
my tastes
—Beulah Marie Power! (Emily, feigning disapproval)
—My Heart! (me, feigning humiliation) & then we three has a bit
of a laugh   I grab Emily's hand again & pull her onto the
floor near where Clare & Kate have paired up together
          WITHOUT my help

This Night was in the cards (or in the leaves!)   Mabel
said so   she said something was to come of this night for
me & for Kate   & I am not sorry I asked about it though
it's Kate's secret, for I wanted to know if she would see some joy
(unlike Father I do not think it is Sin for her to love Clare,
I think it Natural & it is Rubbish that they should have to hide
something so rare as what, right this minute, I can see is A
MUTUAL FONDNESS   Clare got a tender look on
his face, it is not a Cousinly Regard   & My Katey is
Blushing)
          I wink at her but she don't even see me

Swing your Partner, thin little feather in a blue dress
Funny feather, who can be flung faster & further than
The Sister of Mister Tilly (Mr. Myself, Yours Truly:
Billy William Marm A. Duke, Lord of Nothing & Nobody)

Emily's fingers gripping mine cool & bony & her other hand
digging a little into my upper arm as she cannot reach my
shoulder, she is so small   (she is too small to comfortably
sink my nose into her scalp, unless perhaps I were sitting down
          this is a disappointment, I will confess, though I try not to
blame her for what Nature has provided her in the way of Stature,
she cannot help it)

I get a little glimpse of
Clare & Kate now & then as we spin around

Her Hand
In His Hand
& The Other
On His Shoulder

(& he with his jacket off
& his shirtsleeves rolled up!)

April 25, 1915

Dear Bob
She have had a baby BOY we called him ROBERT after you
          Bert for short   Bertie Birthmark I called him
when I saw him for he got a brown mark on the small of his
back somewhat like a muddy thumbprint

Dear God
she have done it & they both are Living
~~is this the joyous payment for my years of TOIL~~

Dear Bob
I named him after you, & I hope he is like you   Strong as
Bruin   One who can keep up his Strength on Nothing &
can Persevere long past the point when I myself would Call it
Quits   I want him to have your Stamina, this new
Robert Tilley, he is the sixth one of our family if I reckon it right

~~God~~

~~If you Interfere with him, Be it to The Good~~

Bob you wrote last time some Awful News & I did mean to write
back sooner but have been quite caught up in our Events at

Home   (I did not know being Husband could be so
Tiring   I can hear you laughing now)   I used to
envy you for your wife & children & could not see why you
should keep yourself so far from them when you had the choice
          though he is but a few weeks old now that baby do squall
some & yes there have been times already when I thought I should
like a wood yard to escape to, a few miles hence   but I do
think him a Blessing to be sure   he is just like Emily in
the face, not Tilleys, for which I am pretty happy   let's
hope the rest of him follows Suit & turns Pure Pearce

Bob now what do you mean the whole camp burnt down
I cannot understand it

the whole first camp   everything   even your bait
        all your furs your gun & the smokehouse cabin the food
the tools it all ALL burnt while you was on the river?   Bob
how long were you on the river why did you not return in time
to salvage some of it?   I cannot see my way around this
          if you was just on the river surely you had time to get
away with something but you says it all burnt to a crisp & you
never even saved the bait to get more lynx with (that is the
worst)   I knows you are still in debt & I am trying what
I can to save something to send you but Father is the one with
the Books he do not pay me for my Labour   I work
toward our place here that he is fixing for us   I got some
furniture stored away in the barn   I am working off what
I owes Him & you see we are all in debt some way   you
to N. C. & C. Co. me to Father & Father to Templeman   it is
a right enough way to be fixed   I do say I know it is no
comfort to you but I would rather be in debt to the company
than Father

he has not made it easy for us here   Emily is sensitive to
his Moods, she thinks he is Cross because he do not like her
          I say he is Cross because that is his Nature   he
been that way long before we were wed, do not pay it no mind

but when you are not used to him from babyhood his Moods
are large & can give a Fright

he have come around to us living here since Jennie left
          he missed a woman's cooking   though I have
made a few dinners in my time as you know & am not too bad a
hand, any Woman can do better   (Emily can   she
is good for that   though now with Baby she is Tired
& I have taken it up again most of the time)

you speak of hunting the Kaiser   I say you cannot think
of that   you got rhumatiz & your ribs where they were
broke that time did not set right   you would not be fit
enough for Them, I am sorry to report   I am not fit enough
with Limp & Hand that do not clench to Fist   we make a
Fine Pair   & anyway it is better to see to your own Life
than fighting over there I think & if that marks me a Coward so
be it   I do not want to be among them what did take
Gallipoli today, our boys among them   you know that
sort of Work comes at a Cost & I am not the type to fare it well
          so I should be half glad to be Lame I suppose

do you joke about the Widows? I cannot tell   there are a
few here now but I do not know if they are ones to suit your
Fancy   yes Minnie Gould is widowed but I do not think
the same for Sis Trask though I don't know her much since she
moved down the Shore   Flora is still married though her

husband is poorly so there's a few prospects if you are serious
about it   if you are I will ask Emily because she knows
more than I do Who is Married Who Died & The Rest

& sure once war is done there shall be several more to choose
from, so sit tight

> I DO NOT MEAN TO OFFEND
> & IF I DO FORGET WHAT
> I HAVE WRIT HERE!

There are things I must Say:

Don't be Angry with me   how was I to write to you about
it when all she said was not to tell you anything   she
wanted to tell all herself   & do not say you only find out
now that I went there   sure did you think I would not see
her & the chillians before I left for good?   what kind of
Uncle would I be to them if that were so?

you had to know I went there Bob

I did not think it would Hurt you   I thought you & she
would talk among yourselves before she Split   Missus
just said to me she was Unhappy   she did not think you
& she were a Good Match from the start & now that the years
have kept on she knows it is not right to stay with you if nothing
changes   I did not say nothing to her   I just
listened to her the way I felt I should as friend to you both
        I did NOT advise her to leave you esp. without speaking
to you first but I DO think Bob it could be for the Best
        you two was like Savages some of the times that I saw &
when you was not you was but Tolerant

is that a Marriage?   I cannot see why you really cares if
she Married a Soldier or not

Soldier MacCoy & her might be happy, you never know
& if they are not he might not last the war

I did not feature she would leave the kids there though
                                        that is a Rough Spot

is Jessey fifteen? ~~I suppose they been used to doing for~~
~~themselves~~   I could use her help here   now that
Emily is nursing she is Tired & don't want to keep house
          she is Sad but I don't know why or how to talk to her
          I know you remembers them days with Eva   she
would get on the Ginger & you on Whisky, you could not talk to
one another but both were sunk into their Misery or if you tried
to talk you'd Shout or Worse   I do not want that for
myself   I tries to be the chipper cheerer-upper but it is a
hard job after working aside Father the whole day, what could
wear down any person's Soul

I know I may not hear from you for another year & that to say
once more that you will not make it Out

I do not fault you for it Bob but you must know I wishes more
          if you can get out of debt at all it would be good to come
here   it have been too long for you up there & now what
have you got to Leave Behind anymore?   go to work for
Quailey or whoever got Concerns there   do not Sweat it
but just get your Bills Sorted so you may return   I would
like Young Bert to meet his Namesake!   if you were here
you would be his God Father but you are not here & we have
Jim instead   a weak Second!

write me all the news from the fellows when you sees them if you have the time to do it

now Bob don't lose hope   I will comb around town for some Pretty Widows & will ask them to send you a Picture or at least their Measurements Written out on a Card

Good Night
Your Brother Bill

P. S. Father says to tell to you that if you want any goods sent from us he will give you the stuff at a good price cheaper than we sells it & write it up against your next payment   he will wait up to a Year No Interest   write him if you want anything   Hard Tack Dry Biscuit Canned Butter or anything we have   it would be cheaper than some of the goods we gets in Tanana even with the cost to ship   I can make a good box to fit it with wood & tin & it will not get Bust Up   just write him with the order he will write down the amount in the Ledger   you got your own page so do I so do every Fisherman on the Shore

April 2, 1895

my Sunday secret is to sit here outside the piano room door while Mother practices for Church   it is our Quiet Time for Studies   Bible or School, Our Choice   though we should not choose School too often or Father will be Cross with us, as Eugenie learned

it is no Secret that I sit here   the Secret is that while I sit here I don't Study   though I have my book upon my lap I do not Study but I Listen Only, I am Just my Ears taking in the sound, & the rest of me is still as Dead People   she plays softer at home & the Hymns sound more beautiful that way, & also without the whole town chiming in with their mishmash of bad voices & good ones until the Music gets drowned out

on Sunday Mornings Before Church it is just Mother's piano & sometimes a soft little bit of her voice, quietly humming the melody despite herself, though Father doesn't encourage that, he thinks it Vulgar for the Pianist to Sing as Well

from here also I am right next to the porch & so can listen with one ear on piano & one on sound of footsteps & catch Jennie

with Baby Arthur when they get back from the Sunday Walk
she takes him on so Mother can have time to practice
   Father do not want her to play for Church if she do not
practice them all beforehand although Mother knows the
Hymns very well she played them all many times before
& it is not Difficult Music I asked her once could she
play some other things she said only if your Father is
Away on Business with no hope of soon returning I said
why is he so Cross with us she said she wished she knew
for sure but it was naught to do with me, I was A Good Boy
—Your Father thinks that unless you are Stern you are Doing
Wrong he doesn't approve much of Taking Pleasure in
Life
—why not
—it's a Sin, I suppose now don't ever tell him I said that
—I wouldn't
—I know you wouldn't
—but is it a Sin, though, to Have Fun
—it depends who you ask I don't think so God
would want you to be happy & have a little fun, don't you think?
(Mother's God is not the same one as Father's, that Judges
What You Have Earned In Life Against The Bad Things You
Have Done, & All Turn Out to be Sinners Somehow, No Matter
What, Even the Smallest Little Babies)

I tries to find my Fun where I can & if listening to Hymn
Practice is not Fun exactly, it is Peaceful & Calm & I Loves
It It is my Favourite Part of the Week besides my time
I looks to Baby (we all take turns, Mother is Tired & Jennie has
to do our Cooking & our Washing) I do not say to
anyone this is my favourite thing for it should suit me more to
say Store or Schooling or even Farm but it is not so, I wants to

be looking to him   he makes me laugh & is a Child of
Fun for sure

& though he is but a Babe, we get on better than I do
with most Folks   I was happy today when Jennie came
in with him, I could take him right quick with excuse that she
should change for Church   Baby Smell on top of head
the Best Smell in the World, his fingers tight around my thumb
          I took him to my room so Mother could keep practicing
          if she heard him she would stop   we could hear
her from upstairs but it was not as clear & I had to listen to
James & Clare's stupid whispering on the other side of the
bedroom   they pretend to study their Maths together
Sundays but look at Comics instead & write Secret Messages &
Clare stays to Dinner & sometimes he stays over at our House
          I said to Mother why can't they stay to Clare's
sometimes instead of coming here   I get no Sleep
when Clare stays over they laugh & whisper all night but won't
tell me what about   she changed the subject   she
don't like talking about Uncle Robert's Family   Clare &
the other cousins comes by but we do not talk to Auntie or
Uncle anymore   something went wrong between Father
& his Brother years ago when I was only four or five so I do not
remember them too much though I sees them on the road
sometimes   they do not go to Church with us   &
you must not ask on it or you gets a knock

but Clare can come before Church Sunday & stay to Sunday
Dinner too every week & sleep at ours as well that night & that
is all right as long as we never speak of his Parents   that is
The Rule & though it makes no sense to me it is not the
strangest one that the Grown-ups have come up with

I sat Babby on my bed   I gave him a toffee to suck
that I had saved inside my mattress   I made a small hole
(no one can see it) that is good for Treasure of this sort   he
likes Candy   we got that in common, the real Sweet Tooth

—Do you think he looks like me   I asked James, but they
did not pay me any attention   I am just The Runt
I am a BOY & they are NOT, not anymore, their voices have
changed & are ringing out lower now with a few squeaks here &
there when you least expect it   me & Kate & Eugenie
love to torment James about it (for several months he sounded
like a Mallard, we couldn't help but let out a few Quacks)

I think Clare got eyes for Jennie although Jennie is thirteen &
he is nearly fifteen now   she is Pretty I have always
thought so since she first came here   do he have Eyes for
her or do he just have Eyes for Every Girl   that is the
rumour at School but Jennie do not go to School she got no
time for that   Clare & James loves to talk on Girls
          they thinks I do not understand it yet, I am but a Kid to
them   I told them I have a Sweetheart   they
laughed at me & turned their backs again & whispered low with
heads bent close together

I will not ignore Arthur like that when he is my age (though by
that time I will be a Man!   by that time I might have my
own Little Babies & my own Wife & young Uncle Arthur could
be THEIR GODFATHER AGE 11!)
(now that's a strange thought!)

Jennie wanted him back from me, I could hear her rushing to
dress in the room next door

she wants him always ~~she had a baby of her own~~

I am shy around her   she is two years older than me &
she has Bosoms

Father do not want us to talk to her   she is not to be part of
the family & we are to remember that although she lives with us,
she is merely Hired Help   Hired on for a Purpose ~~to
Take Over where Mother Cannot~~   Mother is Tired
she is Sickly   she have got not much Energy for Nothing
but Drags herself to Church each week & Plays & she got two
students for Piano comes to see her on Thursdays   she
gets up out of bed for them & does the lessons & then she falls
back down   we do not know how to Help her   Doctor
says it is Weak Nerves Weak Constitution   feed her Beef
Broth & Livers & she must rest as much as possible or she will
get Worse

when I sit outside the piano room door I am imagining her
behind it in her Sunday Dress, but how she was before Baby
was born   I do not like to be there when she leaves the
room   I don't want to see her how she really is now,
stooped & sad   damp with cold sweats   something
got her in its grasp

Baby Arthur sleeps in Jennie's room, who is Not Family but just
Hired Help & Who Lives Amongst Us Only On Account of
Circumstance   & I am forbidden to visit him or to ever
go in that room, as is James, for it is not Proper   —I have
no plans in that direction thank you, James said (he always
been a Sammy-Soft)

I am not allowed in there, especially at Night   but tonight
I am sure I hear her crying out   some panicked strangled
noise

it is coming again   it is a Bad Sound   I goes over
there quick   it is right next to ours   I do not care if
Father straps me for it tomorrow   the sound compels it

Jennie is in the centre of the room, stood by the crib with both
hands over her mouth

I go to him & though it is dark I can tell he is too still
        he was always moving even when asleep   always
kicking his legs or curling his fingers in & out & when I touch
him now his cheeks are cold quite cold what were warm as
anything but hours before when I kissed them   —Jennie
        what happened

I want to shake him but Mother said I must never do that
        did she mean even if he Died? it must be all right then
        Jennie doesn't say anything   she can't say what
happened   got her hands clamped over her mouth &
tears coming down

I go to Kate's room   though she is but eight she is the
best to help me
—Kate get up, there's something wrong with Babby
& she takes him in her arms   she puts his little face up to
her ear & makes us stop our crying so she can listen properly
        we try & hold our breath   I got Jennie by the
hand & I am PRAYING

Kate's face tells All

I knew we was too late

& though she tries to blow air into his mouth to start his breath
it is all for Nothing

—What happened? Kate wants to know but Jennie can't say
anything

Kate hugs her & makes her sit down on the bed   Jennie
is shaking

—Here's what we must do   Duke, go back to your room &
pretend you didn't come here   if Father knows you did,
you'll suffer for it   I'll say I heard her cry out, came in &
found him   Jennie, you'll have to tell us what you know,
but I know Sweetheart you didn't do anything, did you
          you woke up & he was gone already, it wasn't your fault
          I'm sure he didn't make no noise   there are lots
of babies that happens to, you know, they just pass   it
isn't your fault but you will have to talk to Father all the same
          just tell the Truth & he'll Forgive you

Kate quickly lets me hold him but I wish I didn't do it   how
can I erase the feeling of him now, cold in my arms, so much
heavier than before?   no lively wriggle like a piglet, just
the heft of something dead? a baby of stone?

I get back in bed & check that James & Clare did not wake
          this is where I sat with him, this morning   I tried
to teach him to shake hands with me & his little palm was sticky
with my mattress candy

in a few minutes I hear Kate going down the hallway
I hear her knocking at Father & Mother's door   I can hear
whispering & then the sound of Father quickly following her
back down the hallway, Mother trailing afterward

I want to go to her   she should not see this
          It Is Not Right   I lie there & pretend to
sleep   there are gruff loud sounds   Father's
questions Kate trying to answer & Mother keening in Jennie's
room   Clare wakes me up to say something has
happened & he & Jim leave to see it for themselves

I know I must follow but do not know if I can bear it
I am not strong enough to Play the Lie

          Can I not escape?
          Could I take his place?

               I Should Like to Feign Sleep
               Till I Too Pass Over

June 26, 1916

Mr. Arthur Tilley:

Father as you have never offered me that Furniture that you bought from Mr. Butt for me I thought that I might ask you if you were going to keep it or give it to me or pay me the money so as I could buy some myself   you got Furniture enough without that & I got nothing & no money to buy it with & that is mine & you know that it is right that I should have it   if you don't intend to give it to me let me know & come to some understanding about it as I will have to see who it is that owns it when Mr Butt comes for I do not think it is right for me to be drove so tight as this & you to have that Furniture not in use
          I assure you that I would never ask you if I could manage without it but I can't get chairs & tables or anything without money so I believe that what I bought & paid for I got a good right to & if you look at it as you should you will see that you are doing a great wrong to keep it from me   as far as I can find out you have sold the boat & if you have you could well afford to give me my own

Father you have been telling me that you only paid twenty-five dollars of my money for the cow but I can show you by this copy from your own letter that there is more than that as you got the bill made out on the letter as follows

Paid Butt balance on Cow	$40
two tons Hay at 20	$40
then there was ten bags feed	$24
& six sacks oats $3.50	$21
& all the bills that I paid was	
Ben Baker	$20

this is not as it is on your own letter & if I had that much it would help me along all right now

Father I suppose you thought you were doing right by ordering me out with 30 days notice & breaking all your agreements with me & making yourself subject to paying back all that you received from me while I was away   for you were getting money under False Pretenses   for you proved that by ordering me out that you never intended to fix the place for me to live in or anything else   it was all like buying the cow it was all yours & nothing mine   now Father there has got to be some settlement & I want you to remember that the quieter you settle it the better I will like it   I am going to give you a chance to let me know what you intend to do if you intend to do anything but it got to be settled for if I am to lose everything I shall lose it fair & show the world how a Son can be deceived by his Father   up to the time that you ordered me out I thought more of you than I did of myself   now I suppose you forgets when you used to wait for me to come from selling the paper & little things on the wharfs in St. John's to get the five or ten cents from me & how glad I was to be able to give it to you

& then you takes enough from me to make me comfortable for years by lying to me so much as you was making a house ready for me to live in then you buys a cow for me, & a quarter of the stable from Aunt Bettie & the Land & I suppose you thought you was doing right when you sold it to Dick Baker but I think you will have to find the money or the Land & Lumber yet

for I am going to see if there is any Justice in this Country or not or if a man can get money by lying & getting anyone into a mess like you got me into by ordering me out in the dead of winter with a sick woman & an Infant Baby & not a place to go to & only for Strangers I would have no place to sleep or live   you never gave me a chance but the one notice to be out in the month   you offered me that bed but you thought even that was too much & locked the door so as I couldn't get it out

I would come & talk this over with you but there is no chance of us talking it over As Men   & I took this letter as the only way to see what you intend to do & if you don't answer I will see that you don't intend to keep it out of court for I have made up my mind to see this to The End

Because you are the cause of all my Troubles
Your Son Duke

P.S.
This is what the Lawyer says about it   there is the fact that you received the money from me   I can claim this because you broke all the agreements between us

May 7, 1919

Dear Father,
Your letter of Apr 27th received tonight, you say that
I misunderstood you about the hay, yes I know what you said
about the ½ ton that Jim gave me but that was not all you said,
you told me not to let the horse go hungry & I took more than
the ½ ton that Jim gave me & that was what Kate was going to
pay you for but you say I was cheating her I was fleecing Kate &
Alice you think I am a Common Criminal that would steal off
his sisters

Father I think sometimes you do not know me at all

so as I figure it, all I owes you is $10.00 that is left after the
money Kate & Alice gave you that they owed to me from before
& you know that $10.00 couldn't buy a great lot of anything now
anyway   or do you want more Justice to be wrought
between us   I got no stomach for it   can we not just
settle this now   I will promise to get you the $10.00 as
soon as I can but that is all I owe & how you asks me to pay over
what Kate & Alice already put forward on my name is pure
meanness   Father I would never have thought you
capable of it when I was younger but I seen by now you got no
thought for Us, it is all You

you say you think I have got in a Bad Pickle   you are
right but it was not my doings that got me as I am now & it's no
great pleasure to see your own offspring in need especially the
one that stood by you when all the rest failed   I am down
now & can't help myself & you say I am fleecing poor Kate &
Alice   if Alice would pay me the money her & Chandler
owes me I would be able to help you a little   that is what
I would do if she paid me back even though you have not been
a help to me in these past ten years I have been home
you have been not a Help but a Hindrance you have not been
Kind you have not Loved me you have Cast me from you, you
are Mean you make Lies to try & show I am to fault for All

although I do not want to keep a bad feeling between us Father
you cannot say what you like to me without response   I am
sorry I did not ask you to Eva's Christening but you have not
been good to us this past while & in fact Emily says you do not
speak to her when she goes up to Church   that is not a
thing I wants between us

but you can't think I am forgetting all that has come before

if I help you now it is for Peace between us & for my Wife &
Children   they don't deserve this   just trust that if
I take hay it is paid for & that is that   I should think you
would be glad for even that bit of money   I have heard
from some that you are not working, you are not well, the store
will be gone this year & Templeman is winning out
          I heard from one that you may go to a Poor House in
St. John's   do you think that is best when Daisy & Jim
both said to go to them   let them take you on   why
turn from them to die in the Poor House for you know that is what
would happen if you were to stay there for any length of time

that is what they're built for

You got enough Life in you yet for a few Good Summers & you could be happy with Daisy & her Bunch

if I were another kind of Son I would have come calling sooner to see what you mean to do to square with me & Bob our shares if you are selling   you know most Men would ask that straightaway if they were as strapped as I am but I have said nothing because I still respect you even if you have been hard to me & done me wrong many times since I been back
          I respect you & so I do not ask about my third & what you plan to do with it   I am waiting for you to tell me yourself as is proper

if you cannot work then I would like to go back there
          I could buy it from you over time   if you sell to me that is better than Templeman   it is the Family still & I can keep the Tradition   anyway I do not think it is all your decision   there are 3 of Us   I am dead sick of Fishing   I got to find another Living

think about all I have said   I would like to be Civil
let us talk together when you comes down here in June & I will abide by what we agrees on then

we all got some hard luck

Your son
Duke

Date?

The old girl is gone, she's gone
She's gone to God in Heaven

The wife is gone, she's gone
Gone to Her Rest in Heaven

(where I shall never join her,
for which she sighs —God Bless Him!)

I did not think to outlive her & now do not know how to be the
Only Parent   how do I talk to them about it   Mary
is so small   Bob is pretending he got no Mother
        Bert is sullen as anything & hardly home out of it & Eva
already been Nursemaid since spring   how can I ask her
to take it on, all of it, how can I ask them to HELP ME

~~Emily I Never Loved You~~
~~Even Though I Tried As Hard~~
~~As Ever a Man Could~~

~~I Hope You Are Faring Better~~
~~With Your New Holy Husband~~

~~& Now That You've Died~~
~~Life Is Good~~

we were not as we could have been   we were not Pictures
of Wedded Bliss as in the Talkies

you blamed me for It All & for you wasting your Youth when all
the lads around was writing you postcards & telling you how
fetching you were & you could not entertain them for you had
been PROMISED to me   is that my fault?

~~YOU BITCH YOU SHOULD NOT HAVE BEAT ME LIKE~~
~~I WERE YOUR DOG~~

~~YOU BITCH I AM NOT A DOG FOR YOU TO HIT & CURSE~~
~~AT~~

      EMILY DEAR,
      MY SWEET SMALL DOVE,
      HOW SHALL I EVER MANAGE
      NOW THAT YOU'VE LEFT ME?

Dais & all came to the wake   I wanted solitude   Daisy
watched the kids so I could get away up to the barn & START
DRINKING

~~drown me please, pickle me~~   ~~CROSS ME OUT!~~

this life has been a botched, misshapen thing   it makes no
sense to me   did I dream the fucking thing? ~~PARDON~~
~~THE CUSS~~

Emily come back, we'll make it different

I am sorry I kept you waiting so many years but I told you not
to wait, remember that? before I left we only knew each other,
what, a few months?   & then you will wait 8 years, you will
bet all on an engagement by Post   sure Emily we only saw
each other a dozen times at most before I left, & half of them in
church & dances, I were not sure you were my Suited Wife but
was I to turn down your hints & plain directives that you should
like to be married, in all them letters you wrote?
          NO ONE would do it esp. when they is fixed as I was
out in Alaska with hardly a woman at all & most of those taken
already, or Whores, or Indians

when I think on it, what did you see in me that were worth the
wait if you had so many suitors lining up for you?   you
could have broke it off   in fact I wrote to you to say to do it,
two or three times, once the waiting got so long   it were
your Pride that would not let you give it up, you could not bear
all hands knowing of it when for years you been talking Mrs.
Emily Till~~ey~~   (for that you fit right well in this Family,
dear)

we had 3 kisses before I left in '05   they were the first of
my life & I can warrant have been as sweet as any I've had since
(not that I got much to tally)   we will always have that
between us

I never kissed Jennie (not on the mouth) though I dreamt of it
often enough   you got the most of that, though
now that you're dead I can say I gave a few others a peck or 2 to
remember me by   Nell   ~~Mrs. Bob that~~

~~time I stopped on my way Out~~   ~~Kate~~   ~~just once~~   ~~we~~
~~were but Youngsters~~   you can't tell no one now so it don't hurt
to admit it

these lips feel ill-used   when did they last press yours?
          it was at least a year ago   you were
in the sickroom so long

when did we last Cherish one another?
          that is easier to figure: when Mary was born
two years ago this fall   you never wanted nothing from
me Afterward   I don't know why   & now I am A
Widower

the sickroom is being aired out & Eva is burning the rags she
used to bathe you with, her smock & mask & the linens that came
in contact with you these past months, all straight into the fire,
the house reeks of it

~~YOU BITCH~~

I had begun to be fond of you again this past while when I could
only see you through the keyhole of the sickroom door, sitting
on the chair Mother used to leave there for me while she
practiced her piano on those cherished Sunday Mornings
          it is that same chair, Father never did like to part with
Furniture   your little pedal organ is shoved to the corner
of the room & may now be unplayable by any but Sanitorium
residents, since you've shared lodgings with it for so long
          I hope we shan't have to burn it too, I could not go
through with it

for months I could only hear your voice, & lean down to see you through that hole, at a particular angle that made your face look smaller on your body   I watched you slowly wasting thinner, shrinking down to the bone   all greyish sag of skin without no life behind it   & it was gradual enough that some days I didn't notice how strange you looked, as though you'd always been a Skeleton   I grew quite used to our new life where you lay in bed in that room & I watched you through the keyhole   I never felt closer to you Em than in these past months   & maybe that's my fault   I was too busted up inside about my Parents to ever give myself fully when I should have done it, back when we first were married

I never was all Yours   I know this to be True

Emily I don't know how I can Heal & it has ruined not just my life with you but the whole of it   ALL OF EVERYTHING

I did what I could to be a Man for you & I failed ~~I am DOG~~
Although it Numbs me some, even Whisky is no Comfort
& I Drink it half out of Habit

I was hurt I was HURT I AM STILL HURTING
& even though He's dead, He is with me, Forever
& He is Judging

(I think it is true that you loved me once
Did you still, Em, when you Passed Over?)

What is my Hope & Where is my Salvation?

once there was Jennie Chants, Jennie Chants   I'd chant
her name in the barn when she was mucking

once there was Bird Island Cove, Spillar's Rock, Maberly
          her skirts full of mud at the back from going up in the
woods, walking   she keeps a pail out by the privy path to
wash them out, so Father won't see her muddy skirts trailing up
over his stairs, it irks him   he likes us all to be neat, even
Jennie

once there was the attic, three floors up   the ladder for it
coming down into the storage pantry   a nest of
woodpeckers in the eaves, dust falling thick in the beams of
light, the great peaked roof too low to stand under

we'd crawl along the ceiling beams out to the window to look at
the fits of the sea   my eyes on the sway of her from
behind   the way she'd hike all that cloth up above her
knees to keep it from getting dirty   milk pale with softy
down like Fairies   them tough black boots she had to
wear that were too Mannish to suit her properly

a plain girl & one with too much Will   Jennie Chants
would hold me to her breast with the front of her clothes
undone   Do You Understand?   that girl milks our
cow & learned to read from stealing newspapers off Father

she makes our supper, washes the bedsheets, feeds the crackies

her skin so white the veins in her Breast are like tattoos

the pink Miracle I mustn't mention
a wondrous Slip of Skin beneath my lips
Stiffening

Jennie Chants would open up her clothes right down the front
          I'd sit across her lap with her skirt hiked up & fit my
mouth upon her breast   the woodpeckers hammering

we could be up there for an hour like that before she got called
down   just that, my mouth there & no more   otherwise,
we were like brother & sister together

& it was her
the first time
her that asked for it

when she first came to us, it was for Arthur
                    M— was too tired to feed him
                    Jennie's own baby was just taken
                    no one ever said there was a Father

Mr. Chants said she was too young for Motherhood & gave her
child to his Sister in Bauline, who'd been trying   he said

'Auntie' Jennie might name the baby, but instead she up & left,
heading straight for our shop, for she'd heard about M— & what
kind of fix we were in   her sad girl's face & leaking breasts
pressed up against the glass, pounding on the door with her
thin fist till Father finally undid the deadbolt & let her in

I'd just suck, & gently clutch her, & she'd kiss my hair & smooth
it back, & hold her breast up to my mouth as though I was a
baby   like a babe I'd gape past her out the window & take
the rhythm of my suckling from the sea   swallow down
the good that she was making, because someone had to take it,
for the pain she was in

(he died before he was weaned, our Baby Arthur
died in the night with a face gone dark
she was making milk for him & it hurt her when he couldn't
take it
& I was a child of Eleven & she of Thirteen
& I guess that's some kind of Pardon

we had seen a tiny face gone dark
our Hearts were dimmed)

but even after she'd dried, we didn't stop our meetings, though
they have grown more infrequent in the past few years
        Jennie has her Suitors   she do not fancy the old ways

Yes, Lord, It is Perhaps a Strange Sin: Ever since I were
Eleven, I reached my brother through the soft funnel of her
Skin   I never imagined how much you could miss a little
baby, & how missing him was going to last forever, it never quit
        she'd press me close to her & I could smell him, that

sweet smell from behind his ears, could feel his miniature fists digging in

that soft, damp little spray of breath I loved to feel on my neck when M— would let me hold him   M—, whose name is now forbidden   she must've had her heart stolen by the little dead face as well   gone a few months later, no note, no fuss, just gone quite early one morning, chasing after her Genius   this Grief is hers, by rights   Father swore he'd spit on her if she dared come back, & then she did come back, to die   & he did spit on her, because he said he would & is a man of his Word, though afterward he let her in to lie abed in a room of her own

      her old practice room for Sunday Morning piano
      she died there

sometimes the effects of our ritual would leave me strewn out on the beams for half an hour or more, once Jennie'd gone down to answer to Father, calling up his orders from the foot of the stairs   there was a space of time in which I felt a calm sort of Nothingness, like all there was to the World was the sound of my heart & my breath & the gulls & the surf & the dogs

then One Day   I can be Specific—it was November 17th of last year—Jennie led me up to the pantry & pulled down the ladder   probably for the first time since April

that very day Father decided to board up the woodpeckers instead of just cursing their existence every time he spied the hole they had made under the eave   a view he was privileged to behold on his daily walk up to the Church, & the blemish of which was hindering him on the quest for his Soul's Perfection

on November 17th he climbed up the pantry ladder with a hammer & a board   nails sticking out of his mouth like scary dream teeth   he threw down the plank & let his hammer sail   I was sucking at her breast & she screamed before I felt it   it caught me on the ankle   the blow was hard, I thought my ankle crushed at first, & there was blood, quite a lot of it, as the tines did catch the bone

Father came striding out on the beam, half hunched on account of the roof   whipping off his Belt, his face black with anger   he strapped Jennie across the offending Breast & also her legs with her skirts pulled up & the Belt right on her Skin

—WHORE   HARLOT   CHILD OF BABYLON

the Belt hanging from his hand like a dead black Snake

Father turned away as she buttoned her dress, the marks already starting to rise   he gave her his handkerchief   told her to get to work & see to supper & then he followed her down the ladder without so much as looking at me

in their haste she left her apron & I tore it up to bind my ankle, what was by then bleeding into my shoe   trying not to go swoony   & though it do be a neat trick to properly staunch a wound & bind it without looking at it, I managed good enough to stop the flow   & though I felt like to faint or lose my guts I did neither of these, lest Father find me out for a Sissy on top of the rest of my faults

Prayers that night were lengthy & especially thunderous
        afterwards, Father didn't speak & kept the Whisky bottle
by his plate   when he finished with his Fish & Potatoes
he got up & left the house   I went to the porch & watched
him put my boots outside the white front gate, clicking it shut
        then he came inside, fetched the bottle & lay on the
daybed with his face to the wall while Jennie cried quietly into
the scaldy dish water

the next day I left for Leominster   Pretty Plastics City
        Father had as good as told me to follow after the rest:
Ernest, Jim, Bob, Alice, Kate, Daisy, Genie   he put my
boots out by the road & I figured that was pretty clear
Instructions, so I left before breakfast, a letter on his chair:

        Father, gone to Massachusetts after work   I will send
        you all I can as soon as I have got it   Do not work
        so hard you put yourself in the ground before I get back to
        help you with the place   Your loving son, Duke

I went up in the Attic & caught sight of Jennie out the window,
bent over a pail of water on the privy path, scrubbing at the
hem of her skirt   & even from up there I could see the dark
stripes on her calves that Father had made   she didn't
look up, & I watched as though watching a stranger

in her room, I left a cake of French-milled soap I was planning
to give her for Christmas & underneath, a note:

        Remember Me is All I Ask
        But if Remembrance Prove a Task
        Forget Me

I went to the front gate & put on my boots & in the early morning light with the gulls going mad, I carved my motto next to my name on my walking stick, right into the unstripped bark, nice & deep, 3 times for Luck:

Hell & Sin   Hell & Sin   Hell & Sin

& then I limped down the road with my hammer-struck ankle jammed into my boot & so swole I couldn't tie the laces up

I work for Viscoloid like my brothers   Father says that Plastics are not fit for Man, for they do Imitate too well the Finer Stuffs of Life (Marble, Mahogany, Gold, Ivory, etc) & therefore allow any Commoner to Reach Above his Station
          He thinks the Plastics are Sinful   Ernest says the opposite: They are Progress   he has heard some men say that they are Saviours to us now when we are running out of Elephants & Walrus to get Real Ivory from   We need to Innovate & soon enough no man shall rely on the Natural World for his wants in Life   I do not know which side I am on but have noticed that though he may trumpet about it, Father still takes what I sends him, Plastics Money or not   I work the machine for the mock tortoiseshell combs   the secret to the sheen is adding layers of white into the green when you are pressing them   there are many combs made here but I am on the green three-inchers   & oft-times I do daydream of nicking a pair for Jennie   they got a nice shine to them & are stronger than real shell with a design of tiny raised daisies   the work's dull here & the factory's too hot   & though I am not in the drying room proper the fumes still come out this way, it's enough to get you crying some days   the months go by without much to mark them besides the full up & drain of the moon

my brothers are unlike me   they play at cards & dress
themselves too flashy   they go to Church but have no
Higher Feeling   Father writes that he needs money &
they buy more stockings for their wives   he writes he
might have to sell the Store   Ernest laughs & calls him
things that reek to me of Damnation   James says he
shall move to St. John's & open a Public House, Damn the Store
& Damn Viscoloid too   he should like to be his own
man   there is no Future in Elliston   Jennie doesn't
write   I've sent some postcards but can't express myself
(he might read them)   & dare not send her a Letter
(there is not a hope for sealed envelopes!)

if I don't die before I get back home, I want to free them both
          Father from his Debts & Jennie from Father   I see
the good they've got in them   like us all they're poisoned
by Circumstance but the good is there & someday I'd like to
loose it   I ask for extra shifts, even though the work is
hateful   the smell stinks & pounds behind my eyes
& by noon I have to strip down to my strapshirt & overhauls
          I'm suffering for my Sins, suffering now so I can get it
over with   I don't want any Guilt hanging over me as Life
keeps on   I want to come home fresh with a white crisp
Soul full of starch with perfect creases, & that loaded down with
money I can barely stand up   or at least with some small
fortune   a goodly amount, enough to do Father   if
it takes Two Years, so be it

he writes of financial troubles & the farm & how he don't have
enough money to get good oats for Lightning   I send him
what I can, but my wages are only 1.50 at present   I had
to pay Alice $6.50 to get her to send Father her 5 dollars

Alice 5 Kate 5 Daisy 5 Ernest 10   & I am like the man on
the house not in it, asking for money not for myself   I know
it makes them cross for me to be asking at all

I would rather be working in the store   the day is less
repetitive   Ernest says before I can sell I have to sound
like a proper American, not some salt-soaked bumpkin from
N. F. L. D.

—no one will buy diddly from you, Dukey, if you sound like that
        he has a New England accent so thick you'd never know
we were related   he is strong as a bear but pretty thin &
white   anyone that worked Comb City for as long as he
have is not much good for anything else   what is the use
of money if you kills yourself trying to get more   he do
not see my point   I bring him up to my room for a drink
of Nan's Gin, & I finally come around to asking for money for
Father   He says why should he care if the Store goes or
stays, he's never going back to Elliston anyhow   He don't
feel like having a Mortgage at all   If he were to go back
he wants to buy it outright so he would have it all   if I was
Father I would never sell it to him for I would just as soon see a
Stranger have it

Ernest was like royalty when he was young   Firstborn
        little velvet suits & his own horse & buggy   Father &
M— were important then, Church Founders, Community Leaders,
the Prosperous Merchant & his Musical Wife   Arthur Tilly,
with the medal on his mantelpiece from saving that crew, the
Eric, forty men safe & no one died   when we talked it over
a few weeks ago, passing a bottle in my room, Ernest said it was
not so simple

—what could be more simple?   he saved those men
—so did several others, but Father got the credit, didn't he?
          & then he bought the wreck for thirty pounds, figuring
to make a fine profit on the pelts, if not the boat itself
—you never told me that
—well it didn't turn out as he thought   the boat smashed
up on the Cow & Calf until it was no more than kindling, & the
pelts all washed to sea, & all he got out of it was the anchor &
chains, which he sold in St. John's   still made more than
what he paid out, the Bastard
—but he saved those men
—sure he did, of course he did   I'm not saying he's the
Devil, Duke   but still & all, he had it in his mind how he
could profit even while they were out on the ice waiting to get
drug in, you can bet on it

Ernest never had to sell fish down on the waterfront, Age Five,
to bring the handful of coins back to Father, he never had to
pawn off M—'s things to the church women, see them fingering
the fabric of her dresses & remarking on the quality, when a few
months previous they were crowded around Baby Arthur's
casket, offering their pity & weighing us down with little dinners
done up in napkins   four months later they came like
gulls, greedily circling around her Sewing Machine, her Jewellery,
the Vanity   Father asking me to sell it all   & me,
Age Eleven, bartering with Mrs. Chaulk over M—'s Shirtwaists
with the shape of her still there, no matter how many times
Jennie pressed them

Ernest was grown & gone when all the fuss started, when M—
left & Templeman drove us into the Ground, & he laughs like a
New England Prig when I tell him about it

he thinks that Father do Deserve It, though for what I am not sure

I saved up my money to buy Father some Bully Beef for Christmas & even managed a bottle of good Brandy
I write & tell him not to worry about Templeman, we'll scrape together enough to get clear   he writes of Jennie as though nothing happened, & tells me how she scorched a hole in his Sunday Vest   I wish to the Devil I were Home again
        I send Father the money for coal before he has to ask

while I'm living, he'll never want for anything   I'm going to work my way on the boats with Clare, & maybe even out to Alaska to where Bob is, the money's better & it's outdoor work, saner for a man than getting hedged into a factory, stripped down to his Skin & hot as Hades, breathing in the plastics till you can't taste your dinner come quitting time   the Yukon River sounds as good as Massachusetts, maybe better, especially if Bob has the Golden Touch he bragged of in his letters & the two of us can find a fat vein & make of it Our Fortune
        I know he isn't one for frippery like James & Ernest & that we two could work like dogs together & make our riches quick   & Bob will say of me that since I've grown I am turned out to be a Good Man, strong & trustworthy, his Favourite Brother   & he could see these qualities in me, before he left N. F. L. D., when I was but A Sapling

if Clare can make money out there I think I could too, for I know that if I can get money in my hand I won't waste it & Clare is no one to save   if he does what he said for me at the Company I am sure to go   & if I have good health the summer I shall get a start & see Bob   & if it is like Clare said it was then

I shall be able to come home in 2 years time if I don't get sick
or anything & perhaps in less time than that according to what
money I makes   I might catch the Fever   Me &
Bob will get nuggets set into our boots for hobnails & sprinkle
our letters with Gold Dust, to Impress the Addressees!
          (besides, it doesn't matter where I am if I'm not home
I feel Empty most of the time, but not Peaceful—   Hollow
          Sick   Restless   —like a dog without his dinner)

where ever I go I am always The Same
& none of us got a Head to comprehend that
we all wants our Souls to change in relation to new scenery but
it don't work that way, I know that now, being just the same
sorry Duke inside as always,
even in Leominster, Massachusetts

My Little Grief   ~~Jennie's Breast~~   ~~Jennie's Breast~~

Hell & Sin

The Attic above the Store & Family

All that's left is Father now, & Herself
& She Hired On so She Doesn't Count

Now Father's The Whole Family

the empty rooms spreading out around him like mould on
wallpaper as he drowns out the dark with Whisky

I think of him alone like that
& it's like someone is beating me

Acknowledgements

This novel began one day in the summer of 2004, when I went with my father to visit the property in Elliston that he had inherited from his father. The house was mostly empty, and had been that way since I was a child, but there was one cupboard upstairs that was stuck shut. On this particular visit, Dad forced it open, and discovered a mass of family letters, log books, journals, postcards and ledgers, as well as magazines, school primers, medical texts and other documents dating back to the 1880s. Thank you to my father for allowing me to hold onto these papers for years, and to my family as a whole for giving me the space and silence I needed to write a work of fiction from those pages. Thank you to Craig Francis Power for reading the first few drafts, and being a sounding board for the mask process I worked with to write these characters. Thank you to Ian Wallace for the inspiration to experiment with my Pochinko training in this new way, so that by making and wearing masks of Duke and Eva I could sink deeper into the characters and allow their voices to fully emerge. Thank you to Richard Pochinko for the legacy of his clown and mask work. Thank you to Mario Villeneuve, who sent me stacks of images of Klondike life, slightly too under- or over-exposed to make it into the photographic collection of the Yukon Archives, and to Ali Kazimi, who found an album of Tilley family photographs for sale in Vancouver and tracked me down to return it. Thank you to Kathleen Winter, Martha Baillie, Wayne Johnston, Bryhanna Greenough, Mary Macdonald, Ben Jackson, Elling Lien, Audrey Hurd, Shannon Bramer, Ken Sparling, Debbie Crump and the staff at The Rooms Provincial Archives. Thank you to Michelle Butler Hallett, Leslie Vryenhoek and Ramona Dearing for feedback on the first piece of writing done on this manuscript back in 2005 — its ending. Thank you to Beth Oberholtzer for her unerring eye and to John Haney and Carey Jernigan for the cover image. Thank you to my publisher and editor, Beth Follett, for her infinite care with this book, and with this author. Thank you most of all to the authors of the original Tilley family correspondence, especially William Marmaduke Till(e)y and Eva Tilley, whose voices led me into this fictional world, and whose words are embedded within mine throughout this text. I have taken great liberties with the characters and events in this book, writing into the gaps and mysteries in the original documents, and I thank the real people whose words I have used for inspiration, and whose names I have kept intact, even though I have ventured quite far, at times, from the 'truth' of how it all happened.

Many sources were consulted during my research, including: Jonathon Green's *Slang Down the Ages: The Historical Development of Slang*, Eric Partridge's *Slang To-Day and Yesterday*, Partridge and Jacqueline Simpson's *Dictionary of Historical Slang*, and *The Encyclopedia of Swearing: The Social History of Oaths, Profanity, Foul Language and Ethnic Slurs in the English Speaking World*, by Geoffrey Hughes. *Of Boats on the Collar: How it Was in One Newfoundland Fishing Community* and *More Than Fifty Percent: Woman's Life in Outport*

Newfoundland 1900-1950, by Hilda C. Murray, were consulted with frequency, as was *Yukon River, Marsh Lake, Yukon to Circle, Alaska,* by Mike Rourke, and *The Dictionary of Newfoundland English,* edited by W. J. Kirwin, G. M. Story and J. D. A. Widdowson. I also consulted Jeffrey L. Meikle's *American Plastic: A Cultural History,* Donald C. Mitchell's *Sold American: the Story of the Alaska Natives and Their Land 1867-1959,* John S. Makuk Lutz's *A New History of Aboriginal-White Relations,* Eric Nicol's *Vancouver,* Paul Yee's *An Illustrated History of the Chinese in Vancouver,* Mildred G. Winsor and Naboth Winsor's *A Pilgrimage of Faith: A History of the Methodist Church 1814-1925 and the United Church of Canada, 1925-1990, Good Time Girls of the Alaska-Yukon Gold Rush* by Lael Morgan, *Klondike Women: True Tales of the 1897-98 Gold Rush* by Melanie J. Mayer, *Music of the Alaska-Klondike Gold Rush: Songs & History* by Jean A. Murray and *The Songs of the Gold Rush* by Richard A. Dwyer, Richard E. Lingenfelter and David Cohen. Other sources found among the family papers include *The Camper's Own Book For Devotees of Tent and Trail* 1913, edited by George S. Bryan, and *Wellcome's Medical Diary and Visiting List 1904.* Ernest Tilly's column, *Memories of an Oldtimer,* which ran in the Newfoundland Quarterly, was also a wonderful source of material, especially the March 1958 edition, which described Arthur Tilly's involvement in the rescue of the S. S. Eric.

This book was written in part during residencies at Berton House in Dawson City, Yukon, Landfall in Brigus, Newfoundland and Labrador, and the Leighton Colony at the Banff Centre, as well as during my tenure as Writer-in-Residence at the Calgary Distinguished Writers Program, University of Calgary. Unofficial residencies in New Chelsea and Brigus South NL, courtesy of Kym Greeley and my parents, respectively, were also crucial to the completion of this work. I would like to acknowledge the support of the Canada Council for the Arts, the Newfoundland and Labrador Arts Council, and the City of St. John's Arts Jury. The first two sections of *Her Adolescence* were published together in a slightly different form as a single short story titled *Her Adolescence*, included in the anthology *Hard Ol' Spot*, edited by Mike Heffernan (Killick Press, 2009).

Sara Tilley's work bridges writing, theatre and Pochinko Clown Through Mask technique, with each discipline informing the others. She's written, co-written or co-created eleven plays, including new work for She Said Yes!, the theatre company she founded in *2002*. *Skin Room*, her first novel (Pedlar Press, *2008*), won both the Fresh Fish Award for Emerging Writers and the Percy Janes First Novel Award, and was shortlisted for the Winterset Award and the Thomas Raddall Atlantic Fiction Prize. Sara writes fiction, plays and nonfiction, teaches mask and clown technique, and acts, directs and designs for the theatre. She lives in St. John's, Newfoundland and Labrador.